HEADCOUNT

About the Book

Management consultant Frank Stein gets blackmailed by his boss Monica "Mo" Hussein into joining a secretive group of vigilante killers. The group is called the Network, and its members target civilians that use corporate influence to enable and support genocide, hate-crime, and anti-democratic activity.

As Frank is forced to turn himself into a murderer, he struggles with his conscience at first. But when he begins to understand Monica's reasons for doing what she does, he finds a way to justify his own actions.

Soon Frank comes to the awful realization that he's actually beginning to enjoy his new lifestyle, and not least because he's falling in love with the woman who's blackmailing him.

About the Author

Prior to becoming a writer, FRANK STEIN spent almost a decade working as a management consultant in New York City for one of the world's largest consultancies. He holds an undergraduate degree in philosophy and an MBA from Columbia Business School.

www.frankstein.net

HEADCOUNT

a thriller

FRANK STEIN

4CP FOCUS
MINNEAPOLIS

Headcount: A Thriller

Copyright © 2012 by Frank Stein
All Rights Reserved

If you'd like to reproduce, transmit, sell, or distribute any part of this book, please obtain the written permission of the author first.

This is a work of fiction. Names, characters, places, businesses, organizations, events, brands, and incidents either are the product of the author's imagination or are used fictitiously with no intent to malign or misrepresent. Other than that, any resemblance to actual persons, living or dead, events, businesses, or locales is entirely coincidental.

Book Design by Jack Straw
Silhouette Illustration © Shannon Fagan | Dreamstime.com
Blood Spatter Illustration © Katrina Brown | Dreamstime.com

Set in Caslon

Published by 4CP Focus
Minneapolis, Minnesota, 55408
First Edition, 2014

ISBN: 978-0-692-02607-6 (alk. paper)

10 9 8 7 6 5 4 3 2 1

www.frankstein.net
@FrankSteinBooks

HEADCOUNT

PROLOGUE

My name is Frank Stein. There is a middle initial but I never use it. I'm too close to actually being a monster to carry it off. Just call me Frank. Frank will do. Frank is a good name. It describes me just fine. I may be a monster, but I'm straight up fucking honest.

Or at least I will be with you.

I'm not a writer. I'm a consultant. Yeah, I know that word doesn't mean shit now. Everyone's a goddamn consultant these days. This is the new world of the non-permanent job—you find what you're good at, and then you take it from company to company. Like a mercenary. A virus. A parasite. A bacterial infection. A leech.

No, you say, that's not right. Be nice, you say.

To hell with that. I know what I'm talking about. I'm one of the originals. A management consultant. Remember us? The business doctors. Corporate SWAT teams. Self-professed experts in whatever it is you do. We come in, clean up your shit, and get out. We don't care if your shit stinks. Actually, we like it when your shit stinks. If it didn't, you wouldn't bring in asswipes like us.

But this isn't some memoir with cute anecdotes about

my life and career. It's not some goddamn insider look at the industry. And while I hope some of you read all the way through, the truth is I'm not writing it for you. I'm writing it for me. To convince myself that I'm still sane. To remind myself that I'm still human. To trick myself into believing that there's still some good left in me.

Even after what I've done.

I

It begins with a laptop. All stories about management consultants begin and end with a laptop. The laptop is everything to the consultant. It is what the rifle is to the Marine. It is what the handgun is to the street cop. The vodka to the Siberian prison guard. Your blanket in the cold. The flickering dim light in the deafening dark. We are one with our laptops. We are sub-human without our laptops. I think you get the idea.

This laptop didn't start off as any of those things. It wasn't the standard issue given out to new consultants or the upgrades given to managers or the slim sexy machines given to partners and directors. I had only just noticed it sitting there on the generic office table in that long flat unnamed office complex in the sterile office park in one of those dead little towns that you're always surprised is the global headquarters of that eleven billion dollar company. I stared at the laptop and then looked away when I heard Simone behind me.

She walked around me and pushed the laptop away and leaned on the edge of the table. I sat down and lowered the chair and used my face to gently push her legs apart. After a while she made a sound and then I stood up. When we were finished she turned and I leaned in to kiss her, but she raised a hand to stop me.

"Gross," she whispered.

I laughed and licked her hand. She smiled and then we stepped outside for a smoke.

We smoked and then Simone went directly to her car. I watched her tail lights disappear around the corner and then walked back inside. The place was dead. Goddamn clients. In at six, out at three. Little Timmy has baseball practice. Precious Jenny has a soccer game. We're hosting a Tupperware party. To hell with them and their perfect little lives.

We curse like sailors when we're alone or with each other. It's a spontaneous release of all the withheld swear words that only partners can use around clients and not expect repercussions.

Not just any partner, of course, but certainly the one who currently owned my ass: Monica Hussein. Mo Hussein. Smart as hell. An amazing salesperson. Ripped like a triathlete. A wonderful mentor. Clients loved her, which says a lot when you bill out at seven hundred an hour. And yes, you know where this is going—a total nightmare if you have to work for her every day.

But she had been exceptionally chilled that day. It wasn't even Thursday. Not that our four-days-at-the-client policy seemed to be holding up. New York was a distant memory. I didn't know why I even kept an address there. How long did I have to be away before the rats took over my shithole on the Upper Upper Upper West Side? No, I'm not kidding. Most consultants don't get paid enough to live in the fancier areas of Manhattan. At least not middle of the road consultants like me. I was good, but I wasn't the best.

Maybe that's why Ms. Hussein hadn't bothered to hide that she had been staring at a client-issued laptop all day. She couldn't imagine I'd notice. And even if I had, why would I think anything of it? Why would I know that our client,

Walker-Midland, didn't allow an outside consultant to go anywhere near its in-house computers? How could I know that all client machines had pre-installed software keys that allowed access to the company intranet? And not just the company intranet. If you plugged into a wall network jack, then depending on where you were located, different areas of the castle opened up. And we happened to be in an administrative building. Sounds benign until you realize that payroll is an administrative department. And Walker-Midland was one of the few global conglomerates that hadn't outsourced the processing of its three billion dollar payroll.

But we weren't there to consult on their payroll process. At least not yet. Actually, I wasn't quite sure what we were doing. For now it was some pro-bono scoping work. In other words, Ms. Hussein had offered Walker-Midland her team's services to help put together a list of possible projects for consultancies to bid on. Of course, with the implication that she'd get to pick the juiciest ones from the list.

Worked for me. There wasn't much pressure. All I really had to do was make sure I was in by nine and not out before eight. The client wasn't paying, so they couldn't care less about me. And Mo wasn't riding me too hard. As long as I looked busy she didn't bother me. So it wasn't surprising that she didn't notice that I had noticed the laptop. And she certainly wouldn't have guessed that I knew what it could mean.

Of course, I wouldn't have known if not for Simone, Walker-Midland's Chief Human Resources Officer and the person responsible for bringing us in. Simone was forty-six. She had two grown kids out west. She also had three ex-husbands, one of whom was underground. As in dead and buried. Yes, Simone had left her perfect little family-life far behind. And she didn't want to go back down that path.

Fine with me. I'm too much of an asshole to be husband material anyway. And I don't know about being a fourth husband. Especially when husband number three dies in a boating accident. Boating accident? Reminded me of that story about that guy who had four ex-wives. Four divorces must be rough on the wallet, someone asks him. The man sips his drink and replies: I don't believe in divorce; I believe in boating accidents.

But I didn't take that seriously, of course. Simone was a cool woman. Besides, I just wanted to use that story about boating accidents. So, back to Mo and the client-issued laptop. Now, it was possible that she had special permission to use the laptop. I didn't know the Walker-Midland policy by heart. But I did know that a laptop could not be checked out overnight. Even Simone didn't have a company laptop. Walker-Midland was old school. Everyone had desktops at work. If they traveled, they could use shared desktops at satellite locations or check out a machine for the day.

So it had been strange to see the client-issued laptop blinking at me before Simone came over. It sure looked like the one Mo had been using—I had noticed the big white numbers: 451. Why had it not been checked back in? Why had it been on after hours? And plugged into a wall network jack?

I walked back towards the desk and wondered if I should look at the laptop. But when I got there it was gone. I shrugged. Must have been security or some IT guy on the late shift. So I packed up and I left.

And that's how the story begins. With a laptop.

2

The next morning my BlackBerry warned me of an e-mail from Mo Hussein before I had even left the hotel. Not too many words, as was her style: *See me - Mo.* So I did.

"What's up," I said. I walked into the empty spare office that Simone had assigned Mo.

"You tell me," said Mo. She didn't look up from her computer screen.

I glanced at the back of her laptop. Chadwick & Company standard issue. One of ours. I looked at Mo and shrugged. "Not much. Been picking through some of the documents I got from you and Simone. A lot of reports that don't make sense. There's probably scope for some kind of reporting optimization work. Want me to write up a proposal?"

Mo looked at me. She smiled but I didn't like the smile. "I didn't call you in here for a status update."

I felt my stomach try to squeeze into my nutsack. She had seen me with Simone. Of course. How goddamn stupid could I be? I see my boss staring at a laptop all day, then I see the laptop on a table, and then I have sex with our client at the same table. Simple logic should have told me that Mo had been there. She must have watched us and then taken the laptop when we went down to smoke. Shit. *Shit.*

I smiled back. "Okay. What do you need?"

Mo stood up and walked around me and shut the office

door. As she walked back to her spot behind the table she looked at me over her shoulder. "Simone won't be in today."

I shrugged. "Fine, I guess. I didn't have a meeting or anything with her today." I waited for Mo to say something else but she didn't so I did. "What happened? Is she ill? Or working from home?"

"No. She's missing." Mo leaned back in the cheap office chair and put her hands behind her head.

"Missing?" I looked at the time on my BlackBerry. "Well, it's only nine in the morning. She's probably running late. Or maybe she slept in. Did you call?"

"I didn't call."

I got that feeling again where my gut is down where my balls should be, and so I sat on a chair facing Mo. "What's this about?" I said.

Mo pushed a shiny bit of paper over to me on the table. I flipped it over. Then I jerked my chair backwards and cried out and gagged. I looked at Mo. She looked at me without blinking and with no expression on her face.

"She's dead?" I finally said. I looked at the picture again and turned away. "Where did you get this? How can this be real?" I was almost shouting now. "What the hell happened to her? What kind of animals could have done that to her face?"

Mo smiled. "Careful who you call an animal." She took the photograph back and I watched as she tore it into small pieces. I almost laughed in my panic as I watched her calmly swallow each scrap of the photograph and wash it down with VitaminWater.

"No," I said. I tried to smile, maybe even laugh, but all that came out was a gurgled stream of words. "This is ridiculous. This has to be a joke. This can't be real. This is not happening."

"It is happening. And this is just the beginning," said Mo. "Well, the beginning for you, at least."

I stood up, not sure what to do. I started to move towards the door.

She called after me. "You going to turn yourself in? Or you're going to try making a run for it?"

I stammered. Then I stopped trying to talk.

Mo stood up and moved close to me. "You watch those crime shows on TV, right? You know that when they find your semen and saliva on her they're going to be a little less willing to believe your side of the story. And what's your story? That your female boss admitted to the murder and showed you a picture which she then proceeded to eat? Good luck with that. This is Texas, you know."

I stammered again.

"Of course, they don't have to find anything," said Mo. "In a couple of days people will realize that Simone is missing. And it can just stay that way. Like they say: no body, no crime."

"You're insane," I said.

"Sanity is relative to one's frame of reference. Don't worry, though. I'll help you with the transition."

"What the hell are you talking about?"

"I need some help. It's becoming harder for me to do this work discreetly now that I'm a partner with C&C. I need someone lower down the chain."

"What work? What kind of work involves doing . . . that?" I said. I rubbed my head and looked at the ground.

"Trust me, she had it coming," said Mo. She smiled again.

"Nobody deserves to be murdered. Especially not like that."

"Shut the hell up. You don't know shit about what's going on. It'll take a while for you to get it. That's why I needed to lock you in to start with. But you'll get it."

"Get what? That you're a homicidal maniac? I think I'm starting to see that already."

Mo laughed. "Nice. You speak your mind even when you have no control in the situation. I was right to pick you. And when the opportunity presented itself last night, I knew it was a sign from Allah that you will be the one to accompany me in this holy mission."

"Sign from Allah? Holy mission? Are you kidding me?"

Mo raised her hand and took on an almost comical expression and tone of voice which, under the circumstances, was frightening as hell. "To work the legal dead zones created by international jurisdictions, extradition treaties, and other government red tape. To take out the invisible men and women financing and enabling the mechanisms that brainwash Muslims into becoming foot soldiers in a fake religious militancy. To purify Islam while reconciling it to the promise of democracy and capitalism. You know, regular consultant stuff."

3

"But I'm Jewish," I said. "You're sure Allah wants you to team up with a Jew on your holy mission to purify Islam?"

Mo laughed. "Actually, I'm not particularly religious. And this isn't about Islam. Or religion at all, for that matter. I just said that crap about holy quests and Allah because it sounds dramatic. You know, some self-righteous fanatical bullshit to freak you out a bit. Wanted to see how you reacted. Sorry. I was just playing."

"Oh, okay. So you're just a regular homicidal maniac, not a religious one. Phew."

"You're a funny guy, Frank." Mo smiled and shook her head. "Well, the first part of what I said is true. More or less."

"What? The stuff about legal dead zones or something? What does that even mean?"

"I'm not going to get into it just yet."

"And how does Simone fit into this? Or did you do that for fun?"

"I don't kill for fun. I take it very seriously. As will you." She looked at her laptop screen and then looked back up. "Anyway, I have a meeting soon. You should get back to your desk. And yes, write up something about that reporting optimization shit you were spouting earlier. If we can sell it, you'll lead the project."

I stood up and slowly walked out and found my desk. It took me fifteen minutes just to unpack my laptop and plug it in. An hour later I realized I hadn't even turned it on. I walked to the men's room and locked myself in the handicap stall. I waited until the guy pissing had left and then I turned on the faucet in the sink and broke down. I cried like a helpless baby. I howled like a trapped animal. I whimpered like a beaten dog.

I splashed cold water on my face and hair and waited in the stall until the redness left my cheeks and the swelling under my eyes subsided. Then I slowly walked back to my desk and sat down.

I had to go to the police. There was nothing to think about. I had to go to the police. No question about it. I tried not to think about my options. I had that feeling where I already knew what I would do, but I didn't want to articulate it to myself because it scared me too much. I knew I had to go to the police now, because if I thought about it I knew I wouldn't go to the police. Shit, and I was thinking about it. No, I couldn't go to the police.

So I had to find Simone. But then what? That picture didn't look fake. Simone was dead. And what would I do if I found her? Destroy the body? Make myself look guilty in case I got seen or caught? Risk getting her blood on me and making it an easy case for any prosecutor? No. Finding Simone's body wouldn't do shit for me. It would make it worse.

What would happen if I just turned myself in and explained the situation? An investigation? And then what? A trial? Her word against mine? Prison for life? Wait, we were in Texas. The rape and vicious murder of an upstanding community leader means death row. Ten years of taking it up the ass, and then a needle in my arm. No way. Call me a coward, but no goddamn way.

I could run. But where? And how? I wasn't rich. Besides, how much more guilty could I make myself look if I disappeared? Nope.

Which meant I had to kill Mo.

Wait, what? How could that make any sense? Kill someone to avoid being framed for a murder I didn't commit? Yeah, that would be a real upstanding thing to do, not to mention intelligent.

Then suicide.

Bullshit. I didn't have the balls.

Which meant the decision was made. I had an answer by the process of elimination. Like bullet points that get crossed out with tacky PowerPoint animation, just one option left:

See what this crazy bitch wants you to do.

4

The rest of that first day did not survive in my memory. I vaguely remember hitting the gym that night. The room service woman happened to walk by and she stopped in to say that the dinner menu was about to close and did I want to order my usual—the salmon. I don't remember what I said to her, but she wouldn't talk to me after that and she never brought the salmon to me again.

I didn't sleep that night but it didn't matter. At least I was spared the dreams. I sat upright in bed with all the lights on and the television off. I thought about my mum and dad. No, I couldn't turn myself in. They would never make it through the trial. Not to mention what they'd have to go through if I were convicted. Sure, they'd believe me when I swore I was being framed. But for how long? At some point maybe even a mother will start to believe what the judges and prosecutors and press are saying. After all, I did have sex with Simone. And in theory she would have had the ability to destroy my career if she wanted—enough motive for a jury these days. More than enough motive for a bloodsucking workaholic New York City management consultant. The press would damn well love it. Anyone who knows someone who's been laid off would nod his head and cite the law of karma, even though management consultants almost never decide who's going to get laid off. Damn that movie *Office Space*. And that

George Clooney chick flick. Poisoning every possible jury pool. No way I'm getting into a courtroom. Especially not in Texas. Good lord, I thought, I am so screwed.

Still, wasn't it possible that Simone was actually alive? Sure, that picture looked real, but anyone can fake a goddamn picture these days. But it looked like a Polaroid, not a printout of a digital image. You can't Photoshop a Polaroid, can you? Maybe not, but you can't eat one either, as far as I knew.

So could Simone be in on it? Could she be part of this ridiculous mission or whatever it was that my crazy psycho bitch boss was going off about? No. Simone was a cool woman. We had fun together. She was cool.

I stood up and went to the window and cried. Not for me this time. Now I cried for Simone. Yeah, I was in some shit. But Simone was dead. What had she gone through? And why? So that Mo could set me up? Could Mo be that insane?

She had to be, right? There was no other way to explain it. She was a goddamn lunatic. And she had me by the balls. So my choices were what again? I could cut and run. But I had nowhere to go and not enough money to get there. Plus, I couldn't disappear on my parents, and I couldn't make them accomplices, either. Maybe suicide wasn't that bad an idea. No, it was actually a terrible idea. Not only would my folks live the rest of their days thinking I was a rapist and murderer, but they'd know I was a coward too.

Then suddenly it became clear. The lack of sleep and dehydration seemed to bring me to a state of pure ecstatic realization. What had earlier seemed so insane now seemed obvious.

I'd do it. I'd kill her.

Well, maybe first try and get her to write down or videotape a confession. And if she wouldn't, then I'd kill her. Maybe a knife or something. That shouldn't be hard to get. Just a big kitchen knife would do. But what about her body? Cut it up? Pack it in garbage bags? Or suitcases? Or both? That seemed to work in movies, but I had no idea if it was feasible.

I went to the table and started to make a list on hotel stationery. Then the phone rang. It was four in the morning, but the phone was ringing. I answered. It was Mo.

"Good morning, Frank. Sleep well?"

"Screw you, Mo."

She laughed. "Sorry. That was cruel of me. I remember my first night too. It was hell. Are you at the point where you've decided to murder me? Did I interrupt you while you were wondering what to do with my body?"

"No, I already know what I'm going to do with your body. Slow-cook it like a big slab of Texas brisket. Then I'll take it to the office and treat everyone to a slice."

"Oh my God, I love you. This is going to be so much fun."

"You crazy, crazy bitch. Tell me this is a joke. It is a joke, isn't it? You saw me with Simone last night and the two of you are messing with me, right?"

Mo went serious. "Sorry, Frank. I know how you feel. I've been there. It was tough for me to make the mental shift in the beginning, too. But I'll be there to help. I'll be the only one there to help."

"How do I know Simone is really dead? I need to see her body."

"You're not in a position to make demands, Frank. Just trust me. You may think I'm a crazy bitch, and maybe I am. But I'm in control here, and you know it."

I started to cry again. "But Simone . . . she was slashed all over the face. What the hell is wrong with you? That wasn't just murder. How long before I end up that way?"

Mo was quiet. "Hey. Calm down, Frank. It's not what it seems."

Now I screamed. "Then what is it? What the hell is it?"

"Meet me in the lobby in ten. We'll go for a drive. Bring your cigarettes."

I hung up. I punched the mirror but it didn't break. I dressed and grabbed my smokes and headed down. Mo was already there. She wore black jeans and a red top that had a silhouette of the devil on it. I laughed when I saw it.

She smiled at me. It was a warm smile and I was taken aback. "Come," she said. "I'll drive."

I followed her out into the parking lot. She asked me for a cigarette and I gave her one. We stood outside her car and she lit both our smokes with a single match. She smiled at me again. I wasn't sure what to say or do so I waited and smoked.

Finally she unlocked the car and motioned for me to get in. We drove out of the hotel lot and got onto the highway. After a few minutes she spoke.

"Simone didn't feel a thing. Everything you saw was done post-mortem. She died peacefully and on her own terms. On her own schedule."

I didn't need to say that I didn't understand.

"Carbon monoxide. As painless as it gets. She sealed her house and then brought in a barbecue. We grilled some salmon and drank some wine. And then we said goodbye because it was time."

I looked at Mo. She was crying. Real tears. I was shocked.

"I don't understand. Simone killed herself? And you were there?"

Mo nodded. "Not while she died. But I was there to say goodbye."

"But why?"

"That's how it works in our world. She was my Alpha and I was her Beta."

I stared at Mo.

She continued. "And now I'm your Alpha and you're my Beta. That's how it works in our world. That's how it works in the Network." She turned and looked at me. She was dead serious. "Welcome to our world, Frank Stein. Welcome to the Network."

5

I was quiet. I didn't look at Mo as she drove and smoked. She didn't speak, but I could sense she was waiting for me to ask. I didn't. I wasn't going to give her the satisfaction. I wasn't going to walk into her madness. She'd have to drag me. I waited for her to continue with this Alpha-Beta crap. She didn't.

"What do you know about Walker-Midland's business?" she said.

I looked at her and then looked straight ahead at the white lines on the black road. "I know they're one of the largest US-based conglomerates. They own a bunch of random companies—everything from ice-cream to steel piping to condoms."

"Yes. But do you know where they make most of their money?"

"Not really."

"Fertilizer."

"Fertilizer?"

"Yes."

"You mean like the shit they put on fields?"

"Yes."

"That's literally shit, right? They sell shit to farmers?"

Mo smiled. "Not exactly. Most farms produce their own manure or source it locally. Walker-Midland sells chemical fertilizers. That's most of what goes on fields these days."

"Chemicals. Like nitrogen products."

"Yes. Nitrogen, phosphorus, and potash. The big three. Walker-Midland produces and distributes all three."

"Where? In the US?"

"Of course. And elsewhere."

"Like where else?"

"China, India, Russia—you name it. Walker-Midland is one of the top sellers in almost every country. They're also one of the top employers of union labor in the world. And if you've ever seen the details of a union contract, you'd know this means Walker-Midland has some of the most hopelessly complicated payroll and human resources systems in the history of the universe."

"Okay." I wasn't sure where this was going.

Mo was quiet for the next ten or so minutes. The sky was turning from black to a deep blue. I looked at the clock on the dash—just past five in the morning. I yawned.

"Sleepy? Or just bored?" Mo said.

I lit another cigarette.

Mo put her window down and the smoke rushed out. Then she looked at her rearview mirror before taking the next exit. I looked around. Nothing. Just barren Texas landscape. Mo smiled. "We're here. This should wake you up. Or make things interesting at least."

We drove a few miles down a single-lane road and stopped in the almost-empty lot of a large unmarked warehouse. It had three small windows near the door, but the rest of the building was metal and sealed. We headed towards the door. Mo pounded on it. At first there was no answer and then a buzzer sounded. Mo pushed the door and it opened. We stepped inside the building.

It was dim and yellow and smelled odd, as if someone

had tried to recreate the stench of sweaty armpit by mixing chemicals in a lab. Straight ahead was a large closed door that probably led to the main warehouse floor. To our right was a narrow corridor with a half-open door at the end. I could see the flicker of a computer monitor in the room. Then a large figure opened the door wide and looked at us.

"This way, guys," said the man. He spoke with an Eastern European accent. His voice was coarse but gentle, like that of a father calling his kids inside for dinner.

I followed Mo into the room. She shook the man's hand and smiled.

"Miroslav? I'm Mo Hussein. This is my colleague, Frank Stein. Thanks for seeing us so early."

The man smiled. He nodded at me and then turned back to Mo. "Oh, no problem, Ms. Hussein. It is very slow here at this time. And I am always happy to talk to consultants. Like that movie Office Space, yah?"

I smiled. Fuck that movie.

Mo laughed. "I love that movie. But as I told you on the phone, we're not here to make any sort of personnel decisions or recommendations. You know, most consultants don't do that stuff in real life. Especially these days. Terminating people is the job of the company's managers."

Miroslav nodded. "Yah. You told me. But I never worry about my job. I am the only one who knows the payroll systems for this unit." He dragged two chairs from the back of the room and set them near his desk. He motioned for us to sit. We did. Then Miroslav went behind his desk and sat down hard on the battered cushioned office chair. "So, what you need help with?"

Mo cleared her throat. "We've been engaged to do efficiency audits of some of the operational processes at Walker-

Midland. One of the areas we've been looking at is payroll processing and how the contracts with unions are implemented in the system."

Miroslav didn't say anything. His expression changed for a moment, but I wasn't sure if he was worried, confused, or had simply broken wind into his chair.

Mo continued. "You are the local payroll manager for the Walker-Midland chapter of the nitrogen chemical workers' union in Texas, correct?"

"Correct."

"And you are familiar with the various payroll concessions granted to members of your union at Walker-Midland, correct?"

"Yes. I have to put them into the payroll system."

Mo smiled. "Then you can explain this clause I found built into the payroll system code. The clause that allows escalations in wages and other benefits for Texas workers that do the third shift five or more days a week."

Now Miroslav's expression changed and I could tell he was worried. "Maybe. It was long time back. I try to remember. What is problem with clause?"

"Well, it's probably just a mistake the human resources and payroll operators made while performing data-entry, but I found it odd that fourteen of the twenty-six workers that fall under this clause seem to be based in Texas, but have direct deposit records that route their wages to bank accounts outside of the United States. Bank accounts in Poland, in fact." Mo paused. "Miroslav—that's a Polish name, isn't it?"

Miroslav gulped and looked away from Mo. "I can check up on this. It may be the case that some workers are on temporary assignment in Poland."

Now Mo stood up. "I don't think so. What would they be assigned to in Poland?"

"Probably same work. Poland also uses nitrogen fertilizer. There is lot of work there. Walker-Midland is big company."

"Yes. But Poland's nitrogen fertilizer industry is only just starting to be privatized. It has been government-run thus far. And as far as I know, only a handful of European companies have been given permission to buy some of the Polish manufacturing facilities. Walker-Midland has no fertilizer operations in Poland."

Miroslav shook his head. "Maybe they are there for some other work. I do not know. I do not understand all this." He held his hands up with palms facing out to Mo. "I only type in the numbers. I work with hands, not brain." He cautiously laughed.

Mo walked around to his side of the desk. Miroslav swiveled his chair to face her. She smiled at him and raised her hands to show her palms in the way Miroslav had done. "I can work with hands too."

Then Mo dropped to the ground and in one smooth motion rammed the heel of her palm into Miroslav's knee. He screamed in a way that made me want to scream. I grabbed my own knee in an unconscious act of sympathy. I was a runner, and had found out the hard way that the knee is the most complex joint as well as the one that can generate the most pain if the alignment is upset. And it was safe to say that Mo had upset the alignment. In fact, from the way the big man was now sweating and howling, I'd say she had pushed the patella so far back that his femur was scraping against his tibia. You don't need to know what those terms mean to guess that the result is the kind of pain that makes you forget everything. All you can think about is how badly you want it to stop.

I should have said something but I didn't. I couldn't. I just sat and watched. Yes, I was horrified to some extent. No, I'm not a fan of inflicting pain on anyone for any reason. But yet I wasn't as revolted and freaked out as I thought I would be. I wasn't as upset as I wanted to be. What scared me more than watching my boss smash a random person's knee-cap was that I wasn't as scared as I should have been. What made me sick was that I was looking at Mo in awe. There was something beautiful about her calmness and precision. There was something inspiring about her expressionless determination. Perhaps I was already numb from what had happened to me. Maybe the lack of sleep made me believe I was in a dream. I don't know what it was, but it was something.

Mo looked at me. She didn't say anything. After watching me for a few moments, she nodded and then turned back to Miroslav. He had stopped screaming and was sitting frozen, still oozing sweat and dribbling spittle as he made a whimpering sound that harmonized well with the squeaks coming from his quivering chair. Mo leaned past him and pulled up his e-mail program on the computer. She opened a new message window and typed a paragraph of text. Then she looked at her BlackBerry and copied a list of what I imagined to be names. Probably the fourteen names she had mentioned.

Mo stepped back and faced Miroslav again. "Stop crying, big man. Don't worry, I'm not going to break your other knee." She moved close to him. "But I am going to kill you."

The big man stammered, and I could see droplets of saliva spew from his trembling mouth. "No. Please. I have a daughter."

Mo whispered. "You should have thought of that before you decided to do what you've done. What about the fathers and mothers and daughters of the people your acts have killed? The Romanian Gypsies? Polish Jews? Albanian Muslims?"

"Please. No. I give you anything. I do anything. Why you do this? You are police? Government? You must arrest. You cannot kill."

Mo shook her head. "I'm sorry, Miroslav. I don't like to kill. I know that every life I take makes me less human. But we all make sacrifices. And we all make choices. Someday I will answer for what I have done. But not today. Today is your day. Today you will answer for what you have done."

Now the man leaned forward. He was begging. "No. I do nothing. This big mistake."

"There is no mistake. We have traced the fourteen bank accounts linked with those names. I had hoped it would be as simple as you siphoning money to your poor family in Poland. But you have no family in Poland. Then I hoped you were just a regular greedy thief, sending money to your own secret accounts. That would be fine. Simple embezzlement, and we wouldn't even be here. But it's not that simple, is it?"

Miroslav didn't speak. His eyes had gone cold and he had stopped whimpering. His breathing slowed down and he stared into space. He knew he was going to die.

Mo looked at me. "This man has been funding three separate European genocide groups that are based out of Poland."

"Via those fourteen employees? So those people don't exist? They're phantom employees?"

"No, they do exist. They are real people. And they are all legitimate members of the local union. In fact, they are set up correctly in the system—Texas locals on temporary assignment to a Polish subsidiary of Walker-Midland. It wouldn't even get picked up on any of the audit reports."

"So the problem is?" I was confused.

"The problem is they are chemical plant workers, but have been assigned to a construction-equipment manufacturer, the only Walker-Midland subsidiary in Poland. But no one would notice just by looking at the company name or industry codes. It's too cryptic. But if you know what you're looking for, you'd see that these fourteen workers are pulling in over eight hundred thousand dollars a year in total, if you combine the various overtimes, healthcare reimbursement, paid-out vacation, and so on. A drop in the bucket, and Walker-Midland's records are so disorganized that there was no systematic way to catch it. Simone and I noticed the discrepancies. We traced the direct deposit accounts the salaries were going into. And then we figured out where the money was ending up."

"And the actual employees?"

"Hanging out right here in town. Getting paid a small fraction of the payload in cash by Mr. Miroslav here."

I looked at Miroslav. He didn't blink. Then he turned to me and smiled. "Jew dog. We will remove you from Poland. We will finish what Germany could not finish."

I stood up and hit him in the face. I felt his teeth cut into my fist but I didn't care. "If Germany had finished what they started, there wouldn't be any Poles left either, you ignorant pig. Nothing worse than a bigot who doesn't know his own history." I shook my head and stepped back.

Mo smiled in surprise. Then she stopped smiling and told me to hold Miroslav's arms. I went behind his chair and did what she said. He didn't struggle. I guess I should have been surprised that a man like Miroslav wasn't trying to fight us off or call for help or reach for a weapon, but he seemed strangely resigned to his fate, and I didn't really question it. I was starting to resign myself to my own fate, even though I still wasn't sure what was happening.

Then I saw Mo reach into her back pocket and pull out

a knife. It was a small folding knife—not quite a hunting knife, but not a Swiss Army knife either. Now I felt Miroslav's arms go tight as he writhed in his chair.

He looked up at Mo and began to plead again. "My daughter. She have no father if you do this."

"How old is your daughter?"

"Five years."

Mo nodded. "Then she's young enough to eventually forget you. To forget that the blood in her veins comes from a bigot and a murderer who's too much of a coward to do the dirty work himself. She's young enough that there's hope she will find her own way."

Miroslav opened his mouth to protest but nothing came out except blood. Mo had driven the knife into the side of his neck just beneath the jawline. She had sliced clean across under his chin and was already wiping the knife off before I understood what had happened. I held on to his arms for a few more seconds before realizing there was no need.

Mo leaned close to Miroslav as his gagging became less pronounced. "I had a daughter, too," she whispered.

I stood up straight and stared at Mo. She beckoned to me and I followed her. We walked outside to her car and I blinked in the dim light of the rising sun. She opened the trunk and unzipped a bag and pulled out what seemed to be plastic explosive. Then she motioned for me to follow her back inside.

We went back into the office and Mo planted the explosive and rigged a detonator. I watched quietly.

Finally Mo went to the computer and sent the e-mail she had typed up earlier. Then we walked back out of the room and towards the main door. On the way Mo planted more explosive near the door to the main warehouse and quickly set up another detonator. Then we walked back out to the car and got in.

As she started the car I asked about the e-mail. She looked at me and smiled.

"A note to the global head of payroll informing her of the discrepancy. With a copy to the head of operations. From Miroslav's e-mail account, of course. A last confession from a man apparently racked with guilt and repentance."

"So they'll remove these fourteen people from the payroll and take whatever legal action is needed?"

"They'll make sure new protocols are in place to catch this sort of thing going forward. But they won't have to worry about removing the fourteen from the payroll or making any arrests."

I looked at Mo. She glanced at the time on the car clock and then pointed at my cigarettes. I gave her one. She lit it and smiled.

"It's almost six. I figure we've got about three hours before anyone tries to do anything about that e-mail."

"So?"

"So we have three hours to kill fourteen people. But let's get a cappuccino first."

6

We cruised through a Starbucks drive-through. Mo got a cappuccino and I got a skim latte. She laughed at me for not taking full-fat milk. She said I needed my strength. I stared at her with a mixture of wonder and unadulterated fear. She had just murdered a man, and here she was laughing at my goddamn skim latte.

"*We* murdered him," she said.

I was quiet. Mo was right. I was now a murderer. Sure, I hadn't sliced his throat myself, but I did hold his arms so he couldn't fight her off. Not that he really struggled. It was odd how he just kind of sat there. Miroslav was a big dude. And if he really was a genocidal maniac, why wouldn't he at least try to fight us off? Why wouldn't he try to retaliate against a Jew and a Muslim woman? Okay, his knee was all messed up. But still, wouldn't a man like that have a gun or at least some kind of weapon handy?

I asked Mo. She shook her head. "The people we're after aren't the foot soldiers. They aren't the grunts who pull the triggers or bash the skulls or strap on the bombs. In fact, most of them are so far removed from physical violence that you sometimes get what we saw with Miroslav: they freeze and just accept it. When the violence finally catches up to them, they understand what they are accountable for. And this leads to a kind of spontaneous acceptance. Of course, it's too late for them at that point. Too late for excuses."

"But Miroslav didn't seem repentant in any way. He said some shit about wiping out the Jews even when he knew you—we—were going to kill him."

"I didn't say repentance. I said acceptance. And it occurs at a deep emotional level, not necessarily an intellectual level. Miroslav was a bigot. Years of narrow beliefs resulted in thought habits that made him incapable of speaking in terms other than the garbage you heard him spew. But still, I promise you, there was a moment of understanding before he went down." Mo sipped her cappuccino and stared out of the car window at the empty Starbucks parking lot.

"If you say so. At least someone understood," I said.

She looked at me and smiled. "You could have stopped me if you wanted."

"Yeah, right. I like my kneecaps, you know."

She laughed. "Whatever. You didn't even say anything."

"I was too scared."

"Okay, sure. I get that. But it wasn't just fear, was it?"

"I'm not sure what you're getting at."

Mo looked at me in the way a proud parent looks at a child who has just stood up on his own for the first time. I felt uncomfortable.

"What?" I said.

She smiled and nodded. "You had already made up your mind."

"About what?" I said again. Then I understood.

"Before we even got to the warehouse. You had already decided you weren't going to the police and you weren't going to kill yourself and you weren't going to kill me. You knew what you were going to do."

"That's ridiculous. I still don't know what I'm going to do."

Mo laughed. "Whatever. Who do you think you're talking to? I can read the emotional state of someone as easily and unconsciously as I breathe."

I looked at her and then looked away. Mo was a partner at Chadwick & Company. Homicidal maniac or not, you don't make partner unless you're a terrific salesperson. And you can't be a terrific salesperson without being an exceptional judge of character, which means it's second nature for you to know what a person is thinking or feeling before they themselves figure it out. As Wayne Gretzky used to say, if you want to win, don't go to where the puck is; go to where it's going to be.

So she was right. Although at a superficial intellectual level I was still weighing options and making lists, at a deeper level I had already decided. I had made my choice. I would join the crazy bitch in her insane mission.

And part of that decision meant I needed to stop calling her a crazy bitch. After all, I'd now chosen to follow her. So if she was a crazy bitch, what did that make me? Crazy as well? Was this the mental shift she was talking about? Had I really turned into a goddamn psycho over the course of twenty-four hours?

I finished my latte and sparked a smoke. I looked at her and shrugged. "So what now?"

She laughed and kissed me on the cheek. Then she checked her BlackBerry. "You tell me. We've got two hours and twenty-three minutes."

"For what?" I said. Then I remembered, and suddenly I felt cold and naked even though it was Texas and I had just downed some hot coffee. "You mean you were serious about the fourteen people?"

Mo nodded. She lit a cigarette.

"But haven't we done what's needed? The payments will be stopped, and these guys will be arrested, right? Why do we need to kill them? That seems a bit excessive, don't you think?"

"If arrests were an option, we wouldn't even be involved. A company this size will first launch an internal investigation. In fact, it'll take weeks to even get approval to start the internal investigation. Maybe longer, since these are union members. And then it's anyone's guess how long it'll take to get from that point to an actual situation where arrests can be made. Not to mention the international complications—communication issues, government red tape, confidentiality issues with Polish banks and unions. These guys will disappear the moment Miroslav's death becomes public." Mo shook her head. She looked at me with compassion and perhaps a hint of pity. "Frank, the Network is a group of killers. Killing is all we do. It's not a question of whether it's excessive or not. We're only brought in when there's no other reasonable option."

Now I felt hot and confused. "Brought in by whom? Do we work for the government? Are we some of kind of secret CIA assassins or something?"

Mo laughed. "Nothing so glamorous. The CIA has enough assassins. And compared to us, they are as bureaucratic as any government agency."

"Then what?"

She sighed. "It's complicated. But generally speaking, the Network is a loose collection of connected interests."

"Connected interests like what? Is this something to do with the purification of Islam or whatever?"

Mo laughed again, this time louder. "Oh, Lord, no. As I said, that stuff about Allah and Islam was just to mess with you. I told you, I wanted to see how you'd react. Wanted to make sure I hadn't picked a bigot. No, we are one hundred percent secular. Our only allegiance is to democracy and capitalism. And those are just our values, not our objectives. We aren't stupid enough or arrogant enough to think we can run around and single-handedly spread democracy and capitalism. That can only be done organically—by the natural growth of art and culture and entrepreneurship. That's being done by everyone else."

"So what's our objective then?"

"I just told you. We kill."

I laughed in disbelief.

Mo looked at me. She was angry. "What?"

I shook my head. "It just sounds so ridiculous. On one hand you talk about democracy and capitalism and the spread of art and culture and free markets. And here you are saying that our job is to kill people without allowing them fair trial or even giving them the option to turn themselves in."

"Frank, as we get deeper into this, you'll find that these people would love to get turned in. They know that the systems they operate within will protect them or at least delay the consequences of their actions. Remember, we're not out there chasing the bin Ladens. We're not trying to topple unfriendly governments. That work is being done by the right people: armed forces and intelligence agencies."

"Then whom are we hunting?"

"The no-name people that hide between the cracks. The insects that live in the folds of the flab created when international law tries to merge with international business. The unknown people that provide the legal and financial support for the known groups that are being targeted by the armies and intelligence agencies of the world's democracies."

"But the world's democracies are already targeting these

people, aren't they? Money launderers, corrupt government officials, businesses that manipulate international tax laws, etcetera, etcetera?"

Mo nodded vigorously. "Of course. And we don't generally step in and take out people that are already being targeted. But for every one of these groups that's being monitored or traced, there are ten that are either too buried in legality or appear to be too small or inconsequential to justify major government resource allocation. And then there are the one-off lone wolves, who are the hardest to find and eliminate. No government even tries to look for individuals working alone."

"But how do we know about these people? Is the Network connected with some of these government agencies?"

Mo smiled. "Yes and no. Our members are spread across different industries and professions and countries, so there are certainly some that work for various government entities. But I couldn't say how many or who they are or where they live." She laughed. "I said we were a loosely connected group. That's an understatement. It's probably more accurate to say we're a disconnected group."

"Then how do you get all this information? Don't you have meetings or something?"

Mo laughed. "Like a secret assassins' conference? You need to stop watching those in-room movies in your hotel."

I didn't laugh.

Mo continued. "No. Our structure is closer to that of a terrorist cell setup. Each of our cells has two units: an Alpha and a Beta. The Beta unit knows only its Alpha. And the Alpha is connected to just one other unit: an Omega."

I stared at her to try and figure out if she was serious with this Greek alphabet cloak-and-dagger bullshit. She was.

"So you know only one other member of this entire group?" I asked.

Mo nodded.

"And I'm a Beta?"

Mo smiled. "Not yet. There's a bit of a learning curve."

"Well, I think I've started on that curve. I just helped you kill a man."

She shook her head. "It begins when you kill. And now you're going to have fourteen chances." She looked at the time. "Just about two hours to go. Better get thinking. You're running out of brainstorming time." She laughed. "What kind of consultant are you, anyway? Let's hear some ideas."

I stared at her. "Ideas? You mean ideas to kill fourteen people."

Mo nodded. "In two hours."

I was stunned. I wanted to faint and wake up when it was all over. I blinked several times.

Mo nudged me. "Well?"

Now I got angry. "Screw you. Why don't I just kill you? Just one murder instead of fourteen, and it's over."

She laughed. "Is it? You think it'll be over if you kill me?"

I took several deep breaths. I felt like I was choking. I needed some fresh air, and I stepped out of the car and stood in the empty, dry parking lot and stared at the rapidly brightening sun, hoping it would blind me so I could live out my days twitching in a chair and learning Braille. But then I looked down and turned around and got back in the car. Sometimes when you're in too far, going back isn't an option. Sometimes you need to go in further and hope you make it through to the other side.

"What weapons do you have?" I said. "Any guns?" I couldn't believe what I was saying. I hadn't even held a gun before.

"No. We don't use guns. Too many complications. We don't have the same protections your CIA secret assassins might have." She laughed.

"Then what? We track down fourteen people and hack them to death with your pocket knife?" I was annoyed.

"You tell me."

"How the hell should I know? I've never used anything more dangerous than a goddamn PowerPoint slide. I haven't slept for almost thirty hours. And now I'm supposed to come up with creative ways for killing fourteen people at seven in the freaking morning?" I was shouting now. Luckily the parking lot was still empty.

Mo was quiet. She just sat and watched me.

I lit another cigarette and sulked in my seat. Then I turned to her. "Do you have all their names and contact numbers?"

She nodded.

I spoke slowly. "Maybe we call them to a series of meetings this morning. Similar to what you did with Miroslav. Say we're doing interviews as part of our consulting project. Line them up in fifteen-minute slots. And then . . ." I stopped.

"And then what?"

"You know what."

"Say it."

I swallowed hard. "Then we kill them. We take them out one by one."

Mo nodded. "Okay. Not bad. But where do we do this? Your hotel room? And what are you going to say to interviewee number twelve when he comes in and sees us covered in blood and surrounded by eleven bodies? Or interviewee number two, for that matter?"

I was embarrassed. It reminded me of my first consulting project and getting chewed out for plugging bad assumptions into an Excel financial model. I thought for a bit. Then I nodded and looked up at Mo.

"You have some more of that plastic explosive?"

"Yep."

"Then how about we find a spot and call all fourteen of them to a meeting at the same time? We can just rig the place and take them out in one shot."

Now Mo clapped. "Thank you. Now that's efficiency. Frank, you are a good consultant after all."

I felt pleased but then immediately felt sick.

"So what's a good spot?" said Mo.

"Actually, that warehouse would have been the best spot. Especially since we had to blow the place anyway. And the fourteen probably wouldn't have gotten suspicious at being asked to meet there. They probably come there to collect their cash payments from Miroslav."

"You're right."

"Damn. We should have thought of that before blowing up the place." I shook my head.

"Did you see the place blow up?"

"Well, no. But I saw you plant all that explosive, and . . ." I looked at her. "Wait—"

Mo nodded. "Yep, the explosives are on a timer."

"So now all we need to do is get those people there? How much time do we have?"

Mo smiled. She started the car. "Don't worry about it. Today is payday for them. They meet in the main warehouse area just behind the garage door we saw. They drive in through the rear entrance and gather on the warehouse floor and then Miroslav goes there to meet them." She looked at the clock on the dash again. "And that would have happened, oh, about thirty minutes ago."

She laughed when she saw my expression. "Turn on the radio," she said.

I did. We listened to the local news for a while, and then we heard it:

—and breaking news . . . a warehouse that stored chemicals for Walker-Midland has exploded killing several workers. While the bodies have yet to be identified, authorities confirm they have recovered the remains of fourteen individuals. Initial reports are that it was an accident, but an investigation is underway. We will keep you updated as—

I smiled and shook my head as Mo turned off the radio. "So, what, this was some kind of psychological test for me?"

Mo nodded blankly. She looked pale. She stopped the car at the side of the road and looked at me.

"What?" I said.

"The radio said fourteen."

"So?" I shrugged. Then I realized what she was saying. "Shit, with Miroslav, there should have been fifteen."

Mo nodded.

"Now what?" I said.

She started the car and slowly pulled back onto the road. "I guess your next test is going to come sooner than expected."

7

"I can't do it. I won't do it. You need to let me go. We both know you aren't going to let me sit on death row for a murder that wasn't even a murder." I looked at Mo. I felt closer to her now. Now that we had killed fourteen people together. Close enough that I felt she wasn't a heartless psychopath. Psychopath, maybe. But not heartless. "And you know I'm not going to say anything about what you did at the warehouse. There. We're even now. I have something on you, and you have something on me. So just take me back to the hotel, and we're done. I'll take a nap, go to the gym. Maybe order some room service. And then I'll go in to the office in the early afternoon. It'll be like this shit never happened."

Mo didn't look at me. She just kept driving. She didn't even blink. She just shook her head.

"What?" I said. "Say something."

Mo didn't say anything.

"Look, I know you're a good person. Whatever it is that's driving you to do what you do is none of my business. I'm not going to lose any sleep over the people you're . . . getting rid of." I gulped. "But this isn't me. I can't just hunt down people I don't know and kill them."

Now Mo spoke. "So I'm a good person? And you're nothing like me? Does that make you a bad person? Or am I not really a good person?"

I felt confused. It seemed really hot in the car and I was sweating. I put down the window but quickly put it back up when I felt the warm blast of Texas air hit me in the face. I cranked the air conditioner and took several deep breaths.

"Mo, I don't know what to say. I haven't slept in . . ."

"Yes, I know. Thirty hours. You told me." She looked angry. "You know, there are nineteen-year-old kids carrying sixty pounds of equipment through the goddamn desert after being awake for forty-plus hours. And they get paid about a third of what you make."

I was annoyed. "So now we're soldiers?"

She snorted. "Don't flatter yourself. You have no idea what that term even means."

"And you do?" I laughed.

The car barely swerved as Mo let go of the wheel. I didn't see her hand move, but I felt it smash into the left side of my face. The right side of my head slammed into the passenger-side window. I sat there stunned, gasping for breath. I could feel my left cheek throb and expand as the blood rushed into the swelling.

We drove in silence for several minutes as I slipped in and out of consciousness. I'm not sure if I was passing out or simply falling asleep. It didn't matter. I was in a stupor. I knew I was drooling but I didn't care. Then, for some inexplicable reason, I remembered something Mo had said earlier. I turned to her and tried to speak. I couldn't. I tried again, and the words came out.

"Your daughter?" I said.

Mo was quiet. Then she nodded.

"She's dead," I said.

"Yes."

"She was a soldier?"

Mo nodded again.

I sighed and looked out of the window. Then I turned back to her. "Iraq? Afghanistan?"

Mo smiled. She shook her head. "Westchester County, New York."

I stared at her. "Your daughter was killed when she was on leave? How?"

Mo took a deep breath. She smiled again. "She shot herself in our garage."

"Oh my God. That's horrible. I'm so sorry."

Mo shook her head. "Don't worry about it. As you said, what drives me is none of your business, right?"

I was quiet. I vaguely understood what she meant about it driving her. I had read the stories about these kids coming back stateside with no idea how to reconcile with what they'd seen and done in those god-forsaken places. And as soldiers they are taught to be strong, to handle things, so they bottle up these unresolved emotions. And sooner or later the bottle breaks.

Obviously Mo felt responsible. Any parent would. But she'd be angry too, wouldn't she? So was this her way of seeking revenge? I looked over at Mo. No. She wasn't on a vengeance binge. She was trying to understand. She wanted to know what it was like for a good person to go out there and attack and maim and kill strangers. In her own way, albeit a radical and violent way, Mo was saying that soldiers shouldn't be the only ones that have to live with these choices. These are choices we've made together, and we should deal with the consequences together.

I sighed. So it was my business after all. By saying "It's not me," I was no different from Miroslav. I was enabling, indeed ordering, others to commit terrible acts of violence on my behalf. But I didn't want to get my own hands dirty and bloody.

I sighed again. "So how do we figure out which one of the fourteen is still alive?"

8

"Wait here," said Mo. We had stopped in the outer regions of the Walker-Midland parking lot. "I don't think you want to explain that bruise to anyone at the office quite yet."

I tried to smile but it hurt too much. I winced and lit a cigarette, but then immediately stubbed it out. Those war movies where the dying soldier asks for a cigarette are bullshit. When you're in that much pain, gagging on the smoke of a burning cigarette is not so much fun.

I had fallen asleep by the time Mo got back. She shook me awake. I groaned and looked at her. She smiled at me. "Sorry for hitting you."

I sat up and blinked. I felt slightly better.

Mo started the car. "Some more coffee? Or some breakfast?"

I shook my head. "Just some water would do it, I think."

Mo flipped open the cover of the armrest between the seats. There were several small bottles of water stuffed in there. I grabbed one. It was warm, but it tasted good. I yawned. Then I put down the window and lit a cigarette. I was definitely better, because the smoke tasted good. I was just beginning to relax when Mo handed me a single sheet of paper. It was a printout from Walker-Midland's human resources database.

"John Smith? You're kidding. This is a real name?"

Mo laughed. "It has to be. No one is dumb enough to make up an alias like that."

I shrugged. "I guess so. How do we know he's the one?"

"I went to the HR group. I told them it looked like Simone might be out sick, and since I was working with her, it might be a good idea for me to get a head start on a communication for her to send out to the company."

"And they just gave you the names of the people killed?"

"Yes. They had a list based on the ID cards that were swiped, and were busy working with the police to track down the families of the victims. And they've seen me with Simone often enough to know that she trusts me. Besides, it's not private information. It'll be released on the news anyway."

"Okay. So now what? We're going to this address?" I looked at Smith's home address on the printout. "Looks like an apartment building. We can't just walk up there and murder him. People will see us. And there might be a front desk or something. Or cameras. Or both."

Mo smiled. "You are so paranoid. I love it."

"Should I not be? We're not protected by the government or anything, right? We're just a couple of psycho vigilantes out to kill some dude who may not even know what he's done wrong besides pull a payroll scam."

"No, it's okay to be paranoid. It'll serve you well. And you're right. It's possible that he doesn't know. Unlikely, since no one gets paid in cash for doing nothing, but possible." Mo looked at me. "But if that bit worries you, then consider it part of your job to let him know."

I was silent. Not because I had any issue with letting him know what he was allowing happen. No, that part was okay. It was the other part of the job that worried me. The killing part. The part where I took a life. The part where I played judge, jury, and executioner. And God.

I stammered as I spoke. "So we go up to his place. And then I . . . I stab him?" I choked on the last few words as I fought back a sob. "How can I do that? What right do I have?"

"None. You don't have the right to take a human life. Neither of us does. Each act of violence turns us into lesser human beings."

"Then let's just stop this insanity. Turn the car around. Let's go back to the hotel. Or even the office."

"That isn't stopping. We're still authorizing the elimination of human life. If we go back, then all we're doing is hiding from the truth by passing the buck to a bunch of kids in uniforms."

I suddenly felt she was right. And now I didn't feel so sick anymore, even though I knew I was going to kill a man. What was happening to me? What had I become?

"Frank Stein. You know, that's a cool name. You have a middle initial?"

"That's not funny."

"Sorry. You must get that all the time."

I nodded. "Anyway. So about this apartment building. How do we go in and out without being seen?"

"I'm hoping we don't have to go in and out. I'd like to wait for him in the lot. He's probably about to make a run for it. He's got to have figured out that he was supposed to have been killed at the warehouse with the others this morning."

"Sure. It's interesting that he wasn't at the warehouse. Why is that, you think?"

Mo shrugged. "Maybe he ran late. Or was sick."

"Too sick to collect his cash paycheck? That doesn't seem right."

"No, it doesn't." Mo slammed on the brakes and pulled over to the side of the road. She pointed at the flashing lights of an ambulance and two police cars.

"That's Smith's apartment building?"

"That's it."

"What are the chances some old person just had a heart attack?"

"They don't send two police cruisers for a senior incident."

"You think it's Smith."

Mo nodded. "I'm going to find out."

She got out of the car and walked over to the crowd gathered outside the building. I saw her talk to a man who was standing in his pajamas. Mo nodded and then jogged back to the car. I could tell from her expression that it was Smith.

I waited until she was back in the car. Then I asked her.

"Apparent suicide is what they're saying. A neighbor heard a single gunshot. No one saw anything."

I exhaled and stared at the flashing lights as we drove away. I almost smiled as I lit another cigarette and thought about a shower and the fresh cool sheets of my hotel bed. I turned on a music station and leaned back in the seat. "So we're done. This is the end."

Mo laughed. "If by end you mean beginning."

I looked at her.

She stared at me in surprise. "Wait, did you think that it was just this one job?"

I looked away.

"Frank, I'm not backing off." She looked at me with some pity, but not much. "I know I've turned your life upside down. I know you still don't believe what's happening. But I've thought through this many times. I can live with what I'm doing. I'm not proud of it, but I can live with it. For now at least." She was quiet for a moment. Then she shrugged. "And I've been watching you for a few months now. Simone and I both have. You were too good to be true. Too good to pass up."

"What do you mean?"

"You're smart, and you're in good physical shape. No wife, no kids, no siblings. You love your parents, but aren't in close contact with them. Your recent consulting gigs have been outside of New York, so you've been traveling so much that even your close friends don't really know what you're up to. And you're one of the few senior consultants that has worked across so many different industries that I can move you around to different clients without anyone thinking it odd."

I snorted. "You just described at least fifty other guys at C&C."

Mo shook her head. "You know that's not true. But regardless, there are two other factors that make you different. And ideal for what we do."

"Oh really? What?"

"The first is that although you're a good consultant, the job doesn't fulfill you. You're looking for something more. Something meaningful."

I laughed out loud. "And I'll find it in murder? Killing people is going to bring meaning into my life?"

Mo shook her head. "Sorry for the cliché, but you're missing the forest for the trees. Yes, the details of your work involve killing people. But you need to find a way to put it into perspective. You need to understand that your decisions as a private citizen of the free and democratic world have already authorized the killing of people who threaten our way of life."

"Yes, I realize that. We've talked about it. But that killing needs to be done by the men and women who are trained for this shit. People who've volunteered to do this. Folks that are getting paid to do it."

Mo smiled as she pulled the car back onto the highway. "That's the easy way out. To sit back and say that these other people are trained to kill. It's their jobs, so what's the big deal, right?"

I nodded and shrugged. "Well, yeah."

"Bullshit. That makes sense on paper. But that's not how it works. No one should have to kill another human. No job in a truly free and democratic world should require murder. Or whatever it is they call it when a soldier kills someone."

"Yeah, but now you're the one spouting nonsense that only makes sense on paper. You're basically saying that the world should be a happy, comfortable place where no one kills anyone else for political or legal reasons. That's a fairy tale. Speaking of clichés, that's the biggest one. Like when the genie pops out of the bottle and grants you a wish and you smile and say, 'World Peace.'"

Mo smiled again. She had a look that stank of victory, and I didn't like it. "Exactly. It is a cliché. We're not going to see world peace in our lifetimes. And even if we do, there will be a lot of killing along the way. And that's my point."

I was starting to smell my own defeat, but I ignored it. "I don't get it."

"Yeah, you do. I'm starting to make sense, aren't I? If we accept the premise that no one should have to kill for a living, that taking a human life cannot be trivialized and reduced to a simple job description, that no human can be adequately prepared to deal with the psychological aftermath of killing another, then we have to face the conclusion. The conclusion that as long as we ask our soldiers and agents to kill, we have to be prepared to do so as well. So all I'm doing is asking you to step up. Not for your country or anything like that. It's bigger than that. You need to step up in the name of human decency. You need to share some of the pain. You need to understand what it means to be haunted by the faces of the men and women you've killed, to wake up at night screaming and sweating and begging for forgiveness. Stop asking other people to go through this on their own. Step up and take on some of that burden yourself."

I shook my head. Damn, she was a good salesperson.

Mo looked at me. She laughed. "How's that for some meaning?"

I looked out of the window as the green road signs whipped by. I didn't speak. I just nodded.

"Now you know why it's not going to be just one job? It can't be. This is your life now."

I nodded again. I didn't really think it would be just one job. I knew I wasn't getting out of this without actually killing someone. Or getting out of it at all. The mental shift Mo had talked about was already happening. I had already made two separate decisions to kill. I was in it now. Mo was right: the irrational, emotional, intuitive part of me had already chosen a path. I'm not sure when it happened—perhaps at night in the hotel room; perhaps on the treadmill the previous evening; maybe in the men's room at the office yesterday; or maybe the second Mo had shown me the picture.

Still, I needed to appease the intellectual part of my psyche. So I argued some more.

"That's a noble speech. You almost make it sound like what we're doing is the right thing. But it's not. How can it be? If we try and analyze what you just said, then your argument breaks down."

Mo smiled and nodded. "Go on."

"You've heard of Immanuel Kant?"

Mo frowned at me. "I think so. German philosopher?"

I nodded. "He had a test for whether an action is ethical or not. He called it the categorical imperative."

Mo lit a cigarette. She kept her eyes on the road and gestured for me to continue.

"Kant said that you should imagine a world in which everyone else does what you're about to do. If that imaginary world is reasonable and sustainable, then the action is ethically correct."

Mo shook her head. "I see where you're taking this. No, I don't think a world full of vigilante killers would be a reasonable or moral or acceptable place. It would be a sick, savage place with even more misery and injustice than there is now."

"Exactly." I sat back and crossed my arms. I felt smug.

"Don't look so smug. The reason I said that is because there's no way everyone else could have access to the resources we have for validating our targets."

"But I thought you said we were on our own. Two-person cells where the Alpha unit is connected to one other unit. The Gamma unit, or some shit like that."

"Omega."

"Whatever. So what validation does this super-top-secret Omega person do?"

"It depends. It's a two-way communication. My Omega gives me an initial reading on where to look. Or, if we identify potential targets, I pass that information back up. Then it gets passed through the relevant areas of the Network for validation."

"So what's the validation?"

"Three things. Number one is whether there is consensus amongst the Omega network as to whether the evidence is strong enough to ascertain guilt. Number two is that the group is reasonably sure that legal action would be useless." Mo went quiet.

"And number three?"

"Number three is that we're reasonably sure our targets are not already slated for elimination by a government agency. And please don't ask me how we determine that."

I sighed. My head hurt. "So what now?"

"Well, I need you at Walker-Midland for another week or so to finish up this scoping work. Then I'm moving you to another consulting project. An insurance company. There's an opening on a project with the investment management division of a large mutual insurance company outside Chicago. All-American State Insurance is the company. I need you to get in there and follow the float."

"What does that mean?"

"Figure it out. You're a consultant, after all. I've already told the client I'll be sending out a float allocation expert next week. So you have a week to become an expert."

I swallowed hard. But I wasn't surprised. This was what we did. We became experts. Once we figured out what kind of consultant a client needed, we did what it took to become that consultant. We read articles, studied industry reports, browsed chat forums where experts discussed their work, interviewed the handful of other consultants that actually were industry experts. We reinvented ourselves, driven by the fear of being found out and the guilt of the subtle deception. We often ended up justifying our billing rates simply because we were too paranoid about not being worthy of the obscene invoices that we delivered to clients.

"Okay," I said. "Sounds good."

Mo nodded. "Another thing."

"What?"

"You'll be on your own for the first couple of weeks. I need to finish up here at Walker-Midland before I can spend any time with you in Illinois."

"Okay. So what do I do in the meantime?"
"Do your real job, of course: be a consultant."
"You know what I mean. The other . . . job."
"Lie low until I get there. For now, just follow the float."

9

The float, it turned out, is a common insurance term. Float is where an insurance company makes its money. An insurer takes in money when we pay our premiums, and it gives out money when it has to pay claims. Competition between insurers is so strong that insurance prices usually settle at levels where they balance the money taken in as premiums with the money expected to be paid out as claims. In other words, an insurer can't expect to charge a whole lot more in premiums than it expects to pay out over the long term. If it did, some other insurance company would have room to undercut its price and drive them out of business.

So the real profit for All-American State Insurance came from the float. The float is the pile of money that an insurer holds on to until it has to pay it out in claims. As we all know, we pay premiums now in order to insure ourselves against future events. This means there is a time lag between when insurers take money in and when they have to pay it out. And, as they say, time is money. The insurers take this money and invest it—in stocks, bonds, and everything in between. And when you're talking about billions of dollars of float over several years, the interest and other gains add up quite well.

My job was to follow the float. See what All-American was

investing in. Figure out what stank—from a legal standpoint for my consulting assignment, and from a moral standpoint for my other assignment.

The consulting piece was actually pretty mundane. I was part of a small consulting team that had been asked to study the current allocation of float money and make sure it was in line with government regulations. Not an actual audit, but kind of a check to make sure things were in line for when the real auditors came in.

The government regulations were pretty straightforward. In order to prevent an insurance company from making too many risky bets and perhaps not having enough cash to pay claims, the government simply said that a certain percentage of the float needs to be in cash, some needs to be in high-rated government bonds, and the rest can be in more risky securities like corporate bonds, stocks, real estate, hedge funds, and so on.

The first week was nice. Really nice. The other consultants were a lot of fun—all junior consultants from the Chicago office. Fresh-faced and super-enthusiastic. Reminded me of the old days when I was a motivated and ambitious young consultant just out of business school and ready to climb the ladder and rule the world. The days before I started down the transformative path to self-righteous murderer.

Our client contact was the chief investment officer, Mr. Wesley. He was a nervous sort, which is not necessarily a bad thing for a chief investment officer. You kind of want the guy managing the money to lie awake at night worrying about whether his investment decisions were the right ones. I liked Mr. Wesley. He was a bit jumpy, but he also made these little jokes. The jokes weren't funny, but he giggled when he made them, and it's hard not to smile when you see someone else break out into a genuine smile. I hoped I wouldn't have to kill Mr. Wesley.

The first week passed quickly and with no unpleasantness. We were in a distant suburb of Chicago, and all the consultants went out to Dave & Buster's every night after work. We'd eat bar food and drink beer and play pool. Then we'd drive the quarter-mile to our hotel and have another couple of drinks at the lobby bar before stumbling into the elevators. Life was good.

Then, on the Tuesday of the second week, Mo called, and I remembered that life wasn't good. Life sucked. Life was hard. And it was going to get harder.

"How's it going, Frank?"

"Okay."

"You turn up anything?"

"Anything on what? The asset allocation study? It's going well. These kids from the Chicago office are bright as hell. We're going to be done on time and under budget. A couple more weeks, I think."

I heard Mo sigh over the phone. "Maybe we need to come up with a way to distinguish between what you're doing for C&C and what you're doing for our assignment."

"You mean like a code word?"

"Yes. But something simple. Something that no one would notice if they overheard us."

"Okay. Why don't we just call it a mission?"

"I don't know. That sounds a bit too dramatic."

"Well, it is dramatic. We're killing people." I whispered the last sentence.

"Don't ever say that over the phone. I can't believe I need to tell you this."

"Shit. Sorry."

"Anyway. It just sounds too weird to talk about a mission. People will wonder if they overhear us. So let's keep it generic—when I'm talking about your consulting work for C&C, I'll call it the job. And the other work will be the assignment."

"That's it? Job versus assignment? How crafty." I thought about it for a second. "Doesn't it sound better the other way round? So the job is, you know, the *job*."

Mo sighed again. "No. We stick with what I said."

"What's the big deal? Let's just flip it."

"No. This is better. C&C pays you a salary, so what you do as a consultant is your job. As for the other work, well, I assign that to you. So it's your assignment. Simple as that."

Now I sighed. "Fine. Whatever."

"Sorry. The Network is kind of like the consulting world: not as glamorous once you're inside."

"No shit. Anyway, so as far as my *assignment* goes, I don't have anything. I don't even know what to look for."

"I have a little more information. See if these guys are investing any of their float in one or more of these hedge funds: Charter Capital, The NationFirst Fund, or Macro-Research LLC."

"Okay." I scribbled down the names. "I should be able to do that in the next few minutes. I'll call you back."

I hung up and logged on to the read-only reporting section of the investment database. We had been given guest credentials to look at where the company was investing its float. I wasn't worried about being called out for looking up this information. We were running hundreds of reports and analyses using the same user ID. What I was doing wasn't unusual.

Most hedge funds would fall under the riskier classes of investments: equities and alternative investments. I checked under both those sections, but turned up nothing. I shrugged and called Mo back.

"Did you check the other investment categories?" she snapped. "Check the entire universe of their investment portfolios. It has to be in there somewhere."

I protested. I don't like to be told I'm wrong. "Hedge funds wouldn't be under any other category. That's the whole point of the classification system. All-American isn't investing in these hedge funds. Your lead is wrong."

"It's not a lead. It's concrete information. We know they are investing in these funds. I need you to figure out which investment professionals made these decisions. And to do that, you need to find the records of those investments."

"Fine. I'll look through the other categories and see what I can find out." I leaned back on the office chair and rubbed my forehead. I thought about Mr. Wesley, and I felt scared and sad. "What's the big deal with these funds, anyway?"

"I'll make that part of your assignment. You figure out what the big deal about these funds is and who's responsible for pumping All-American's money into them." Mo paused. "And then wrap up your assignment with those people."

"Okay. But you'll be coming out here, right? I mean, you'll be here for the, er, final presentation." I felt ridiculous using such lame metaphors.

"Nope. Sorry. I have to fly out to the West Coast to help sell a big new project. This one's all you."

"Are you kidding?"

"Of course I'm not kidding. Call me when you get the names of the people responsible. I'll have them checked out, and then I'll give you the final go-ahead."

The air conditioning was churning out freezing air, but perspiration gushed from my forehead. I ran my hand across my brow and drops fell onto my notepad and all over the desk. Then I felt a chill as the sweat rapidly evaporated from my skin. I sneezed just as the realization hit me. Mo never planned to be out here. This was my first solo assignment. My Assignment Zero.

10

I didn't join the other consultants at Dave & Buster's that evening. I just didn't feel up to it. The past week had been relaxing and fun—not terms I'd normally use to describe the first week of a consulting job. When you first get to a project, you're usually stressed out about impressing your clients and proving to them why your billing rate is so high. But I hadn't been worried about impressing anyone. Maybe that's why my client, Wesley, had been so impressed. Go figure.

Anyway, that fun week was over. It was different now. Speaking with Mo had reminded me that my job wasn't my only job. I also had an assignment. My Assignment Zero.

And so I spent the evening doing research for the assignment. The three funds Mo had named were relatively easy to find. I had missed them earlier because I had only looked under the equity and alternative investments categories. It turned out they were included under the debt category. And not corporate debt, but sovereign debt. In other words, the three funds—Charter, NationFirst, and MacroResearch—didn't invest in companies. They invested in countries.

Still, I didn't see what the big deal was. Securities of foreign countries were fine investments. Insurance companies put their float in those securities all the time. Sure, All-American could have bought directly from the central banks of each country and saved the management fee that these hedge funds were undoubtedly charging. Still, the funds were probably investing in a basket of various nations' debt that was optimized based on their own proprietary research and models. That's what hedge funds do. No big deal.

I browsed to the websites of the hedge funds, but there wasn't much to look at—just login screens for current investors and phone numbers for institutional sales. Fairly standard for hedge fund websites. Many hedge funds are run by a couple of people, and they don't waste time building fancy web pages. I knew enough about the hedge fund business to know that neither the size of the fund nor the graphics on its website had any correlation to how well the fund performed. So, as I said, I didn't see what the big deal was.

But like any good dog that's been asked to do something, I now had an assignment, and I wanted to do well. Mo *had* said I'd have to figure this one out. Which meant she knew that something was up with these funds, and she wanted to see if I could discern that myself. She was training me. Or just testing me again. Probably both.

I sighed and picked up the desk phone. I was about to dial the number for Charter Capital, but then realized it would show up on their caller ID as an All-American corporate number. So I picked up my cell phone, typed in that code that lets you block your number from caller ID systems, and then dialed Charter Capital. I was half expecting a gruff man with a strange accent to answer, and was relieved when I heard a pleasant, Midwestern sounding woman.

"Charter Capital Institutional Sales. What extension, please?"

"Um, hi. I'm looking for some information on your fund."

"Thank you for calling. What company do you represent?"

"None. I'm a private investor."

"I'm sorry, sir. We don't take on individual clients. Our funds are only open to institutional investors."

"It's okay. I'm a qualified investor." I knew that hedge funds were only allowed to accept individuals who met certain qualifications: a net income or net worth above a certain level.

"I'm sorry, sir. Have a nice day. Thank you for calling Charter Capital." She hung up.

I cursed at the phone. Then I tried the next fund—Nation-First—and got an almost identical response. I cursed again, and went downstairs to have a smoke. I watched the sun go down over the strip malls in the distance and breathed deeply as the nicotine did its job. By the time I was done with the smoke, I had decided what to do next. Yes, I would lie.

I went to my laptop and pulled up a domain purchasing site. After checking out the available names, I settled on *smokeyhillscapital.com*. It sounded generic enough for a fund-of-funds—a hedge fund that invests in other hedge funds instead of directly purchasing securities. The site cost $7.99 for a year's worth of hosting space. In a few minutes I had put up a generic page using one of the web hosting provider's HTML templates. I set up an e-mail address with the Smokey Hills domain name. All of this took less than fifteen minutes. I love capitalism.

I dialed the number for the third fund on my list.

"MacroResearch. May I help you?" What was it with these Midwestern women answering phones? I was in the Midwest, and it was late here, so their offices must be on the West Coast for them to still be open.

"Yes. I'm a managing director at Smokey Hills Capital. We're a three hundred million dollar fund-of-funds that's just starting out."

"How may I help you?"

"I'm interested in learning more about your fund. Is there a prospectus or some other literature that you can send me?"

"I can connect you to our head of institutional sales. Whom may I say is calling?"

"Um. John Smith."

"Okay, Mr. Smith. Before I transfer you, may I ask how you heard about us?"

I was flustered. I wasn't prepared for these questions. You'd think as a consultant I'd be a better bullshitter, but no. That's probably why I was just a mediocre consultant.

"From a friend who invests with MacroResearch."

"A friend? Sir, we don't have any individual investors. Do you mean someone who invests on behalf of an institution?"

"Yes, of course that's what I meant."

"May I have the name of the institution?"

Now I was stuck. Could I lie about this? I had no idea how many clients MacroResearch had. If the number was in the hundreds, I might get away with making up a company name. But this woman seemed to know at least some details. And her voice was already getting a bit stern.

"All-American State Insurance."

"Thank you, sir. Hold on for just a moment."

"Thanks."

After holding on for almost five minutes, I was getting impatient. What, were they trying to trace my call? And so what if they did? Even if they had a way to get around the caller ID block, all they'd get would be a phone number with a New York mobile area code. My number was unlisted, and relatively new. They wouldn't find out anything about me. After another couple of minutes I checked my newly purchased website logs and noticed that the site had been visited in the last few minutes. So they had checked out my website. Big deal. That's why I set up the damn thing.

Finally a man's voice came through over the phone. He sounded vaguely British, but who knows these days.

"Mr. Smith? Good evening. I understand you were referred to us by Mr. Wesley at All-American State?"

I gulped. "Well, no. I wouldn't say it was a referral. And I don't know a Mr. Wesley. I have a friend from b-school who works in their investment management department. He told me about you guys. He also asked me not to mention his name. Something about confidentiality. You know how it is with these big companies."

There was a pause and then the man continued. "Er, yes. Of course. No problem. How can I help?"

"Well, our fund-of-funds is just starting up. We have almost three hundred million in capital, and we're researching placement opportunities."

"I see. Well, we're not really open to new investors right now. Why don't you give me your number and I'll make sure someone calls you if something does open up."

"Sure. But in the meantime, would you be able to tell me a bit about your fund? Or perhaps there's a prospectus or literature that talks about your investment strategy?"

"I'm sorry, Mr. Smith. You're in the industry, so you can understand that the details of our strategies are proprietary. All I can tell you is that we invest solely in sovereign debt, and we actively rebalance our portfolios based on our own research as to the relative creditworthiness of our target nations."

"Yeah, I get it. You guys are trading in and out of emerging market debt? Or other high-yield stuff—Russia, Greece?" I knew that hedge fund people were secretive, but it was worth a shot to see if he'd talk. Some people just can't help talking about themselves and what they do. Unfortunately, this guy wasn't one of them.

"Good day, Mr. Smith." He hung up.

I sighed and shook my head. John Smith. Could I not have come up with something better than that? Now what would I do? I knew nothing. And I'd already used up any potential sources of information by not being prepared when I spoke to them. I leaned back in the cushioned office chair. Now what?

Wesley. The guy from MacroResearch had asked me if I knew Wesley. He had mentioned Wesley. So he knew Wesley by name, if not face. Wasn't that meaningful?

I shrugged. Perhaps, but only if I could figure out the problem with these funds. They seemed to be as legit as any other fund. The secrecy wasn't unusual. The people answering the phones didn't sound like stereotypical Jihadis, although I know there's no such thing as a stereotypical Jihadi these days.

Then it hit me.

I leaned forward and typed a few words into my web browser. I looked at the list of countries that came up. Two were at the top of the list. I grabbed my cell phone and dialed Mo's number.

"Hey, Mo. I've figured it out."

"I don't have much time now, Frank. Go ahead."

"The funds are buying the debt of rogue states."

"Go on."

"Countries like Iran and Sudan. They've figured out how to get around the US sanctions on these countries, and are buying the treasuries that these nations are issuing. Because of the sanctions, these countries are starved for capital, and so they're happy to pay very high rates to anyone willing to lend them money. So that's it. These hedge funds are essentially facilitating loans for Iran and Sudan and other blacklisted regimes via the All-American State Insurance Company."

"Good job, Frank. How did you get to that answer?"

I smiled. I wanted to say that she just gave me the answer. I was only guessing. I didn't really know. But I didn't say that. "A gentleman never reveals his secrets."

"Um, I don't think that's a thing."

"Sure it is."

"Whatever. Anyway, you're right. These three funds are channeling billions of dollars a year into Iran, Sudan, and several other countries that aren't even official nations. And since hedge funds don't have to reveal their strategies or investments to even their clients, there's no easy way to figure it out. Or even a legal way to stop it, really, since these funds have complex international corporate structures that are more or less legit. But legal or not, it's wrong."

I nodded. "I guess it is a bit sick that when an American pays her home insurance premium, part of it is passed on as a loan to an authoritarian regime which can use it to buy weapons or attack US interests. And since so many of All-American's customers are from army families, in some way parents could be unwittingly lending money to people that are trying to kill their kids."

"Yes. And the insurance company profits from the interest paid on the loan."

"But the hedge fund gets a management fee for investing the money for the insurance company. They're essentially setting up the transaction. They're the bad guys, not All-American. You just said that All-American probably doesn't even know where the money is going." I spoke fast as I thought of Mr. Wesley. No way did he deserve to get killed. "For all they know, MacroResearch and the others are just buying the treasury securities issued by friendly European or Asian countries."

Mo was quiet for a few moments. Then she spoke. "Do you have the names of the All-American managers that made the calls to invest in these funds?"

I thought for a second. "Mo, it doesn't matter. They aren't the ones responsible."

"I asked you a question. I didn't ask for your opinion."

I bit my lip hard. "Wesley."

"Then you know what to do. So do it."

"No way in hell."

"This isn't a choice. I'm not sure if you're suddenly feeling safer because you're in Illinois and I'm in California, but remember: your only choice is between this and death row in Texas."

"But I thought you were going to check it out first and only then give me the final go-ahead." I was trying to delay the deed.

"Consider this conversation the go-ahead."

"So you already knew it was Wesley? Or are you just not going to get him checked out through your super-secret assassin information network?" I was pissed.

"Just get it done, Frank. You have two days before the police break down your door and hand you a one-way ticket to Texas. So just get it done."

11

I felt like kicking myself for not recording the end of that conversation. I would've had her, or at least had something on her. She didn't quite say she had killed Simone, but she came close. Note to self: record every future conversation with Mo.

But wait, I could do that now, couldn't I? Just call her back and get her to say something incriminating. I scrambled to find a mobile phone app that allowed me to record the conversation to a digital file. I tested it out, and then I called Mo back.

"What is it, Frank? Done already?"

"No. I won't do it."

"Okay."

"What do you mean, 'okay'?"

"I mean okay. Don't do it. Thanks for letting me know."

"So that's it?"

"That's it. I mean, you still have the two days, but that's it for now."

Dammit. She was smarter than me. I didn't say another word. I just hung up. I slammed shut the lid of my laptop and shoved it into my bag. Then I left and went back to the hotel and ordered the salmon. I ate and watched a little TV.

Finally, I grabbed the hotel stationery and began to make a list of options.

1—Stab
2—Strangle
3—Push from height
4—Car accident
5—Club

I stared at the surreal list I had just written out. I was glad it was on paper. Anything that takes electronic form these days is bound to live forever. This would be a tough blog-post to explain.

Accident sounded good, and since you don't hear of many stabbing or clubbing accidents, car accident was the best option. It also seemed the most hands-off. Of course, I didn't know shit about car engines or brake lines or any of that stuff. I'd lived in Manhattan for over a decade now. All I knew about cars was how to hail one on Amsterdam Avenue. Sure, I had driven rentals for years when on out-of-town jobs, but those years of business travel had only taught me how to call the rental car office and ask for a new car to be driven out to me because mine seemed to have a flat.

I could look up some information on the web, but I didn't want my browsing history filled with sites describing how to cut someone's brake lines or loosen the axle or whatever else you do to cause a fatal car crash.

Clubbing was out. No way I was smashing poor Mr. Wesley's head with a baseball bat or something. Plus, it'd be loud and messy.

Strangling would mean no blood, but that's cold. Staring into someone's eyes as you squeeze the life out of him? Nope, I wasn't at that level of psycho just yet.

Pushing from a height sounded easy. Everyone knows that when you fall from a tall building or something, you're dead before you hit the ground. Of course, I'm not sure exactly how we all know that—the only people who could confirm that are dead, right? I thought about All-American's office building. No, that wouldn't work. It was a classic suburban office building, wider than it was tall. All-American had only four floors. That's vegetable height, meaning you're more likely to be paralyzed than killed. And paralyzed people can still identify the bastard that pushed them. No, that wouldn't work. Besides, the windows didn't open, and there was no roof. Same thing with my hotel.

So we were back to the knife. I'd have to stab Wesley. But it would still be noisy and messy. Unless I drugged him first. That was it—knock him out somehow, and then just stab him.

That made me think of another option: poison. If I could drug him, then I could poison him, right? But with what? Rat poison? Liquid Plumber? Sleeping pills? I didn't want to look up poisons on the web, either.

Goddamn it. You'd think Mo would have sent me to a training session or something. Maybe I should just ask her, I thought. It was still early in California. I turned on my recording application and called.

"Hey."

"Yes, Frank."

"How should I kill him?"

"Excuse me?"

"You heard me. How should I murder Wesley?"

"That's an insane question. Call me when you're sober."

She hung up. I shouted in frustration. I wasn't sure before, but I was now: she had guessed I was recording the conversations, which meant I'd lost access to the only person who could give me useful advice. I really was on my own now.

I smoked another cigarette in my non-smoking room.

Then I slipped under the covers, turned off the light, and let my subconscious think about how I would commit my first murder.

12

I woke up with the answer. Somehow it made me feel at peace, and I bounced out of bed and got ready for work. I drank my skim latte and checked the morning's e-mails with a lightness that I hadn't experienced in what seemed like a long time now. I was at the office before nine.

"Good morning, Frank. How're you today?"

I swiveled my chair around and looked up. It was Wesley. "Morning, Mr. Wesley."

Wesley smiled. "I've told you guys to call me Tim. You consultants are so formal. I guess that's partly why your rates are so high." He seemed to think he had made a joke, and he laughed with glee.

I stared at him. I should kill him just for that. I smiled and shook my head. I really was a monster.

Wesley continued. "What if I called you Mr. Stein? Or Mr. Frank Stein." He paused. "Hey. Oh my god, I just got it—Frank Stein! Tell me you have a middle initial. Is it—"

"No. I don't have a middle initial." I smiled and made it a point to enunciate the next word. "Tim." I looked him in the eye. This joker was going down.

"Sorry, you must get that a lot," said Wesley. "But it is funny. Especially for a consultant to have that name."

I sighed. "You know, Mary Shelley's monster actually didn't have a name."

"Oh my, the monster can read!" Wesley made some ridiculous gestures with his hands and then danced off to his office.

I shook my head and almost smiled. Thanks for making this easier on me, Wesley, I thought.

I wasn't going to make my move until about eleven. At around ten I hit the restroom and then scoped out the area. First I took a stroll down the hall and located the one fire alarm that wasn't covered by a camera. Then I took the stairs down to have a smoke, double-checking that there were no cameras in the actual stairwells, and taking special note of the unusual height and steepness of each set of steps. I was back at my desk by ten-thirty, and then I just sat and waited.

I thought back to the fire drill that we had all been forced to participate in during my first week at All-American. I had noticed that Wesley was the fire marshal for the entire wing. I had also noticed that he had emerged from the stairs almost fifteen minutes after the last person had been evacuated. Part of his duties must have been to check that no one was still up there. These memories had been buzzing in my head when I woke up, and it had all come together in a neat little plan involving option three: PUSH FROM HEIGHT.

I figured that even if falling down the first flight of stairs didn't kill Wesley, it would at least immobilize him. Then I could just roll him down the next set. If that didn't work either, I'd have to hit his head against the edge of a step a few times to finish it. That last thought make me feel weak, but I told myself it wouldn't come to that. Regardless, it would look like an accident. All I had to do was make sure I was the last one into the stairwell. I was also counting on the fact that Wesley wouldn't take the full fifteen minutes to search the floor before heading for the stairs. After all, this was a real alarm, so the fire department would get there pretty quickly. Hopefully the timing would work and the firemen wouldn't walk in on me bashing poor Wesley's head against the second floor landing or something. I gulped and took a deep breath. Think positive, I told myself.

I looked at my computer screen and saw that it was almost time. Eleven in the morning is the one time of the day when almost everyone is actually sitting at his or her desk. It's that wonderfully productive time when the morning coffee has already worked its way through the system and lunch is just far enough away that you're not already getting ready for it. It would be my best shot for pulling the fire alarm without anyone seeing me.

I walked back out into the hallway and looked around. There was no one. I wrapped a piece of toilet paper around my fingers and quickly walked to the fire alarm and yanked hard on it. At first there was nothing, and I froze. Then I heard the bells go off and those big lights along the hallways started to flash. I got back to the main work area just in time to see Wesley dash out of his office and start to direct people to the stairwell. I noticed my colleagues walking in my direction, and I turned and ducked into the men's room. The men's room was empty, which was good, because I immediately went to a stall and threw up all over the toilet seat.

I waited in the stall for what seemed like forever, but was only three minutes according to the clock on my cell phone. Everything was quiet, and I knew it was time. If Wesley was doing a check, then I couldn't let him catch me in the restroom. I had to get to the stairs first, and undetected.

After slowly pushing open the door and making sure I was still alone, I jogged to the stairwell. Yes, I was probably caught on film, but my actions were quite explainable. Not that anyone would ask—it would be a simple case of Wesley slipping and breaking his neck or whatever on the stairs.

When I got to the stairwell, I froze again. I was too close

now. Soon there would be no turning back. Once it started, it would have to be finished. I listened for sirens, and exhaled when I didn't hear any. I leaned up flat against the wall near the door and got ready. I didn't want to push too hard; just enough so that he fell. The more steps he hit, the better, right?

Now the door opened and I saw a hand on the door knob. It was Wesley. He stepped out into the landing without noticing me. Incredibly, he stood at the top of the stairs and checked his phone. It looked like he had been timing himself or something. I stepped forward and went up behind him.

And of course I stopped. I couldn't do it. Wesley didn't deserve to die. And I wasn't ready to kill. I sighed and then I cleared my throat.

Wesley shrieked and jumped up in the air. Then he cried out again as he lost his balance and tumbled down the stairs.

13

My mind performed decision-related calculations at record speed as I raced down the stairs after Wesley. He was bleeding from his nose and lip, but he seemed all right. I helped him to his feet, and we slowly made our way down to the landing between floors.

I'm not sure why I started questioning him, but I did. "Mr. Wesley, do you remember making investments in MacroResearch, Charter Capital, and NationFirst?"

"Sorry, what?" Wesley slurred as his lip bloated up.

"They invest in sovereign debt. Do you remember investing in these funds?"

"What? Why . . . why are you asking me this now?"

"Just want to keep you talking so you don't pass out before we make it downstairs. Come on, Mr. Wesley. I mean Tim. Answer the questions and don't look at the stairs. Lean on me." I stared at the long bumpy drop from the landing down to the third floor. I could still do it. I thought about what Mo had told me—there were people half my age committing murder on my behalf. Was I going to step up and take responsibility for my choices? All I had to do was let this guy drop. It was almost an obligation. Maybe my earlier hesitation had been a blessing in disguise. I had forgotten that it was important to let Wesley know why he was being killed.

He needed to know why the violence had tracked him down and entered his life, why it was ending his life.

"I don't know, Frank. We don't spend much time researching sovereign debt funds—those are usually the safer instruments. It's the stock and real estate and private equity funds that we worry about the most. Why, are we out of compliance on our allocation weighting? Did you find something in the reports?"

We were now on the second floor. Just one more flight of stairs. One last chance for me. I stopped at the top of the flight and took a deep breath. "Let's wait for a minute, Mr. Wesley. I'm tired. I don't want you to fall down the stairs again."

Wesley nodded. He looked pale, was breathing irregularly, and appeared to be close to passing out. It would be so easy now. I wouldn't even need to push. All I had to do was let go. I thought about death row in Texas, but that seemed so unreal, so far away. Too far away, in fact. No way I was killing Wesley.

I carefully took him down the last flight of stairs. He was almost unconscious now. I pushed open the door to the parking lot, and heard the sirens as I walked out into the sun. A few people saw me stagger out with Wesley almost on my back, and they ran up to us. They laid Wesley down on a patch of grass while I waved my arms to get an ambulance over to him.

The paramedics put Wesley on a stretcher. He was barely conscious, but managed a smile as they took him past me. As the ambulance door closed, Wesley pointed at me and spoke in a surprisingly loud voice.

"That man—Frank Stein. He saved my life. He's not a monster after all."

I smiled as I heard Wesley's silly laugh ring out from behind the red metal doors. No, I wasn't a monster yet. But I knew that soon I would be. It would only be a matter of time before I crossed that last line.

14

She was waiting for me in the hotel lobby when I got back that night.

"Mo? I thought you were in California."

"Well, I'm not." She smiled. "How are you, Frank?"

"Fine."

"Good." Mo was sitting on one of the cheap multicolored couches in the lobby. She pointed at the thinly cushioned armchair next to her. "Let's talk."

I sat down without making eye contact with Mo. I was scared, maybe even a bit guilty, like I had done something wrong. Good lord—guilty for *not* committing a murder.

"I flew in when I heard that Wesley was injured." Mo paused until I looked up at her. "Frank, did you try to kill him?"

I wasn't sure what to say.

"The truth, Frank."

How does she do that? I shook my head. "No. I couldn't do it. I waited for him at the top of the stairs. I was going to push him, but I chickened out."

Mo exhaled. "So Wesley getting injured was an accident?"

I nodded. "I startled him, and he fell."

Mo smiled. "Whew."

"What?"

"I was starting to think I had made a mistake with you."

I stared at her.

"Remember when I said there were two other reasons you were perfect for this work?" said Mo.

I thought back to the conversation in Texas about job satisfaction and the meaning of life. "Yes."

"This is the second reason."

"What is?"

"Your conscience. The fact that you have one."

I was quiet. I wasn't sure if it was conscience or cowardice that had stopped me from killing Wesley.

Mo continued. "Wesley didn't deserve to be killed. He had no clue where that money was going. And once he finds out, he will drop those funds from his list."

"How will he find out?"

"He'll get an anonymous but credible tip. You don't need to worry about it."

"So that's it for this assignment? What about those hedge funds?"

Mo shrugged. "They're still targets, but we don't have access to them at this point. Another cell will pick them up." She nodded. "Yes, so that's it for this assignment."

"So it was another test?"

Mo nodded. "You can call it that. Conscience is important in this work. We've had too many cases where an Alpha or Beta loses it and becomes an undiscerning killing machine. Remember, our members are driven, ambitious, highly-capable men and women. When they do something, they do it well. When they start learning something new, they are motivated to become really good at it really fast. And that works with killing, too, unfortunately."

I let out a short laugh. "So it's a good thing I chickened out?"

"You didn't chicken out. You made a call. Your gut told you that he didn't deserve to die, and you held back."

I shook my head. "Thanks for the vote of confidence, but

I made no such self-righteous call. I was scared, pure and simple. I even puked in the restroom before going out onto the stairs. The same fear would have stopped me from killing Miroslav or one of his cronies."

Mo leaned back on the couch and gave me a long stare. "Let me ask you this. As you were helping Wesley down the stairs, did you still think about killing him?"

I waited before answering. Then I spoke softly. "Yes."

"And why didn't you?"

"I asked him about those funds. He didn't seem to remember them. And I don't think he could have been lying—he was too woozy."

Now Mo leaned forward. She was smiling. "What if he had said that he knew about those funds? And what if he said that he didn't care where they were putting the money as long as they got their profit?"

I thought for a moment, but I didn't say anything.

"Would you have pushed him?"

"I don't know. Probably not."

"But it's possible."

I sighed. "Yes, it's possible."

"So then you did make a decision."

I nodded. She was right. I rubbed my eyes and yawned. "Fine, you win."

"I always win." Mo laughed. "Anyway, you didn't really believe I would send you on your first kill just like that, did you? Without any guidance or training or instructions? What kind of operation do you think we're running here?"

I was almost offended. "Actually, I think I had a pretty good plan. It would have looked like an accident."

"You'd be in jail right now, I guarantee it."

I thought about the security camera footage of me jogging from the bathroom to the stairs. I thought about emerging into the parking lot from the stairwell a good ten minutes after everyone else. I thought about Wesley's blood that had stained my poorly selected white shirt without my even noticing. She was right again.

Mo stood up. "Anyway, I'll let you get some sleep."

I nodded.

"Oh, and change your flight plans. I'll be here through the weekend, and you should stay too."

"Why, what's going on?"

Mo smiled. "We're going to do a little training session."

15

The rest of the week was uneventful. Wesley didn't come in, so I didn't have to deal with my own guilt by acting normal around someone I came so close to murdering. Mo didn't show up at the All-American offices at all, and I didn't hear from her until Friday evening.

She was waiting for me in the hotel lobby when I got back from work on Friday. She wore a dress—something I hadn't seen her in before. She smiled at me. "Hey. Drop your stuff off upstairs and meet me in the lot in ten minutes."

"Okay. What're we doing?" I was apprehensive. The last time I had met her in a parking lot the trip had ended with fourteen murders.

"Relax. We're just going to dinner." She smiled again. "I promise."

We went to an Olive Garden down the street. The food wasn't bad, and the conversation was surprisingly light and engaging for the entire dinner. Then we ordered some coffee, and when it came, Mo took on a serious expression.

"Three things for this weekend: contact, communication, and covertness. We call it the three Cs."

I rolled my eyes. "Sounds like the Network is run by management consultants."

Mo smiled. "I admit, those terms are a bit hokey. Here's what they translate to: how to kill; how and when to explain why you're killing; and how to get away with it."

I nodded. That sounded less hokey. I looked around at the families gorging themselves on Olive Garden's free salad and breadsticks. I somehow felt powerful and heroic, like I was sacrificing my own peace of mind so these people could continue to stay fat and happy.

Mo sipped her coffee and then continued. "Let's start with weapons. First, no guns. Too much crap to deal with—getting licenses, transporting them, leaving bullets and casings. Not to mention the noise."

"Okay. I think you mentioned that before. But explosives are obviously fair game."

Mo nodded. "Yes, but we don't use them much. They're also hard to transport, and they can be traced. The warehouse in Texas was a special situation. Besides, most Beta members don't handle explosives themselves."

"Fine with me." I smiled as the waitress refilled my cup.

Mo waited until the waitress left. "Obviously knives are good, and you'll need to learn how to use them."

"Like that folding knife you use? Or do I get to pick my own favorite one?"

Mo shook her head. "I wish I could say that you should find a kind of knife that suits you and then stick with it."

"No pun intended," I said.

Mo paused. She didn't get it.

"Sorry." I cleared my throat and nodded. "Right, we don't want to make it easy for someone to find a pattern connecting a bunch of unsolved murders." I thought for a moment. "But what does that mean? Should I buy a wide range of knives and then use them randomly?"

She laughed. "You really need to stop watching those ninja movies or whatever it is that you get these lame ideas from."

"Sorry."

"No, you won't have a set of state-of-the-art killing blades. Good lord." She laughed again. "You'll find it's best to use cheap knives that are easily available at either a hardware store or a kitchen supplies store. That way you can inconspicuously buy a new one in every town you visit. Cash always, of course."

"So I'll buy a new knife for every job?" I felt a chill run up and down my spine. What scared me was that it wasn't fear; it was excitement. Like a child being told he could buy a new toy every few weeks.

"Something like that." She nodded. "We can go through some knife techniques back at the hotel, but to the point about not leaving a pattern, you won't want to use a knife every time."

"Okay. That makes sense."

"You'll need to learn some free-hand techniques."

"You mean like how you smashed Miroslav's kneecap?"

Mo nodded. "Yes. I'll give you a rundown on the best spots to target for immobilization. Or worse. And then we can talk about ad-hoc weapons."

"Which are what?"

"Stuff that's not really designed to be a weapon, but which can be used to kill, depending on the situation."

"Like what?"

Mo shrugged. "Almost anything. Let's see . . . I've used umbrellas, knitting needles, mechanical pencils, the wire from a spiral notebook, stainless steel water bottles, tablecloths, forks, a tennis ball—please don't ask me about that—pillows, and . . ." She looked down at her feet. "The heel from one of the shoes I have on right now. I saw that in an old movie, and was curious to see if it could really work. Turns out it's not very efficient." She smiled at what must have been an indescribable expression on my face. Then she shook her head and commented on how she should probably get rid of those shoes, but she knew she looked hot in them.

I could feel my breathing quicken, and I felt flushed and panicky. I pushed the cup of coffee away from me and leaned back in my chair. After taking several deep breaths, I stood up and walked outside. Mo joined me a few minutes later.

"You okay?" she said.

"Of course not."

"Sorry. It'll get easier. Soon this won't appear surreal to you. Soon it'll be normal."

"That's what's making me sick," I said. "It's already starting to appear normal."

16

We spent that night holed up in Mo's hotel suite talking about things that two management consultants shouldn't have been talking about.

Mo started with knives. She laid out maybe thirty different blades on the glass coffee table—it looked like she had raided the entire knife section of some kitchen supply place. Later she told me that she had made several trips to a bunch of stores in the Chicagoland area. No patterns.

"Knives are obviously messy," she said. "So you only use them in situations where you can get cleaned up afterward. But if you follow the rule of buying cheap knives that you get rid of quick, they are virtually untraceable, so it's not a bad trade-off."

I nodded.

"Stand up," she said.

I did. Mo spent the next two hours showing me the most lethal strike zones for a knife attack. She told me what to expect in terms of blood spatter, victims' flail reactions, how long before unconsciousness, how soon to death. I was wired by the end of it.

"These strike zones are what you should aim for even when using an ad-hoc weapon," she said. "But remember, don't play favorites. You don't want the police to suddenly notice a string of murders committed by umbrella or lightbulb."

"Lightbulb?"

Mo shrugged. "Sometimes a situation gets messy and you need to improvise."

I gulped. I didn't like the images associated with an improvised murder.

"That's why it's good to know some immobilization techniques. Stand up again."

Mo showed me a series of moves that targeted the more sensitive parts of the body: throat, eyes, joints, ears, groin, chin, temple, and kidneys. She also gave me a run-down of certain holds, throws, punches, and kicks. I had taken a couple of months of mixed martial arts while in business school, so some of the moves were familiar. But I took them a lot more seriously now. After all, if I was going to do this, I would do it well. If I was going to become a killer, I'd damn well better be a good killer.

The next C was communication: guidelines for how and when to explain why you are killing your victim. Of course, the idea was that the victim should understand why he or she was being put down, especially since our targets usually hadn't had much exposure to physical violence. Most of them lived peaceful lives while other people suffered for them and because of them. So yes, it made sense for them to experience a bit of realization before the end.

"But there are limits to the risks we will take," said Mo. "Remember, each target has been vetted and validated, so if you're in a situation where stopping to explain your actions could compromise the kill, then screw it. Our first responsibility is to get rid of these people. We're doing them a favor by taking the time to point out their crimes. Don't ever forget that."

I nodded. "So if Wesley had really been a target, it would have been okay to have taken him out without a discussion about those hedge funds?"

"Yes." Mo was quiet for a bit. "But you'll have to see how

it goes. See what works best for you in the beginning. Maybe it'll be easier for you to try and explain your actions first. Or maybe it'll just be easier to first kill and only after you've gained some confidence take the time to pontificate. Again, our job is physical and practical first, and only then spiritual or moral."

"Okay," I said.

Mo smiled. "Which is not to say that the physical act has no spiritual or moral significance. You are sacrificing your own humanness for the sake of humanity. And that is profoundly significant."

"Okay," I said again as I stared at the row of knives on the table.

Mo yawned and sat back down on the red sofa. She lit a cigarette and looked up at me. "I think we're almost done for tonight. We'll go through most of this again tomorrow, and then again on Sunday. I'll also write down a practice routine for you to do on your own every morning and evening."

I nodded. "What about the third C?"

Mo laughed. "Covertness? We've covered some of it already with the attention to not creating a pattern and so on. Yeah, we'll talk about fingerprints and cleaning up the crime scenes and handling the bodies and some of that crap tomorrow. But the general rule is this: paranoia is king. When in doubt, follow up on the doubt. If you are worried that something might go wrong, then assume it will go wrong, and account for it. If something doesn't feel right, then get the hell out and save yourself for another day or another kill."

"Great. That rule pretty much guarantees that I'll never do anything."

Mo nodded. "You'll be nervous and hesitant at first. That's normal, and it happens because you haven't started to trust your own instincts. But soon you'll know how to distinguish between the normal adrenaline-fueled anxiety and the feeling that something is really off. Like what some people call 'jungle sense'—when you can tell what's hiding in the bushes even though you can't see or hear it."

I didn't say anything. I suddenly felt tired and drained, and I wanted to go home to my parents and hug my mum. I looked at Mo and thought about her daughter. I tried to imagine what it would be like to go to your garage and find your child with her head blown off.

And then I didn't feel like a baby anymore. I felt like a man who had made choices and who was about to step up and pay the price for those choices. And that price would be my sanity, freedom, and the ability to sleep through the night.

17

I was a new man after that weekend. I felt powerful and righteous, and at the same time disgusted with myself for feeling powerful and righteous. But I was also a management consultant who was being billed out at four hundred and sixty dollars an hour, and so I sucked it up and went in to work on Monday morning.

Mo called that afternoon. "Hey. I'm at the airport. Heading back to California to finish up that sales pitch."

"Okay. Anything for me to do here?"

"No. You should be wrapping up at All-American this week. I've already got a new project for you starting in ten days."

"New job? Or new assignment?"

Mo laughed. "Both. Along with a promotion."

I was confused. C&C had just promoted me to Senior Consultant, and I wasn't due another bump for at least a year. "Promotion to what?"

"Beta."

I wasn't sure if I should be happy. "But I thought you said that I would need to . . ."

"I think you're there. You've made the right choices so far, and I think you're ready." She paused. "You'll have to be. This next assignment is going to be the real thing, and it's going to be hard. I need you to be confident going in, so I'm promoting you."

"Okay. Well, thanks, I guess. What's the assignment? Or job. Whichever. I can't keep this stuff straight."

Mo laughed. "We're going to be advising a Japanese firm that wants to set up a motorcycle manufacturing facility in Wisconsin."

"Japanese?" I shivered as I envisioned chunks of my own flesh being hacked off by smiling sushi chefs.

"Don't worry. These aren't samurai we're talking about. Still, it's going to be a little tricky. I'll be with you all the way on this one."

"Okay. So what do I do?"

"Nothing for now. Think about what we learned this weekend."

"Okay."

"And have the C&C travel department book us into the Milwaukee Hilton for two weeks starting next Tuesday."

18

The Milwaukee Hilton was an old, once-grand building with superficial renovations. It was exactly what one might imagine the Milwaukee Hilton to be like, if that makes any sense: excessively ornate staircases and yellow chandeliers, old red carpeting, odd-shaped rooms, and lots of people with beards hanging around at the bar. I loved it.

Mo called to say she'd be flying in late that day, and since the Japanese company didn't really have any offices in Milwaukee yet, we were going to be working out of the local C&C branch in combination with some conference rooms at the Hilton. Our first client meeting wasn't until the next day, and so I stayed in my room and watched television.

Since I was technically working that day, I did a little thinking about the consulting job I was about to start. A Japanese company setting up a motorcycle factory in Milwaukee? I checked the web, and immediately felt like a fool for not remembering that Harley-Davidson was headquartered in Milwaukee. There had to be a connection. Maybe the same logic that results in similar businesses getting clustered together? Like New York's diamond or fashion districts? Did the Japanese firm think it would be easier to find skilled and experienced labor by starting up next door to Harley? Perhaps even a long-term plan for a merger or an acquisition? Or maybe figuring all this out was part of the reason we were being hired.

Okay, that was enough thinking about the consulting job. My head hurt. It was late afternoon already, and so I hit the gym before it got mobbed by the pre-dinner crowd. The workout didn't help my headache, so I ordered the salmon and some fruit when I got back to my room. Mo called me just as I was finishing.

"Hey," I said.

"I'm here. See you in the lobby in ten?"

Too many meetings with Mo in random hotel lobbies. But if you're a consultant who doesn't like hotel lobbies, then you're in the wrong freaking line of work. I sighed and told her I'd be down.

The lobby was packed. It looked like some kind of convention was going on. Lots of people with nametags and that nervous smile you get when you're surrounded by people you're supposed to be networking with. I looked for Mo, and saw her sitting at the lobby bar. I went up to her.

"What's up."

"Hi, Frank. You want a drink?"

"No."

"Good. Let's step outside and talk."

"Okay."

We walked outside. The sun had just set. We went around the building and stopped in a courtyard that had a couple of empty benches.

"So what's the deal?" I said.

Mo lit a cigarette. She offered me one and I took it.

"This one is going to be tricky," she said.

"You mentioned that. What does 'tricky' mean in the context of murder?"

"Stop using that word. It gives me the creeps."

"Like it doesn't give me the creeps? But that's what it is, right?"

"Technically, yes. But I still don't like it."

"Welcome to my world."

Mo looked at me as she blew a puff of smoke into the reddish blue Wisconsin dusk. "You know what your problem is?"

"What?"

"You still think you have a way out of this. Maybe it's because you haven't killed anyone on your own yet. Or maybe it's because you think you're going to somehow get through this without taking a life."

I was quiet. I stared up at the illuminated hotel building. I could see flashes of light as the convention-goers entered their rooms. I sighed as I thought about the delicious humdrum of their lives. If only I were a mid-level sales manager from South-Central Iowa with nothing to worry about but my ten local customers and my two chubby kids. But no, here I was, possibly living my last week as a somewhat normal human being. My last few days as a non-murderer.

Mo watched me for a few moments. "I don't care what you think of me, Frank. I know you must hate me. I know you're constantly thinking about a way to prove that you didn't kill Simone and that I'm setting you up. I know you tried to record our calls, and trust me, I would know if you were wearing a wire. I'm pretty good at this, and you're not going to find a way."

I turned and looked at her. She almost looked sad as she sat there alone on the concrete bench, her dark hair shining under the rising moon. But I could see that she wasn't kidding. She had made up her mind a long time ago. As grotesque and awful as her actions might have been, she had found a way to live with them. And I would have to do the same.

Mo shifted in her seat as she stubbed out the cigarette. The sadness and vulnerability I had seen in her for that instant was now gone. Now she was the stoic warrior-queen who had killed god-knows-how-many people. The woman who had taken my freedom from me, and the only one who could give me my life back. Like a demon slowly wears down its human target before possessing it, Mo was pushing me to the point where I gave in, the point where I said, "Yes, I am with you. I am committed. I have killed, and I will go on killing."

Mo smiled and shook her head. "You will have to kill. Whether it's me or someone else, your road to freedom passes through the life of another human being."

I flinched. I knew she was right. Whether I moved forwards or backwards, I would have to kill.

"Sorry," said Mo. "But I'm going to keep saying things like this. You need to be mentally prepared. You need to have gone through it in your mind so many times that when the moment comes there is no hesitation. In your mind, you will have already killed. The physical act will just be a technicality. It'll just be the paperwork."

And then just like that, the moment of self-pity passed for me. I didn't feel sorry for myself anymore. I knew I had a conscience. I knew that if I killed, it would change me. It would torment me in my sleep, invade my daydreams, poison my personal relationships. But that's why it would be a sacrifice. I had to remember, there were nineteen-year-old kids doing this for me. They had consciences too. They couldn't sleep either. They were no longer capable of stable and healthy emotional relationships. Those things weren't part of their job descriptions. I got paid more than they did. To hell with my selfish arrogance. Why should I take it for granted that I didn't need to live with the guilt and self-hatred that comes with taking a life?

I looked at Mo, and realized that she had been watching me. She had an odd smile on her face, a smile I didn't really want to interpret. It embarrassed me. It was something like admiration, and that made me uncomfortable. Nothing about me should be admirable. We weren't heroes or people to be admired, but she was right in that we weren't remorseless murderers either.

"Fine," I said. "I won't use that word anymore."

Mo smiled some more.

I continued. "We're killers, pure and simple. I don't want to glorify it by saying we're vigilantes or dramatize it by saying we're assassins. But I also don't want to degrade it by saying we're murderers. We're just killers. That's as neutral a word as I can think of right now."

Mo nodded. "I can live with that." She smiled. "If you can."

I laughed and shook my head. It was still unbelievable to me. Maybe it would stay that way even after I had killed. Maybe I would never really believe I was a killer.

"You ready to talk some specifics now?" said Mo.

"I'm ready." I sat next to Mo on the bench. The courtyard was still empty, the moon was now bright as hell, and the hotel building was glowing like an upright tubelight. "Tricky, you said. What's going to be tricky about it?"

"Well," said Mo. "Our targets are three Japanese men. They are also US citizens, but they don't spend much time here."

"They work for the firm that hired us?"

"Yes. But this isn't a project like the one at All-American, with a bunch of consultants working with a bunch of client-employees at a huge company. We're the only two consultants on the job, and these three men are the only clients we're going to be working with."

"Ah. That is tricky."

"Yes. So although we might get plenty of alone-time with these guys, we have to be careful."

"So it'll have to be an accident. Maybe explosives again?"

Mo shook her head. "Nope. Firstly, it'll take us a while to get access to untraceable explosives in Wisconsin—I obviously didn't fly here with the remaining plastique from Texas. And second, all our meetings are either going to be in the hotel or at the C&C offices, and there's no way we can pull off an explosion without risking other lives."

"Then what? Something more subtle? Like poison, maybe?"

Mo smiled. "No poison. No accidents. And nothing subtle. In fact, we'll have to go to the other extreme."

I stared at her. "Which is what?"

"It's going to have to be an obvious, over-the-top murder scenario with a clear set of identifiable suspects, but not enough evidence to actually convict anyone."

I laughed. "And you have a plan for this?"

Mo nodded. "Of course I have a plan."

19

Mo didn't tell me the plan that night. Instead, she told me our first meeting was to be at the C&C offices in downtown Milwaukee at eight the next morning. Good enough for me. I was in no hurry to learn Mo's definition of an over-the-top murder. Wasn't any murder over-the-top?

Before bed I went through the practice routine Mo had set for me—multiple repetitions of certain martial arts moves and knife strikes. She had also showed me how to detach the closet pole without breaking it, and I went through a number of attack moves with the metal pipe. I know this sounds laughable, and I actually did laugh a couple of times when I initially caught sight of myself in the mirror. But after a week of twice-daily sessions, the moves had started to become second nature to me, and I began to appreciate the sense of peace that the motions brought to my daily routine. In some way, I knew I was going to be good at this, and it calmed me down.

Mo drove us to the Milwaukee C&C office the next morning. We booked a conference room, and parked ourselves in it. Our three Japanese clients came in just as I finished booting up my computer and setting up the projector to show the PowerPoint slides that Mo had put together.

Mo had been right: these guys didn't look like samurai warriors. I gave them a warm smile, its genuineness drawing from my relief that our victims looked like they would be easy to put down. The oldest one, Mr. Takahashi, was about five-and-a-half feet tall and maybe three feet wide. Who says fish doesn't make you fat? The other two looked like they might be brothers, and I don't mean that in a racist way. In fact, it turned out they were indeed brothers—not twins, but fairly close in age and facial features. They went by Yoshi and Aki, and I immediately liked them. They were both just under six feet tall. Yoshi was thin as a twig. Aki was a bit more filled out; not fat, but he looked soft and squishy like a bean bag.

Their company, Chimura Industries, was a typical Japanese family-owned conglomerate, albeit a fraction of the size of Mitsui or Sumitomo. Most of Chimura's profit came from farm machinery and other motorized items used in rural Japan. Since rural space in Japan was limited and also shrinking, Chimura was looking to get into a different industry and also branch out internationally. And since Harley-Davidson was one of the most popular and successful brands in Japan, Takahashi and Yoshi and Aki had been charged with developing a plan to imitate Harley-Davidson's designs and production methods so that Chimura could produce similar motorcycles both in the US and Japan. Of course, the idea was that Chimura's versions would sell at less than half the price of a Harley.

This didn't seem particularly unreasonable to me. I knew that much of Harley-Davidson's high price-point came from a keen understanding of the psychology of its customer. After all, most Harleys aren't used as primary transportation vehicles—the reasons for buying one are more emotional and symbolic than practical. And you're always willing to pay a little more for something that makes you feel and look good. You were paying up for the privilege of riding a Harley-Davidson product.

I didn't have much to say or do in that first meeting. It was really just introductory, with Mo going through some slick PowerPoint slides about how C&C had worked with Harley-Davidson before and would bring deep knowledge of the industry to Chimura. I gave them stern professional looks to convey my seriousness and expertise as I clicked the mouse button to switch slides at Mo's command.

Takahashi, Yoshi, and Aki left just before lunch. We had agreed on an approach to the project and a schedule for the next two weeks. Mo and I were to prepare an initial report based on the expertise we could glean from C&C's insider knowledge of the motorcycle industry in general and Harley-Davidson in particular. Then we would discuss market-entry strategies for Chimura, and eventually summarize everything in a final report. The entire process would take two weeks, and C&C would be paid a total of ninety-three thousand dollars plus expenses. Of course, if Chimura liked our work, they might hire us for more detailed planning work. I was curious to see how the follow-on work would pan out once Takahashi, Yoshi, and Aki were murdered soon after delivery of the first report.

"So we're going to wait two weeks before doing this?"

"Of course," said Mo. "We have jobs, you know. If our clients disappear before the project is done, it's hard to collect our consulting fees."

"Of course," I said. I put on my serious professional look for a moment.

Mo laughed. "I like your client-face. It makes you look serious and professional, and well worth the four hundred bucks an hour these guys are paying for you."

"Four hundred and sixty, thank you very much."

"Well, excuse me." Mo smiled. "Come on, let's get some lunch."

We walked out into the sunny street. Downtown Milwaukee wasn't a bad spot. The river added a nice touch to the place, and there were small pockets of office-goers and tourists loitering near the waterfront. I smiled at an old Italian guy who was walking around shouting, "Pepperoni-Cannoli, Pepperoni-Cannoli!"

Mo called the old Italian guy over and ordered a stick of pepperoni and two cannolis. I ordered three sticks of pepperoni and a single cannoli. We sat on a white wall near the river's edge and stared at the murky water as we ate.

"So these guys don't look so tough," I said.

Mo crunched her cannoli. "This is a great cannoli."

I looked out at the river, and my gaze followed it down to where the wall ended and there was no barrier.

"You know, we could just go out drinking with these guys, hit them on their heads, and push them into the river," I said. "I'm sure people fall in all the time."

"I'm sure they do," said Mo. "Which is why there's probably someone patrolling the river around the time the bars close. Besides, there's no guarantee they'll actually drown, and there's almost no way we can knock three guys out without at least one of them seeing us."

I nodded. "Okay."

Mo finished her second cannoli and lit a cigarette. "I told you I have a plan."

"Yes, you did tell me that." I was annoyed that my idea had been dismissed so quickly.

"And so I do."

"Well, what is it? Or do I just keep guessing?"

Mo smiled as I got progressively more irritated. "I like the guessing game," she said. She blew a puff of smoke at my face and winked.

"Go to hell," I said, and then lit a cigarette of my own.

"All right, here it is. Quite simple, really. Next Friday, after we're done with the report, we're going to take Takahashi, Yoshi, and Aki out to dinner. I've already confirmed this with them, and I have reservations at the place."

"Okay. Go on."

"It's a place called Fifth Base. Quite an interesting joint—I've been there before. Most of it is a cross between a sports bar and a biker bar, but they also happen to serve gourmet food in the back. I'm talking lobster, swordfish, steak—you name it."

I nodded. "Sounds good. A bit of the Milwaukee scene plus high-end cuisine."

"Yes."

"So what's the plan? We're going to kill them in a restaurant? That's pretty over-the-top, I guess."

"No, you ass. We're not going to kill them in the restaurant."

"Then what?"

"We're going to set up the scenario at Fifth Base. You're going to start a fight with a group of guys."

"What group of guys?"

"I don't know yet. A group that's drinking. Some dudes who look like they could be capable of violence."

"So you want me to start a fight and hope these guys come over and beat our Japanese clients to death? Doesn't sound like a very good plan. How do I stop them from bashing *my* head in?"

Mo looked up at the sky. "Ya-Allah. You need to start thinking a couple of steps ahead. No, you want to get to a point where things get heated, but nothing violent actually happens."

"Okay, then what?"

"Then we leave and head back to the cars. Fifth Base has a rear parking lot that's quite secluded and usually empty—it's only used for the overflow when there's a ballgame."

"Okay."

Mo was quiet. She looked at me and smiled. "You finish the scenario now."

I thought about it. It was obvious now. "We kill them in the lot and then take off? Or we injure ourselves a bit and say we were all attacked by a bunch of drunk biker-thugs?"

Mo nodded. "That's about right. We can work through the details over the course of the next few days, but that's generally right."

I flicked my cigarette into the river. A young woman in jeans and a tie-dye gave me a look that would have killed me if looks could do that.

I turned back to Mo. "You know, with all this talk of death plans and cannolis and swordfish, I just realized something."

"What?"

"I don't even know what these guys have done. I mean, why are we killing them?"

20

"Yoshi and Aki are part of a group called the Japanese Young Patriots," said Mo.

We strolled along the Milwaukee River as we discussed the reasons why we'd be murdering three relative strangers who were trying to set up a business in America's heartland. I wanted it to seem out of place, but somehow it didn't.

"So what?" I said. "Japan is an independent democratic nation and one of our closest allies. I can't imagine we need to be worried about patriotic Japanese youth. I mean, come on—Japanese kids soak up American culture."

Mo nodded. "You're right, for the most part."

"So correct me." I lit another cigarette and nodded at a group of teenagers drinking beer at an outdoor table.

"You know our history with Japan, I assume?"

"You mean World War II?" I looked at her.

She nodded.

I smiled. "You're kidding, right?"

Mo shook her head. "That wasn't so long ago."

I laughed. "This is absurd. You're saying that Japan wants revenge for losing in the Pacific?"

"Not Japan per se, no. The Japanese government itself is staunchly pro-American."

"Then what? Some old timers that are still pissed about

Hiroshima and Nagasaki? We had no choice, you know. We would have sacrificed hundreds of thousands of our soldiers if we had to fight the Japanese one island at a time. So this group is just some faction of hardliners, like there must still be some old Nazi sentiments alive in Germany?" I thought for a moment. "Wait, but you said Japanese *Young* Patriots. So these are Japan's neo-Nazis?"

Mo smiled. "Not exactly. JYP is actually a peaceful group that is probably closer to something like the Young Democrats or Young Republicans in the US. Basically students and activists with mainstream political ambitions. No big deal at all."

"Then why are we about to butcher two of their members?" I was getting sick of Mo's roundabout explanations.

"Japan is a unique country. The people are a product of an island nation mentality combined with a historically powerful imperialist culture. I'm talking about thousands of years of military dominance in the region. Remember, some people argue that World War II actually started when Japan sailed up the Yangtze River to invade China in 1937."

"Okay. Get to it, Mo."

"This is important," said Mo. She stopped walking and sat down on a bench overlooking the river. I stood in front of the bench and looked out across the gently flowing water.

"Fine. Go on," I said.

"Anyway, the imperial culture of Japan runs so deep that after World War II, the people literally looked to the United States as their new ruler. General MacArthur, the American who oversaw Japan's transition to democracy after the war, was thought of as a king." Mo paused to light a cigarette. "So, in some way, Japan subconsciously believes itself to be a dominion of the United States."

"This is getting a bit heavy," I said.

Mo smiled. "Let me finish."

I nodded.

"And now that more young Japanese are studying their history, these subconscious beliefs are bubbling to the surface and manifesting themselves as feelings of inferiority and subjugation. The Japanese are used to being the dominant empire, and these needs are deeply ingrained in the country's psyche."

I shook my head. "We're psychoanalyzing an entire nation now?"

Mo took another drag on her cigarette and quietly watched the smoke hang and then dissipate in the hot Wisconsin afternoon. "My point is that now there's a growing faction of young Japanese men and women who sincerely believe that Japan must effect some kind of military victory over the United States. It's an idea that satisfies this old need for dominance."

"So it's revenge." I shrugged.

Mo shook her head and sighed. "No. It's deeper and more complicated than that."

I was quiet. Some of this was going way over my head. Not all of it though—there was something in Mo's conspiracy theory that rang true. Still, I was having a hard time connecting this abstract analysis with the very specific and practical act of killing two men in cold blood.

"So you're saying Yoshi and Aki are part of this fanatical youth faction that wants to go to war with the United States?" I said. "But, if what you say is true, there must be hundreds of people like them."

"Yoshi and Aki are two of a small group of people who are taking real and measurable steps towards creating a military infrastructure for this underground movement," said Mo. "Their work here is part of a larger scheme. A pretty ambitious scheme that, quite frankly, I don't think could ever work." She smiled and shook her head. "But regardless, we have to take it seriously, because no one else is."

"What's the scheme? They're going to start a biker gang that invades US cities on cheap Harley knock-offs? We already have gangs running most of our cities. Good luck to Yoshi and Aki. They wouldn't get past Ohio." I laughed.

Mo smiled. "You're not so far off base. They are looking for ways to begin stockpiling heavy military equipment in the United States."

I stared at her. "And this motorcycle company idea is going to be a cover for hiding military equipment that the Japanese underground youth will eventually leverage to launch an attack against the US? That's absurd."

Mo shrugged. "I know it sounds ridiculous, but that's their plan. This new company will eventually build heavy duty motorcycles as well as all-terrain-vehicles. Part of their plan would be to import manufacturing equipment from Japan."

"So they can smuggle in parts for military equipment by disguising it in shipments of random other parts and machines?"

"That's one aspect of the plan."

"What's the other?"

Mo shook her head. "Apparently, their US manufacturing facilities will contain basement areas dedicated to actually building tanks and other armored vehicles."

I laughed so loud that some people on the deck of a passing tourist boat looked up at us. "You are not being serious." I looked at Mo. She was serious.

"Look," I said. I had to wait for a minute so I could stop

laughing. "Even if this is true, then why not just hand over these so-called plans to the FBI or Homeland Security? They can watch for any signs of it and then bust it up the legal and nonviolent way."

Mo shook her head. "Even if our government takes this seriously, they will likely launch an investigation. Which might scare off Yoshi and Aki."

"Well, good. Then we won't have to kill them. And the USA will be safe from the angry Japanese kids." I shook my head and lit another cigarette.

"Frank, I promise you these guys are serious. This plan may sound like a joke to us, but these guys are not joking around. If they get scared off, they will find another way." Mo shook her head and got up from the bench. "No, we have a chance to take these guys out, and we have to do it. In fact, the longer we wait, the more likely it becomes that our government will get wind of their plans, and then these guys will disappear and we'll have missed our shot."

"Okay. But even if we do take them out, won't some other leader of this youth movement just step up?"

"Maybe, but they won't have the same resources at their command. Yoshi and Aki are part of the Chimura family—rogue members, but secretly so. With them gone, the movement will not be able to use the Chimura group of companies as a vehicle for their plans." Mo started walking back towards the office. She looked back at me and spoke over her shoulder. "Remember, people with far-fetched plans but a shitload of cash are more dangerous than those with great plans but no means to implement them."

I jogged to catch up with her. "Okay. But what about Takahashi? He certainly ain't no youth."

Mo laughed. "No, but he's in on it with Yoshi and Aki.

No doubt about it. All three have to go. We do it now, so our kids in uniform don't have to do it later and at greater risk to themselves and civilians."

I shrugged. "I guess it's fitting enough for potential enemies of the US to be beaten to death outside a sports bar in Milwaukee, Wisconsin."

"Yes," said Mo. "There's something poetic about that."

I nodded as I felt a blast of adrenaline race through my system. I didn't say another word as we walked for almost twenty minutes along the river. I was thinking about the next few days and how I would talk through PowerPoint presentations and financial models with the men I would be killing at the end of the week.

21

The rest of that week flew by. I worked with Mo in a small corner office at C&C's downtown building. I only saw our three clients once—they stopped by to meet with Mo. No PowerPoint needed, so I was left in the small office alone to figure out which sets of optimistic assumptions to plug into our ludicrous Excel financial models.

We didn't speak about our end-of-project plans at all. There was a lot of work to be done on the strategy report, and it was just the two of us working it. Mo was surprisingly hands-on for a partner, and she embarrassed me several times by pointing out errors with my revenue and profitability calculations. With everything else going on, I had forgotten how good a consultant Mo was, not to mention how focused you had to be to work with her. By Friday night, I was exhausted both mentally and physically.

I got back to the hotel and collapsed on the bed and lay there for what must have been close to an hour. After I blinked away the recurring images of spreadsheets and pie charts, I stood up and changed. I contemplated the gym, but instead simply went through my evening routine. I had found that to be almost as good as a workout, with the added benefit of the odd mental peace it gave me. What I had only suspected earlier was now clear to me: that feeling of tranquility was in fact confidence. I was learning to accept what I was becoming.

I slept well that night, which was good, because Mo called my cell at seven on Saturday morning.

"Good morning, Frank."

"Hey," I mumbled.

"Breakfast in ten?"

"How about fifteen?" I rolled over and reached for my cigarettes.

"Ten," said Mo. She hung up.

Twelve minutes later I was downstairs. I saw Mo sitting at a table in the hotel coffee shop that overlapped with the lobby. She was surrounded by a plate of fruit and a cup of coffee and a newspaper, and it looked like she had been there for a while.

"You're late," she said as she folded the paper and dropped it onto one of the three empty chairs near her.

"Not that late," I said. "Not late enough for you to have finished the newspaper and drunk your coffee and eaten breakfast already, if that's what you're implying."

Mo smiled. "Well, well, well. Aren't we in a perky mood this morning. Slept well?"

"Actually, yes."

Mo nodded. She smiled again.

"What?" I said, and smiled back at her. It had been a long hard week working in close quarters with Mo, and we had gotten to know each other pretty well. Not well in the sense that we talked about childhoods or personal lives. More like we were getting used to being around each other. I kind of liked it—and her. She was tough and demanding, but she also had a sense of fairness and straightforwardness that made you want to do well and please her. She was an excellent leader, and she must have been a wonderful mother.

I went to the breakfast buffet and filled up my plate with a small portion of the heavily buttered scrambled eggs, two Wisconsin sausage links, and a large bowl of fruit and oatmeal. I ate quickly and in silence, not in the least bit self-conscious about the fact that Mo was watching me shovel the food into my mouth. As I said, we had eaten every meal together for the past week now, and I pretty much expected her to be around at any given time.

Mo waited until I was done with everything but my coffee. "Okay," she said, "should we step outside for a smoke?"

I nodded and gulped down the rest of my coffee. We walked outside down to the end of the block facing the Milwaukee Convention Center, which was not being used that weekend. There were a surprising number of birds flapping about and chirping away, and it was only when I noticed how low the sun was that I remembered it wasn't even eight in the morning yet.

Mo lit both our cigarettes and then put on her sunglasses. "I think we're going to do separate cars this Friday."

"You mean you and I will drive to the restaurant separately?"

"No. I mean we'll tell Takahashi and Yoshi and Aki to meet us there. I checked with them, and they have a rental car that they've been sharing."

I shrugged. "Okay. That makes it easier for us, right? I mean, we won't have to fake any injuries to ourselves this way. We can just do the job and leave in our car and tell the police that we left before they did, end of matter."

Mo nodded. "Yes, that part is easier. We just need to make sure they park in the rear lot along with us."

"Right. So we need to meet beforehand and get them to follow us there. Shouldn't be a problem."

"No, I don't think so. They're staying at the Hyatt, which is pretty close to the C&C office." She dragged on her cigarette, took a look at the burning butt, and then dropped it into the gutter near the curb. "We'll just have to remember to have one of us step outside during dinner to move our car."

I looked at Mo. "I don't get it."

"It's going to be a messy scene. We can't afford to have our car dirtied or dented by accident."

I thought for a moment. "Oh, I see. Since they'll be following us into the lot, they'll probably park right next to us." I nodded and smiled. "Damn. That's what I call detailed planning."

Mo smiled. "Remember, paranoia is king."

I shook my head and looked at the ground. I would have to learn to think like this. This was almost more important than practicing my slasher moves in the hotel room.

"Don't worry," said Mo. "It'll come to you. Soon you'll be going over these situations from every angle as often as you breathe."

I nodded. My cigarette had burned halfway through the filter and it smelled awful. I threw it into the street and lit another. "You said messy. What are we going to use? Knives?"

"I'm not sure yet. It kind of depends on the group of guys we pick on at the bar."

"Yeah, I guess." I looked down the empty avenue. "Seems like our plan still depends on a random group of guys being there. And me being able to rile them up enough that other people notice."

Mo followed my gaze down the deserted street. "Yes. But there's a plan B."

I turned and looked at her. "Which is?"

Mo sighed. "If we can't pull off the scene in the bar, then you and I will have to stage a mugging in the lot. And then we'll use knives."

I felt cold even though the sun was moving higher and getting brighter. "Okay," I managed to say.

Mo looked at the ground. "I don't want to have to go to plan B, though. It'll be a lot more complicated."

"Because we'll actually have to rob them? Which means we might leave evidence on their clothes or on their wallets or watches or whatever?"

Mo nodded. "That, and also because the police will pay a hell of a lot more attention to something that looks like a pre-planned robbery-murder."

I paced on the sidewalk and then stopped and crossed my arms across my chest and nodded. "Whereas if they find these guys killed in what seems like a bar fight that ended in the parking lot, they're more likely to chalk it up to a one-time thing and give up on it if they don't find much evidence up-front."

"Exactly." Mo smiled. "But I think we'll be okay. What are the chances of a bar in Wisconsin being empty on a Friday night?"

22

The chances, it turned out, were zero. In fact, we wouldn't even have gotten a table if Mo hadn't made reservations in the dining area at the back of the bar. The bar itself was overflowing with people wearing everything from standard Harley leather to ballroom gowns. Wisconsin truly was the heartland of the melting pot.

The rear parking lot was almost empty, just as Mo had predicted. It hadn't been a problem getting Takahashi and gang to follow us and park in the farthest corner of the lot. They didn't question Mo's spot selection, but just in case, she made it a point to mention that she liked to park as far away as possible so she could walk a bit after a heavy meal. Takahashi seemed to love the idea, and praised her sharp consultant's mind. I realized that this is what we would tell the police if we were asked about parking in the rear overflow lot instead of up front like every other chunky diner.

Mo, being a partner at a consulting firm, got phone calls at every hour of every day, and when one came in just before the swordfish arrived, she took the opportunity to step outside and move the car. She winked at me when she came back inside. I smiled, and marveled at how smoothly things were going. Then I felt my stomach seize as I realized that I was up next.

I excused myself and stepped into the main bar area, ostensibly looking for the restrooms. The crowd had thinned out a bit as the diners had all been seated, and the bar area now only contained the serious drinkers. I scanned the room, trying to scope out a group of tough guys who wouldn't take kindly to a New York Jew talking a bit of smack on their home turf. I paused when I noticed a table in the back with five big guys who looked a bit like those Hells Angels dudes who killed that fan at the Altamont Rock Festival in 1969, but I wasn't sure if I could get them riled up without having it erupt into violence. I walked past them and entered the restroom.

As I stared at the urinal, I started to go over what we were about to do, and I began to question everything yet again. How could we justify taking three lives today? How could *I* justify it? After all, I hadn't seen any proof of these insane plans to build tanks in secret basements hidden beneath motorcycle manufacturing plants that didn't exist yet. And whatever evidence Mo could produce to convince me would also convince Homeland Security, right? After all, those agencies were paid to be paranoid and suspicious about this stuff, no matter how far-fetched and insane. Besides, these guys hadn't really done anything yet, had they? So we were going to bash their heads in for something they may or not have said or been serious about?

A crazy idea popped into my head as I zipped up. I nodded to myself, and felt a wave of relief, as if a fever had just broken. I felt elated as the plan unfolded in my mind. I knew there would be no time to get into another philosophical debate with Mo—not that I'd win it. I'd have to voice my opinion in action. I'd go along with her plan, but once we got out into the lot and Mo started the attack, I'd make sure that no one got hurt, and hopefully one of the Japanese men would get a chance to dial 911. Then, once we got arrested, my story about being blackmailed might actually hold up if Yoshi and gang testified that Mo tried to kill them and I stopped the attack.

Sure, I had come to like Mo a bit. Hell, I even understood what she was doing. To some degree I bought into it myself. But I knew I still had a chance to stop before I crossed that last line. I'd probably do some time for being involved in Miroslav's death, but I deserved that. I mopped my forehead with a towel and stared at myself in the mirror. I was ready.

As if on cue, the door swung open and one of the big biker dudes walked in. He wore a red bandana, a Harley racing jacket, and had one of those chains that linked his wallet and keys to his heavy leather belt. He looked like a mean redneck, and though I loathed homophobes, I knew it was a good guess that this sucker would not react well to being thought of as a homosexual. At first I considered just calling him a faggot or something, but that just didn't sit right with me. So I tried an alternative method of implying he was gay.

"How're you?" I smiled at him.

"Good," he said, and stood at the urinal.

"Nice jacket."

"Thank you."

"You ride?"

"Yup."

I gulped. "Um. You looking for a ride later?" I had no idea if gay men actually spoke like that, but I was betting this guy didn't either. As long as he got the message, and as long as it pissed him off.

The biker looked at me. I'm not sure which one of us was more surprised—he at being propositioned by a skinny Jewish guy in the men's room, or I at seeing his smile and the matching look in his eye.

"You're cute," he said, almost embarrassed, "but I'm seeing someone. And he's here with me tonight."

I raced out of the restroom, red as a beet. I wasn't sure whether to laugh or cry, and headed straight out the front door to suck on a cigarette. I shook as the nervous tension left me, and I had finished half my smoke before realizing that I was rocking back and forth on my heels and shaking my head and smiling with embarrassment. I looked around self-consciously, but no one seemed to be taking any notice. I relaxed and lit another cigarette just as two younger guys and a woman stepped outside to smoke. They nodded at me and stopped a few feet away to light up.

When I noticed they were talking about baseball, my ears pricked up. Sports is always a good reason to fight, and I knew that Mo had stowed a couple of baseball bats as well as a tire iron or two in the trunk along with the knives. But I was a football fan, and I didn't really follow baseball. I knew the Milwaukee team was called the Brewers and that they weren't very good, but I couldn't see these guys getting too worked up about me poking fun at a losing team.

As I listened closer, it turned out they were talking about softball. Apparently the woman played in a local league and they had all just come from a game. Now this sounded more promising—nothing riles up a bunch of guys like some asshole disrespecting the woman they're with. Call me old fashioned, but I knew it would rile me up if some stranger said something rude to a woman in my presence. So I took one last deep drag on my smoke and then walked up to the group.

"You play softball?" I asked the woman.

She nodded. "Yeah, just for fun."

I swallowed hard. "You a dyke then?"

"Excuse me?" The woman stared at me. The two guys froze.

I wanted to sink into the ground, but I went on. "Those bats must get used quite a bit after practice, if you know what I mean."

"You fuckin' serious, man?" said one of the two guys.

All three of them stayed calm. Maybe they were still in shock, or perhaps they were just used to homophobes and misogynists talking shit at the bars. Still, now I had started it, and I had to go on.

"Stay out of this, buddy," I said. "I'm talking to your pussy-munching friend." I turned to the woman. "What's the matter, these guys don't have enough cock to suit you? Or do they just get each other off?"

Now the second guy, a well built, clean cut twenty-something moved close to me. "Look man, I don't know what your deal is, but you need to shut the fuck up."

"Come on, Mark," said the woman. "We're done here. Let's go back inside. The dessert must have arrived." She grabbed the guy's arm and pulled him towards the door. He reluctantly turned, and the three of them put out their cigarettes and walked back into the restaurant.

I followed them in, and gave it one last shot. "Yeah Mark, go finish up your fruit tart with your dyke sister." I sneered loudly. "Faggot."

And then Mark turned and hit me in the face. It was a perfect shot, got me just beneath the eye, and it happened right in front of the cash register in plain sight of the wait staff and a bunch of customers. I went down with a yell, so the folks who hadn't noticed would turn around. Several waiters dropped their trays and jumped into action, some of them holding Mark back while others helped me to my feet.

Within a few minutes I had an ice pack pressed against my face and could hear the worried manager's voice in my ear.

"Just relax. We've evicted the other party from the restaurant. My bouncers are holding them outside. Should we call an ambulance? Should I have the police meet you directly at the hospital?"

I waved him away. "No, don't worry about it. It was my fault." For a second I was worried I had taken it too far. I didn't want the authorities on the scene just yet. If the police got here now, my plan wouldn't work. "And don't worry about those guys. I'm drunk and I've had a bad day. I was talking shit."

"I'm sorry, sir, but I'm going to have to call the police," said the manager.

"No, please don't." I pushed away the ice pack and turned to the manager. "Look, I'm with my boss and some clients, and we're in the middle of a very important meeting." I pointed towards the opening to the back room, and made sure the manager got a look at the Japanese guys with Mo. "I need to get back to my table. I could lose my job if I mess up this meeting. They're already probably wondering what the hell I'm doing." The manager looked hesitant, but he was close to giving in, so I pushed. "Come on, man. I just got hit in the face. Now you want me to lose my job as well? Please understand. If you need me to sign a waiver saying I won't sue your place, then I'll do it. Here, hold on to my business card."

The manager sighed and nodded. "Okay, sir. Go ahead." He smiled. "Dessert will be on the house."

23

We skipped dessert and went straight from entrée to coffee. Needless to say, the rest of our meal went quickly and quietly. I explained my rapidly-blackening eye and swollen face with a shrug and a simple, "Friday night in Milwaukee."

That drew a nervous laugh from Yoshi, but Takahashi and Aki just exchanged serious glances. When the coffee arrived, Mo picked up her cup and excused herself, saying she wanted to have a cigarette. She tapped me on the knee, and I followed her.

Mo didn't speak until we were outside the restaurant and far enough away from the handful of other smokers.

"Nice work," she finally said. "I don't even want to know how you did it."

I tried to smile. "I am never doing something like this again."

"I know. It's messy with so many people around. But I couldn't think of another way to get to these guys. According to my sources in the Network, these men are paranoid to the extreme, and would be very suspicious of anything unusual. Believe me, I would have liked to have suggested a trip to the Northern Wisconsin woods or something, but that would have spooked them for sure."

"Wait, so you think they're onto us?"

"No, of course not." She smiled. "We're too damn good as consultants for anyone to believe that we do anything else."

I almost laughed. "So what now?"

"Follow me," she said. Mo walked around the back to where our car was parked. She popped the trunk. "Well?"

I looked inside and shrugged. "I guess we go with the bats. The folks that punched me out had just gone to a softball game."

Mo shook her head. "Well, then we go with the tire irons."

I looked at her.

Mo sighed. "If we use bats, then the police will wonder why they weren't the bats that belonged to that group." She reached into a cardboard box and pulled out two sets of disposable surgical gloves. "Here. Put these on discreetly when we walk out of the restaurant. They're sheer, and in the dark you can't really see them." She put on her gloves and reached into the trunk and pulled out two tire irons. After hesitating, she also grabbed a long sharp kitchen knife, the kind you'd use to slice a watermelon. Then she placed all three objects under the car, just near the left rear tire.

We went back into the restaurant. The wait staff looked at me and whispered, but I barely noticed. My attention had narrowed down to a single point in space and time. I couldn't see, hear, or think of anything but what was about to go down. I was too wound up to even try and systematically rehearse the plan in my mind, and I prayed that I would know what to do when the time came.

Takahashi was on his feet when we got back into the dining room. He looked impatient, almost annoyed. I wasn't sure if it was the food, or if he was shaken by the oddness of me getting punched out for no apparent reason. Aki was quiet and stoic, and he sat and stared at the table like he was meditating. Yoshi was the only one who seemed to be in a mood fitting for someone who had just eaten a nice dinner.

I smiled at them as Mo signed the credit card receipt. We allowed our three clients to walk out first, and then Mo and I followed. I was so tense that I had to clench my fists and whisper and remind myself to breathe. As I felt my fingernails cut into my palms, I remembered the gloves. We were just leaving the restaurant as I pulled them out of my trouser pocket. I looked around to see if anyone was watching—some people were, but I could tell they were focused on my colorful facial bruise, not the colorless rubber gloves in my hands.

Mo was ahead of me when we got to the lot. She put out her hand to indicate that I should wait and let the Japanese group move a few more steps ahead of us. They were walking slowly, talking in Japanese. Takahashi and Aki were in an intense discussion, but Yoshi was lagging behind and strolling with his hands in his pockets. Aki said something to Yoshi, and Yoshi jogged up to him.

I felt a tap on my arm and looked. Mo had raced to our car and grabbed the tire irons. She handed one to me, and in my panic I dropped it. As Mo saw me fumble the club, she ran full tilt ahead to the group, and just as my iron clanged on the black asphalt, Mo's struck the back of Aki's head with a sickening dull sound. He went down immediately, and Yoshi and Takahashi turned and cried out.

"Stop!" I shouted, not sure whom I was addressing.

Mo didn't even flinch. It was like she was expecting me to betray her. She swung at Takahashi, but he dropped himself backwards in a surprisingly agile move for a short fat man, and Mo's tire iron swung harmlessly through the air above his massive raised gut.

As Takahashi fell, he raised his right foot and kicked at

Mo, getting her just around the armpit. She shouted in pain, and yelled for me.

"Okay, everyone just stop this," I said.

Mo turned to me for an instant. "You piece of shit." Then she swung once more, this time getting Takahashi on the leg but missing the knee. Takahashi yelped, but was on his feet again, and he tackled Mo, pushing her against the car. Now Yoshi pulled out something from his pocket, and I saw a whipping flash of silver as he drove a blade deep into Mo's side. I was close enough now to see her eyes widen in surprise and then glaze over as her blood poured out and rapidly began to gather in a shiny black pool on the parking lot.

I screamed and rushed forward with my iron rod held high above my head. I must have moved fast, because Yoshi didn't get out of the way in time and I swear I heard his skull crack right down the middle. He didn't go down, but just stood there, held in place against his rental car, eyes open and unblinking, fluids oozing down his forehead and dripping off his nose. He would be dead soon, and I didn't give a shit.

And then everything slowed down for me. It was one of those periods when you understand that time as we think of it is meaningless. What happened next couldn't have lasted more than five or ten seconds, but if you had told me it took thirty minutes to kill Takahashi, I would have believed you.

I calmly and deliberately took the knife from Yoshi's limp hand and wiped it on my trousers to get rid of Mo's blood. Then I remember actually squinting to read the fine print on the side of the blade. *Stainless – Japan*, is all it said. I remember smiling and nodding as if in acknowledgement to the gods of war, as if I was thanking them that my first kill would be done with Japanese steel, thereby linking me with one of the greatest traditions in the art of death-dealing. I remember looking up at the half-moon and feeling a cosmic connection to every other man or woman that has ever taken a life for a reason that in the moment seemed justifiable.

But most of all I remember looking into Mo's eyes as I plunged the knife into Takahashi's back. As I felt the clean metal slide between his ribs and into his soft, unsuspecting lung, Mo's eyes gently closed and then opened again. I knew she was thanking me. I also knew she was sorry for what she had done, for what she had made me do, for what she had made me become.

As Takahashi's heavy body dropped to her feet, I put the knife down and held Mo upright. I looked around. No movement. The lot was still empty. I lifted Mo and carried her to our car and laid her out in the back seat. I ripped off my shirt and tied it around her waist to slow the bleeding. Then I got behind the wheel and started the car.

"Antifreeze. There's some in the trunk."

"What?" I looked back at Mo.

"Antifreeze," she whispered. "My blood."

I stared at her, and then I understood. I popped the trunk and grabbed the bottle of antifreeze and ran over to where Mo's blood had pooled on the ground. As I unscrewed the cap and prepared to dump the green toxin all over Mo's blood, I surveyed the scene and promptly replaced the top on the bottle.

The scene was perfect. Yoshi's knife had been a blessing. With three messy dead bodies, two tire irons with no identifiable prints, and a knife with Yoshi's prints, it would look like these guys had simply had it out with each other. It wouldn't be too hard to come up with a scenario that sequenced their wounds and didn't require anyone else to be present. And there was so much intermingled blood, there'd be no way forensics would test it all. No, pouring antifreeze would make Mo's blood untestable, but it would also signal that others were involved. Either way was a gamble, and I had to make the call. I didn't hesitate, but just ran back to the car. I took another look at Mo before driving. She was on the phone, of all things. I assumed she was delirious.

"Stay awake," I said. "I'll have you at the hospital soon."

"No. This address." She handed me her phone.

A text message window was open, showing an address in Port Washington, a somewhat distant suburb of Milwaukee. I punched the address into the GPS and drove. I didn't question Mo. I was done questioning her. I was done betraying her.

"Hold on, Mo. We're on our way. It'll only be a few more minutes. Stay with me."

"Relax, Frank. I can tell that no major organs have been hit. I just need antibiotics and stitches. It'll be a cool scar." Her voice was soft, but steady, and I relaxed.

Once I was on the highway and on the way to our destination, I reached up and twisted the rearview mirror so I could see Mo's face. She caught me looking at her, and she smiled. I nodded, and gave her a look that said: Don't worry, you have nothing to be sorry about. I've made my own choices. I've crossed that line, and now the only direction I'm going is forward. Forward with confidence, forward with you.

24

The address in Port Washington turned out to be the sprawling house of a doctor. Chester was the only name he gave me. Of course, it wouldn't have been hard to figure out his real name, but I didn't really care. I figured we got hooked up with him through Mo's Omega contact or whatever. I was pretty impressed, actually, that Mo could make a call and get immediate private medical attention in the middle of Wisconsin. It almost made me feel proud of being promoted to a full Beta member of the Network. It was kind of like qualifying for a premium membership in a hotel or airline program where you get privileges that aren't available to the riff-raff. At the very least, it dispelled any lingering doubts that Mo was just insane and had made up the entire secret-assassins-network story.

Chester was a plastic surgeon, which was actually perfect, because it meant he had basic facilities and equipment in his home. He was expecting us, and met us at the edge of the driveway. He pointed to his open garage, and I drove in.

Chester and I carried Mo into a clean room that seemed to be connected to both the house and garage. It was almost a professional quality operating room—at least to my untrained eye. It seemed like he could perform heart surgery there if he wanted to. Unfortunately, it turned out that the one thing he couldn't do there was replace the blood Mo had lost on the way.

Chester looked at me. "I try to keep some blood here for these types of situations, but it's becoming harder for me to do it these days. The information technology in the healthcare industry is improving dramatically thanks to you consultants, and they track this stuff much better." He shrugged. "I've almost got the bleeding stopped, but we're going to have to get her to a hospital for a transfusion. Unfortunately, since I do so much of my work in my own clinic, I don't have deep contacts at Port Washington General. We'll have to roll the dice and try and explain it away as an accident and hope the ER staff don't call the police."

I looked at Mo. She was barely conscious. I knew we couldn't go to the hospital. The police would want to talk to us anyway, and we had to hold to the story that Takahashi and Yoshi and Aki were arguing in Japanese when we left them, and that we didn't see anything else. If it came out that Mo had been stabbed with a knife that had Yoshi's prints on it, things would get too complicated. We'd have to make up something about being attacked by Yoshi and gang. And even then, two of us killing three attackers in self-defense might look a bit suspicious, especially since the attackers had eaten dinner with us. Plus, how to explain having two tire irons on hand? The way it was, the tire irons could fit with some creative cop's interpretation of the events: maybe Takahashi and Aki used the tire irons to attack Yoshi, who fought back before stabbing Takahashi. Then Yoshi dropped the knife and picked up a tire iron and got into a clubbing contest with Aki, during which the bleeding Takahashi also took a few hits? Or maybe Yoshi was already hit and the knifing was his last act? Or Takahashi double-crossed Aki by knocking him out first and then Yoshi and Takahashi killed each other in a death-match? There were enough permutations and combinations to keep the Milwaukee homicide group focused on the three Japanese victims. And if the case got a lot of press, the feds or the spooks might pick up on it, and perhaps even uncover some of the information that the Network seemed to have access to. Then the feds might inform the local police that Takahashi and Yoshi and Aki were potentially violent extremists, and perhaps liable to be involved in shady dealings that could lead to a parking lot bloodbath. I liked how that situation could play out.

I took another look at Mo. "If we had blood, could you do the transfusion here?"

"Of course," said Chester.

"Then let's do it." I took off my stained undershirt and sat down on a painted metal chair and held my arm out. "Well?"

Chester smiled. "We don't know Mo's blood type. I don't have any bedside test kits, either." He looked at Mo. "And I don't think she's answering any questions right now."

"It doesn't matter. I'm Type O." I remembered that O was the universal donor, so Mo's blood type was immaterial.

Chester warned me that blood compatibility involves more than the simple blood type, but I shut him down and so he got to work. In less than an hour we had enough of my blood to begin the transfusion. I sat on the chair in a semi-trance and watched the dark red blobs drip down and pass through the clear tube and into Mo's arm. She was still somewhat conscious, but didn't seem too aware of what was going on. I smiled when I thought of the symbolism of that moment. If I were a writer then perhaps I'd bore you with some cheesy emotional description of how the night had started with a plan to betray Mo and was ending with . . . well, you get it.

25

But that was not to be the end of the night. I was shaken awake and looked up to see Mo standing in front of me. I had fallen asleep on the chair, and not for long, it turned out. I don't know what Chester had pumped into Mo, but she was awake and upright and alert as hell. She moved slowly, but you couldn't tell from looking at her that she had been stabbed and had almost bled to death just a few hours earlier.

"We need to get back to the hotel," said Mo. "Now."

I nodded and stood up. She didn't need to explain that we needed to be at the hotel when the police showed up.

Mo slowly walked to the door that led to the garage. "I figure we have until early morning at least. My hope is that the restaurant will be closed by the time the bodies are found, so it'll take a while before anyone figures out Takahashi and gang were with us at dinner."

I nodded again and let out a huge yawn. "Sorry." I looked around. "Where's Chester?"

"Cleaning the car," said Mo.

We walked into the garage. Mo wasn't kidding about Chester cleaning the car. I almost laughed when I saw him. The man was in full surgical garb—I'm talking mask, robe, elbow-length gloves, and even rubber boots. Several industrial size—and I guessed industrial strength—cleaners and disinfectants sat on the floor near the car. It looked like Chester was just finishing up, and when he saw us he stood back and put his hands on his hips and smiled and nodded towards the pristine back seat of the rental car.

I clapped, and Chester bowed. It was a funny scene, perhaps the most surreal moment of the evening.

Mo laughed and shook her head. She held on to the edge of the car roof and lowered herself into the front seat. As Chester shut the door for her, she looked up at him and nodded. She didn't say anything, and neither did he. They were both professionals. And I was one of them now.

I walked over to the driver's side door and opened it. Before getting in, I looked over the car and nodded at Chester. Then I smiled and shook my head. "You saved us, man. I don't know what else to say. I don't know how to thank you."

Chester laughed. "You'll be seeing me again tomorrow. Once the police are done with you, I want Mo back here. She can stay here for a few days until we're sure there's no infection." He walked towards the garage door and pulled on the lever. As the wooden panels whirred open, he looked at me and smiled. "And don't worry. You'll have a chance to thank me."

26

"What did Chester mean by that?" I asked Mo. We had been on the highway for over twenty minutes, and I could see the lights of downtown Milwaukee on the horizon. It had been a smooth ride, not least because our paranoia hadn't been fed by any flashing lights on the highway.

"By what?"

"About me having a chance to thank him."

Mo laughed. "Are you worried he was trying to hit on you? I didn't peg you for a homophobe."

"Go to hell. I'm not homophobic."

"Jeez. Sorry." Mo shook her head. "Anyway, for what it's worth, I don't think Chester was hitting on you. I'm pretty sure he could tell that you aren't gay. Besides, you're not his type."

I looked at her in surprise.

"What, you're shocked that Chester is gay?" said Mo.

"No. I'm surprised that you seem to know him. I thought he was just a hookup through your Omega contact." I paused to check my blind spot before taking the downtown Milwaukee exit. "Is Chester not part of the Network?"

Mo sighed. "It's complicated."

I laughed, but not because anything was funny. "And the rest of this isn't?"

"Calm down. I'll explain everything. Just not all of it right here and now, okay?"

"Sorry. I almost forgot you had a knife in your gut five hours ago." I smiled at Mo and lowered my voice. "It can wait."

She nodded. We both tensed up as I pulled into the hotel driveway. It looked quiet, and we both exhaled at the same time, and then laughed in relief. I drove into the covered lot and found a spot next to the elevators.

Mo stopped me from opening the car door.

"What?" I said.

"Let's smoke a cigarette."

I stared at her. "Okay." Then I hesitated. "In here?"

"Yes. And keep the windows closed."

I slowly took out two cigarettes and handed one to Mo. I still wasn't sure where she was going with this.

Mo smiled as I lit her smoke. "The smell."

I was mortified for not thinking of it. I sighed. "Shit. You're right. It smells like a freaking hospital in here. We need to smoke it up a bit just in case the police want to check it out."

Mo nodded. "Remember, Frank . . ."

I interrupted. "Yes, I know. Paranoia is king."

27

My fears of sleepless nights haunted by the faces of my victims seemed unfounded, because the first things I saw when the phone woke me were the big red numbers on the digital hotel clock-radio informing me that I had been asleep for a solid ten hours. My body felt stiff, which I took to mean that I had been neglecting certain muscle groups in my daily routines.

I reached for the ringing phone, expecting it to be the police, but it was just Mo.

"Hey," she said.

"What's up. How do you feel? Are the police here?"

"Okay. Nope."

"Odd. Should we be worried?"

"We should always be worried."

"You know what I mean." I lit a cigarette and lay back down and watched the smoke gather in the afternoon sun that streamed in through the sheer liner curtains.

"No, I don't think it's necessarily a bad sign. They may not have connected Takahashi and gang to C&C yet. It's not like we get any press for a small consulting job. When the cops make the connection, we'll probably hear from them."

"Yeah, but I'm pretty sure the restaurant manager knew that I was with a bunch of Japanese people. And he has my business card, not to mention your credit card number." I sighed and heaved myself out of bed with a groan. Those muscles were stiffer than I thought. "I can't imagine why they haven't called yet."

I heard Mo say something to another person. It sounded like she was in the lobby.

"Are you packed?" she asked me.

"Basically. It won't take me long."

"Good. See you downstairs. We're checking out and heading back to Chester's."

I showered and dressed and packed and was down in the lobby within a half hour. Mo was lounging on a sofa. She looked tired and pale, and I felt a chill run through me when I remembered how close she had come to dying. I winced in sympathy when I thought about how much pain she must be in right now. Psycho blackmailer or not, she was a tough woman, and I couldn't help but admire her. I had no second thoughts about what I had done the previous night. Any doubts I may have had about the innocence of Yoshi and crew had been washed away when Takahashi held Mo down and Yoshi stuck her. I had given them a chance to stop the attack. They didn't need to try and kill her. Their lack of hesitation gave them away as men who had thought about killing, if not already killed. And such men would almost always kill again. I knew, because I was now such a man.

I carried Mo's bags out to the car. She didn't object, which meant she was really hurting. I wanted to ask about Chester and why she was connected to him if the Network used only a strict two-person cell framework. Maybe she herself was an Omega? Perhaps every Alpha was also an Omega, but had to keep it a secret from their Betas? I shook my head to get the Greek out of it.

We pulled out of the parking garage, and I drove to the highway, making sure to take the turns slowly so as to minimize any pressure on Mo's wound. I glanced at her as I took the exit, and could see a spot of blood on her green blouse. I was glad we were going to Chester's, and I was glad the police hadn't tracked us down yet. It wouldn't do to have Mo bleeding all over the place while the police asked about why her dinner companions were found beaten and stabbed outside the restaurant.

It being Saturday afternoon, the highway was busy but not packed. There were just enough cars around to give us a feeling of inconspicuousness, which was nice. We didn't say much during the thirty minute ride to Port Washington and Chester's. I got the sense that Mo was doing everything she could to not break down and cry in pain. I gently pushed down on the accelerator, which was the only thing I could do to help her—just get her to Chester's faster so he could change the dressing, give her some antibiotics, and let her rest for as long as was needed.

I wasn't too worried about work, and not just because it was the weekend. Most C&C consultants got some downtime between projects, and they usually weren't asked to account for their whereabouts during that timeframe. Consulting is a business where even a low-level professional has an extraordinary amount of freedom when between projects. I guess it makes up for the absolute lack of any personal time when you're working a job. Plus, I was with Mo, and at C&C it wasn't unusual for a partner to work from pretty much anywhere, as long as there was cell phone service and internet access. Neither was it odd for a partner to have a senior consultant or manager come out to some god-forsaken spot to help them with a sales proposal or whatever. So, as far as

C&C went, we were covered until the next project came up.

I had Chester's address in the GPS, and we got there without a hitch. I was worried that there'd be a line of cop cars outside the place, with forensics geeks checking the trash for swabs of blood to match what they found in the restaurant lot. But no, there was nothing except for Chester's spotless driveway and virgin lawn. I sighed. This seemed too perfect. Something had to go wrong, right?

It was only when I heard Mo cry out in pain as Chester and I helped her into the house that I realized something *had* gone wrong. One of us had almost been killed. This wasn't supposed to happen. *We* were the killers. I gnashed my teeth when I remembered that Mo wouldn't be in this situation if I had done my job. Mo hadn't brought it up, but the fact remained that I had betrayed her. She had gone in expecting me to be with her, and I had stood back and waved my hands like a goddamn pansy. How lame. Never again. No, this was my life now. No more pleading to stop the violence. Now I *was* the violence.

I stretched out on Chester's white leather couch in the massive living room of his house and sighed. I was just starting to reflect on how quickly my mindset had flipped from thoughts of escape to virtually complete acceptance of my new lifestyle, but was interrupted by Chester.

"Tea?" he said. "Or something else to drink?"

"Sure. Tea is fine." I stood up and walked towards the front door. "Just going to step outside for a cigarette."

"Oh, you can smoke in here," said Chester. He pointed at a ridiculously ornate piece of cut-glass that I hadn't recognized as an ashtray. It was some kind of angel holding a deep, thick glass bowl.

"That's an ashtray?" I took a closer look and saw that the

glass bowl was lined with subtle grooves to hold a burning cigarette. "Oh, I guess it is. Wow."

Chester nodded. "Yes. My ex-partner's choice. Too baroque for me, but that was Tom." He smiled, and I thought I saw him tear up before he turned and went towards what must have been the kitchen.

He was back with a loaded tray before my cigarette was done. I watched him pour the tea, and nodded when he asked me if I took milk and sugar.

"So," he said, sitting on a leather chair that matched the white sofa, "you're Mo's Beta. That's good. It was time for her to move on." Chester sipped his tea and leaned back into the armchair. "It was time for Simone to move on too."

"How can you say that?" I hadn't thought about Simone for a while now, but hearing her name aroused mixed emotions in me. "Who are you to say that it was time for Simone to die?"

"Wow, you are really pissed." Chester laughed. "Simone said you were a great lay, and I can see it now. All that fire." He laughed again.

I remained silent. Chester's laughter upset me, but I figured it was just a matter of time before I'd be desensitized enough to make jokes about dead people.

Chester put down his cup. After he was done with his laughing fit, he wiped his mouth with a yellow paper napkin. "Oh, come on, Frank. You must have guessed that Simone isn't really dead."

My foot hit the tea tray as I jumped up. The steel and china rattled and cackled, but did not drop or break. I stared at Chester, but I could neither move nor speak—not that it mattered, because I wouldn't have known what to do or say. Of course I had guessed it, but then I had convinced myself that the photograph had been real and Mo was telling the truth.

But had I actually been convinced? Or did I not really care? Was I already a killer? A dormant murderer just waiting for an excuse to cast away the shackles of conventional morality? A monster who leapt at the chance to become what he was born to be?

My psychological self-evaluation was interrupted by Chester getting up and walking out of the room. As he left, he looked over his shoulder and winked at me. "Don't worry about the couch. It cleans off really well."

I was confused, and was about to go after him when I heard someone behind me. I turned just in time to catch Simone as she flung herself at me. She dragged me to the couch and threw me down and kissed me furiously as I laughed and cried and cursed and then kissed her back.

28

"So, yes, I am indeed an Omega now." Simone leaned over to light her cigarette from my burning match.

Simone, Chester, and I were sitting out on the back porch. The house was truly a mansion. A marble-trimmed path wound through an immaculate garden, and I had to stare at the flowers for a while before I was convinced they were real. The path ended in a cul-de-sac, at the center of which stood a working fountain, apparently also marble, and somewhat reminiscent of the cut-glass ashtray.

The varied greens of the grass and trees that lay beyond the flower garden were mesmerizing, and I didn't want to drag myself back to the conversation. I nodded at Simone and didn't say anything. I just smiled. Then I slowly refocused on the distant greenery, my smile widening as the smoke from my cigarette found its way into my line of sight, adding a soothing touch to the view.

"His mind is mush right now," said Chester. He laughed and nudged Simone. "What did you do to him?"

I smiled and leaned over the round glass table to grab the ashtray. "Sorry. It's just been . . . I don't know." I laughed and shook my head. "You're right. My mind is mush right now. What did you do to me, Simone?"

We all laughed. Then we shared a perfectly unawkward moment of silence.

Simone broke it. "I'm sorry, Frank."

I shrugged. "Don't worry about it. I like it rough sometimes." We all laughed again, but I knew what she meant. Perhaps later I would be angry, but right now I didn't give a shit. Something had changed in me. A switch had been flipped, and I could feel a steady, burning line of electricity flowing through me like a slow and consistent adrenaline rush that wouldn't go away. Not that I wanted it to go away. I felt alert and alive, almost superhuman. I couldn't articulate why, and I didn't want to. My life suddenly felt right, and I loved it. If this was what becoming a monster was like, then, well, maybe I would start using my middle initial more often.

"Hey, I just found out that your last name is Stein. That's funny. Do you have a middle initial?" Chester refilled our glasses with the cold white wine we had been drinking. He emptied the bottle and placed it on the floor and then looked up at me with a grin.

"Don't go there," I said, and smiled. I looked over at Simone and gave her a tiny nod, just enough to make sure she knew that an apology wasn't needed. After all, I hadn't bothered to check for news about Simone being missing. I hadn't tried to see if she had contacted Walker-Midland about not coming in to work. Hell, she could have been going to work like normal and I wouldn't have known. Looking back now, it would have been so easy to call Mo's bluff. In fact, I'm certain that any normal person in my situation would have spent all their time and energy validating that Simone was actually gone. But I didn't. At some level I guess I didn't want to know. Maybe deep down I had already decided. Maybe I had always known what I would become. All the logic I had used to rationalize my actions simply represented the death throes of the superficial part of my ego that had been confined to the belief that morality and the law were one and the same. But now those last bonds had been broken. Now I could see that morality and the law, although they overlapped to a large degree, were independent of each other. Now I could see that I would no longer be using the law to draw the line between right and wrong. I would have to find that line myself, and I would have to walk it. But I wasn't worried, because I knew I wasn't alone.

I looked at Chester and then Simone. "So what's the deal here? Obviously the rules about two-person cells that never interact and Betas that never meet their Omegas aren't so strict, right?"

"They are strict," said Simone.

Chester nodded. "Rules are what keep this thing going. And they're what keep us alive."

I waited for them to go on or start laughing, but neither of them did. I sighed. "Okay. I'll just wait for you two clowns to explain why we seem to be breaking these unbreakable rules."

Simone smiled. "Because there's a rule that allows us to break the rule under certain circumstances."

"Like with Mo getting injured last night?"

Chester nodded. "Yes. Going to a hospital for treating an injury sustained on an assignment is the single biggest risk to our people."

"But that's not why I'm here," said Simone.

"Okay," I said. "Do I have to keep asking?"

Simone laughed. "There are a couple more rules that allow for two or more cells to connect. And both of those rules are in play here."

Chester nodded, but didn't say anything. He leaned on the table and looked out past me. I turned briefly, and realized that he was staring at the fountain.

Simone continued. "One of them, of course, is when a job

needs more than two people. But that's quite rare, because we're not really designed to launch massive offensives. Our soldiers and government agencies are better equipped and trained for coordinating that stuff."

"So what's the other rule in effect here?" I lit another cigarette and followed Chester's gaze out to the fountain.

"Well, I think Mo's explained how and why we pick most of our targets."

I nodded. "Yes. They're basically picked and validated through the Omega network." Then I turned and looked at Simone. "But Mo did tell me that it's a two-way communication, so an Alpha or Beta can identify potential targets. Still, that's part of the process, isn't it? So why is this an exception?"

Simone smiled. "Individual cells are always looking for potential targets for Omegas to validate, but that's not what we're talking about here. We are also allowed to pursue cases where a target gets . . . how should I put this . . . *requested* by a member. It still has to be approved by an Omega, of course. But it comes from a member." She looked at Chester, who seemed entranced by the fountain.

I glanced at Chester and looked back at Simone. "You're saying that an Omega can approve a personal target—a target with a deeper connection to one of us. That's what's going on here."

She nodded. "Yes."

"And we need more than one cell for the assignment? More than two people?"

"Yes."

"And we're the two cells? Is Chester your new Beta or something?"

Simone leaned back in her chair. "No. Omegas don't have Betas. In fact, we are Betas in some sense. Every Omega does field work, and so I report to an Alpha Omega." She smiled as I shook my head. "Anyway, no, Chester and I aren't in a cell. This is kind of an improvised team." She paused and reached for the pack of cigarettes. "Chester is an Alpha in his own cell, and I'm his Omega contact. The original plan was to have another local team come in to help Chester, but when Mo called me after getting injured, I sent her here and took the next flight in. When a coincidence like this occurs, I don't like to pass it up." She smiled and leaned over and kissed me. "Besides, I heard you made your first kill, and I figured you didn't need to grieve over me much longer."

I pretended to push her away. "How sweet of you. But I didn't give a shit about you. I'm a cold-blooded killer. Grief isn't part of my vocabulary."

"How nice for you." Chester, who had been frozen in silence for most of the conversation, suddenly spoke. His voice wavered, and that teary look I thought I had seen on him earlier was now back.

I was embarrassed at my own insensitivity. It should have been clear to me when Simone mentioned that the next target was personal. I looked at Chester and placed my hand on his shoulder. "I'm sorry, man. This is for Tom, isn't it? Your partner."

29

Janesville, Wisconsin. A nice town that had gotten a bad rap after being associated with a small but highly publicized Ku Klux Klan rally. And even though most of the KKK members had been driven out by the residents years ago, the reputation, unfair though it was, had stuck. This so-called tradition of white supremacy, combined with the abundance of low-rent housing, had led to a couple of blocks in the town being taken over by neo-Nazi transplants from Milwaukee and Madison. These transplants were our targets.

This made more sense to me. Although I had no doubt that KKK members weren't particularly supportive of the gay community, I didn't think they specifically targeted homosexuals on a high-priority basis. Neo-Nazis, on the other hand, are leaders in anti-gay violence. The term "curbing a fag" is one of their contributions to the English language.

The term refers to one of the most brutal ways of killing someone. As the phrase implies, a street curb is involved. The victim is told to lie on the ground and open his mouth and bite down on the edge of the sidewalk. Then a steel-toed heavy combat boot driven by a Nazi foot comes down hard on the back of the head, smashing the jaw and often the skull.

Curbing.

Tom had been curbed.

It had happened late one night when Chester and Tom were driving back from a party and had stopped in Janesville for gas. They had paid at the pump, but Chester wanted to use the restroom, so they had locked the car and gone into the station. Chester had been the designated driver, and Tom had been all too happy to drink enough for both of them, putting him in a condition that prompted a remark on the cuteness of the tattoo that graced the side of the gas station attendant's shaved head. The attendant, somewhat bored and not especially sober himself, took offence and called a couple of buddies.

Chester was pulled out of the bathroom by three young skinheads. Tom had already been taken out back, and was doubled over in pain and bleeding from his ear when Chester saw him. Chester tried to fight off his captors, but was knocked unconscious. When he awoke, the place was crawling with police. It took the detectives several attempts at explanations before Chester understood what had happened. A passerby had called 911 and the cops had arrived just in time to save Chester's life. But they had to have a closed-casket funeral for Tom.

The sun was gone and we had been outside drinking white wine for several hours now, but Chester's story sobered us up.

After several moments of silence, I lit a cigarette and spoke. "So the cops didn't catch the bastards? You must have seen some of them at least, right?"

Chester nodded. "Eight people were eventually arrested. The trial took two years. One of them is doing twenty-to-life. The others are at home."

"You're kidding. What the hell?"

Chester sighed. "The skinheads took off when they heard the sirens, so the cops didn't see them. And the guys who called 911 couldn't identify anyone." He reached for one of my cigarettes, the first time he had done so in the twenty hours I had known him.

"Yeah, but that doesn't mean shit. You picked them all out of a lineup, right?" My voice was loud and peaked with wine and indignation.

Chester took a deep drag and silently watched the smoke hang in the yellow light of the anti-mosquito torches that lined the edge of the back porch. "I screwed up with one ID. Picked the wrong guy. The District Attorney said the defense would have used my one mistake to cast doubt on all the other IDs. And since no one else saw them and there was no other hard evidence, the DA made a deal. The others testified against the gas station attendant. He got convicted, and the rest of them were never even tried."

"Screw that." I looked at Simone, who had been quiet. "You know about all this?"

She nodded. "Heard about it when I was vacationing in Door County in northern Wisconsin around that time." She smiled at Chester. "Of course, being the cut-throat human resources bitch that I am, I saw it as a recruitment opportunity." She touched her cheeks. "And we could use a few more plastic surgeons in our group."

Chester laughed. "You are an ageless beauty, Simone. I wouldn't mess with your face if my life depended on it." He looked at me. "What do you say, Frank? Is she a forty-six-year-old hottie, or what?"

"Forty-six? I thought she was twenty-seven," I said with an incredulous expression. But I couldn't hold the look and I started laughing, which got all of us going.

"What the hell is going on out here?" Mo was standing in the doorway in a long nightgown, her slim body silhouetted by the living-room lights behind her. She pointed at the table. "Give me a cigarette."

We all cheered in delight. I stood up and lit her cigarette and then helped her to a chair.

"How's the battle scar coming along?" I asked.

"It doesn't feel too bad, actually," said Mo. She looked at Chester. "Pretty good work for a Botox jockey."

"Hey now," said Chester. "Be nice or no more morphine for you."

We all laughed again. This felt good, like we were some kind of family. A family with problems, but with problems that we all knew about and had accepted, just like any other healthy family.

Mo smiled as she picked up her cell phone and checked her messages. Then her expression changed.

I stopped laughing and took a sip of wine. "What is it?"

"There's a message on my cell from a Milwaukee police detective."

I almost choked on the wine and quickly put the glass down. It wasn't like we didn't know this was coming. It was just that it seemed so far away now. It was hard to believe I had stabbed Takahashi less than twenty-four hours ago.

"What did the message say?"

"That they were interviewing everyone who ate at the restaurant that night. They must have gotten my name from the credit card receipt. Or from the reservation." Mo shrugged. "In all honesty, it shouldn't be a problem at all. We just need to act appropriately shocked that our clients were beaten and stabbed to death just a few minutes after we drove away. And you need to mention your bar fight. Hopefully the cops will just assume those guys followed us out and, after realizing you and I had left, vented on poor Takahashi and crew.

And maybe one of the attackers got cut, and so they poured antifreeze on the blood so there wouldn't be any evidence."

I gulped again, but this time there was no wine in my mouth and I let out an odd sucking noise. I had just remembered that Mo didn't know about the call I had made—the decision to leave the scene as it was and hope the police would see it as a self-contained massacre. My mind raced, and I suddenly felt very drunk.

"What?" said Mo.

I sighed and looked out across the dark lawn. The fountain lit up well in the night—red and green with flashes of yellow as the jets squirted water out of the marble angel's upturned hands.

"He's wasted," said Chester. He laughed. "Maybe we should switch to red wine."

Mo ignored him and continued to stare at me.

Finally I gave in. "I didn't use the antifreeze."

"You didn't use the antifreeze." Mo spoke slowly, and it scared me.

"I can explain," I said.

"I'm waiting."

I looked at Chester and Simone, but neither of them made any move to interrupt the conversation.

My voice trembled. "The way it was, I figured the cops would think that Yoshi and Takahashi and Aki were in an argument that got out of hand. And there was so much blood, I didn't think they'd test all of it." Once I said that, my confidence returned, and I rattled off a long list of points that backed up my decision.

When I was done, Mo was almost smiling. "Not bad. It's risky, but it may have been a good call. At least it explains why the police took so long to get in touch with us."

I nodded. "Yep. If they're not looking for anyone else, they can afford to take their own sweet time writing up the report."

Simone smiled at me. "Good stuff. Maybe you are worth your billing rate after all."

Chester raised his glass, and the rest of us did the same. Mo raised her fist in a copycat gesture.

"Here's to looking ahead, but not forgetting the things behind us," he said. The words came out slurred, and I didn't try to read too much into his awkward toast.

"Speaking of looking ahead," I said. "What's our plan?"

30

"Our targets live in three adjoining houses on the same block," said Chester.

We were inside Chester's house now and in the basement, all of us sitting on matching brown leather beanbags facing a massive LCD screen on which Chester had pulled up a street-view map of Janesville. The houses he pointed at were the only ones on the block—the other lots were vacant and overgrown. Not a bad setup from our perspective, especially if we could somehow get them all in one house. But that seemed unlikely. Explosives, I was thinking.

"Explosives?" I said.

Chester shook his head. "Too risky. I've scoped these guys out, and at least two of the houses seem to have kids living in them." He turned to me. "Besides, I want these guys to see my face. I want my face to be the last goddamn thing they see."

I nodded. His anger worried me, but I understood. Still, there were only three of us, since I assumed Mo would sit this one out. "Okay. So what then? You're saying there are at least seven guys, right?"

"More likely ten or twelve total."

"Spread out across three houses? And with children in at least two of those houses?" I raised my eyebrows. "Look, I know you guys have been doing this stuff for a while, but I'm not sure my skills are at a level where I can just walk into a house and take out three or four militant dudes with a knife."

Chester smiled and shook his head. "None of us are that good. We're not Navy Seals or anything. We'll have to use guns."

I looked at Simone and then at Mo. "But I thought one of our rules was no guns." When Mo didn't answer, I looked at Chester again. Then I sighed. "How many guns do you own, anyway?"

"None."

"Okay." My head hurt. I reached for my glass of ice water and took a long drink. I put the glass back down on the unfinished pinewood coffee table, and then sank back into my beanbag and stared at Chester. My next question was obvious, and so I didn't even ask it.

Chester smiled. "But these guys have a nice stash."

I leaned forward. "We're going to use their own guns to kill them?" Then I leaned back again and looked around. "Can I smoke in here?"

Chester slid an ashtray across the coffee table. "I've been scoping the houses out for several months now, trying to figure out all the routines, who lives where, etcetera." He waited until I lit my cigarette. "And it turns out they have an armory in one of the houses." He snorted. "Well, more like a room where they stash their weapons. They aren't particularly sophisticated."

I nodded slowly. "Why do they have an armory, anyway?"

Chester shrugged. "It's just part and parcel of being a neo-Nazi in this country. The movement is militant in nature, and even though most members never actually commit an act of violence, the idea is that they're always prepared to do so. And guns are fun toys to collect. Especially weapons that you can't buy legally without attracting some attention. So it's almost like a badge of honor if you add a cool weapon to the collection."

I tried to laugh but only managed a cough. "So we're going to break into this room, steal the guns, shoot everyone, and then run away? That's your plan?"

Chester smiled. "Yup."

I wasn't sure if he was serious. Simone looked serious enough, but I couldn't tell if she was just zoned out on too much wine or if she actually thought Chester's plan was good.

Chester stood up and moved away from the computer monitor. "There is one more thing that'll make it easier for us, though."

"What?" I said.

"Looks like they have some kind of meeting once every two weeks. Monday mornings. Just the men. They get together in the basement of the house at the end of the street and stay in there for maybe an hour."

"And where's this gun-room or whatever?"

"Same house."

"And same basement." I shook my head. "This is crazy."

Chester smiled. "Sorry, I'm not explaining this well. But it's fun watching you get all worked up." He sat down on the thick red carpet and propped himself up with his arms. Then he looked up at Mo. "How's your long-distance shot these days?"

Mo looked insulted. "Do I really need to answer that?"

Chester laughed. "Okay then. Sorry." He turned back to me. "Your boss here will be in position behind a rest-stop on the highway. The rest-stop is on an elevated section of road, and there's a clear line to our targets' house from there. When the meeting starts, she'll take a couple of shots at the empty living room. You know, shoot the windows, TV, a couple of lamps and shit."

I nodded. "Okay. And so all the skinheads will run to the armory, grab their weapons, and head upstairs?"

"Hopefully," said Chester. "Maybe not immediately, but Mo can stop firing after the first few shots, and then I'm pretty sure they'll all creep up there. Or almost all of them."

Now I smiled. I was getting into it. "And the armory will be unlocked, and everyone will be focused on what's happening upstairs. So we sneak in, grab a couple of guns, and surprise them. It'll be like we're flanking them on a goddamn battlefield."

Chester laughed. "Easy there, boy." He looked at Mo, who was holding her side and laughing at me. "Looks like your pick was a Spartan in his last life."

I smiled. I was embarrassed, but in the way that you're embarrassed when someone says something nice about you. I took a sip of water. "Of course, if these guys take every single gun out of the armory, we're all dead."

"No," said Chester. "I've been taking a rough inventory. They have over thirty weapons in there. And I haven't noticed them removing any over the past week."

I stubbed out my cigarette and looked at Mo. "And you have a sniper rifle somewhere?"

Mo just pointed at Chester.

I looked at him. "I thought you said you didn't own any guns."

"I don't. I stole this one."

I shook my head. "Let me guess . . ."

He laughed. "Well, I had to get a closer look at the armory to make sure we didn't waste time looking for it on Monday." Chester went into a storeroom attached to the finished basement area and came back out with a sleek black corrugated box. "The damn armory was unlocked, and this beauty was just sitting there." He looked at Mo. "I know this will turn you on."

Mo leaned forward as Chester flipped open the case. She gasped. "Oh my God, it's an A2."

I smiled. I had no idea what the hell an A2 was. But I didn't bother to ask, and I didn't need to, because Mo rattled off the specs like a tech geek describing the latest superfast gaming chip.

"Remington M24-A2. The military sniper weapon system, but enhanced with side-mounted rails, a ten-round magazine, and a sound suppressor." She looked up at Chester. "You're going to have to pull me away from this. Those guys don't have a chance."

Chester smiled. "You're only there to create a diversion and monitor the situation in case we need backup. I don't want you taking one of us out by mistake."

"Watch it with those insults," said Mo. She smiled and caressed the gun like it was a child. "When are we moving on this?"

"Monday," said Chester.

Simone had been watching the interchange, and now she stared at Mo with a distant smile. Then she turned to me. "What do you think, Frank?"

I looked at her and shrugged. "Well, it seems like a good plan. Except . . ." I paused and gulped while Chester turned to look at me. "Except, today is Saturday, and I've never even held a gun before."

31

The sound of curtains being pulled apart woke me. I was in a guest bedroom on the second floor, and Mo was standing in the window in that same nightgown. I remember noticing how awesome she looked outlined in the morning sun. Then the hangover set in, and Mo's voice blared like an alarm clock.

"Big day today, Frank. Gotta head downtown, lie to the police, get back here for lunch, and then Chester's going to take you out to the range."

I yawned and rolled out of bed. There was a warm glass of water on the bedside table, and I downed it in a single gulp. It didn't taste good, but my dehydrated body welcomed it. After showering and dressing I felt much better, and gladly followed the smell of fresh coffee down the stairs and into the large open kitchen.

The entire gang was there, everyone hovering around the center island. It really was like a family. I smiled and nodded at my new kin.

"What's for breakfast, Mom?" I said to Chester.

Mo answered. "A bagel in your hand while you drive us into Milwaukee. I called the police back this morning. Turns out there's an FBI agent on the case. I spoke to her briefly, but she wants to see us, and we're already late."

Instantly I felt tired and cranky. "What did she say?"

"Not much. She was pretty chilled. I told her I was shocked and dismayed about Takahashi and Yoshi and Aki, so at least we won't have to pretend to be surprised about it. And I told her that we stopped outside the restaurant for a smoke, and that's the last we saw of Takahashi and crew."

"Did you tell her about my fight in the restaurant?"

"No." She looked at me. "But maybe you'd better bring it up. That bruise on your face needs to be explained somehow. Besides, I bet she already knows about it."

I nodded. "What about you? Are you going to be able to hold up without them noticing?"

Mo touched her side and nodded. "Chester wrapped me up pretty well. And I'm wearing black, so even if I bleed through they shouldn't notice."

"Okay. I'm ready." I downed my coffee, drank another glass of water, and grabbed an onion bagel on the way out.

32

Thirty-three minutes later we were in the waiting area of the Milwaukee Police District One building. The place was surprisingly quiet, and it looked like any other government office. I guess I was expecting gang-bangers and hookers and sleazy lawyers to be all over the place, but maybe since it was late Sunday morning they were all in church. After all, this was God's country.

FBI Special Agent Ramona Garcia walked out of the back room at a pace much too fast for the placid atmosphere of the headquarters. She had that look in her eye which tells you that she's smart like a buggy-whip, and I tensed up with a sudden panic as I became sure she would see right through our bullshit.

I smiled and shook her hand, and was relieved when the greeting ended without her slapping cuffs on me.

"Please, this way," said Garcia. She held the waist-high swinging door open for us to walk through.

She took us into an interview room, and I have to say that it did look like what you see on TV: steel table, steel chairs, grills on the high-mounted window, and a mirror on the wall. Contrary to what you see on TV, though, Garcia didn't let me smoke.

"You get that in the bar fight?" she asked me, pointing at

my eye. She flipped through a small black notebook. "With Mark Baylor?"

"Yes. I'm not sure if that was his name, but I think I heard his friend call him Mark, so yes."

"Mr. Baylor said you were really trying to push his buttons there," said Garcia. She paused and looked at me without blinking. "Almost as if you were trying to start a fight."

I shook my head and looked at the table. "Yeah, it's embarrassing. I was just drunk and it had been a rough week." I looked at Mo and smiled and then turned back to Garcia. "My boss here had been giving me a hard time about screwing up at work, and I guess I had one too many at dinner and wanted to vent."

"So you were drunk?"

I nodded. "I'd say so."

Garcia pulled out a photocopied piece of paper and slid it over to me. "This is your dinner receipt. Can you tell me which drinks were yours?"

I gulped, because I knew that I had only had one whiskey with dinner, and no one else at the table had been drinking. "Well, just that one scotch with dinner. But on my way outside to smoke, someone was buying shots at the bar and I ended up doing two or three."

"Oh, cool. I love when that happens," said Garcia. "What kind of shots?"

"I'm not really sure. I don't do shots much these days. Maybe tequila?"

Garcia nodded. She started to write in her little book. "Okay. Thank you, Mr. Stein."

"Sure. Any other questions?"

"Yes, plenty," said Garcia. She looked down at her notes again. "Which one of you was driving?"

"That'd be me," I said. "I get the chauffeur duties."

Garcia didn't smile. "Any reason you parked out back in the overflow lot? They have enough parking out front to handle an average Friday night crowd."

I thought Mo would offer up her story about parking far away so she could walk a bit after dinner, but she didn't say a word. I was about to go ahead and answer, when I realized what Garcia was doing. I spoke as casually as I could. "We didn't park out back."

Now Garcia smiled. "Okay. Any idea why your Japanese clients would do so?"

I shook my head. Let Mo take this one, I thought.

Mo gave a sad smile and then nodded. "Takahashi was always complaining about his weight, and earlier that week in a meeting, one of his colleagues—I can't remember if it was Aki or Yoshi—suggested that he should start walking more. And Takahashi joked that the only way he'd end up walking more is if he parked far away when he went to restaurants." She shook her head. "That poor man. This is so surreal. I can't believe he's . . . I can't even say it. What do you think happened?"

Mo was good, and I thought Garcia's sympathetic smile was genuine.

"We're not sure," said Garcia.

I wanted Garcia to ask us if our Japanese clients appeared to be having a disagreement when we left, but she didn't.

"Maybe they got into a fight or something?" I said. I felt Mo tighten up, and I realized I had made a mistake.

Garcia looked at me and nodded. "Yes, that's a possibility. But it's very rare that an impromptu fight ends up with all participants dead. Especially when there are no guns involved."

I remained quiet.

Garcia continued. "It's possible that Mark Baylor came back with a few buddies. Maybe he didn't see you there, but ran into your dinner companions and went to town on them." She shrugged.

I nodded. "It's scary to think that, but sure, I guess that's probably what happened."

"Anyway," said Garcia, "we should be able to clear it up pretty soon. We're comparing Mark's DNA with the blood found on the scene."

My hangover returned with a screaming vengeance and it was all I could do to not pass out at the table.

Garcia went on. "This is just a formality, but would both of you be willing to volunteer your DNA? Just so we can rule you guys out, of course."

33

"I think you need a warrant for that." I knew I was in the clear and could afford to get a bit combative. "Do you have one?"

Garcia smiled. "No. This is just an invitation for you two to volunteer."

Mo interrupted me just as I was about to whip out my ACLU card. "Frank's seen a bit too much *Law and Order*. It's all those nights watching TV alone in random hotel rooms." She laughed. "Of course we'll give you what you need. Do you actually need a blood sample?"

"Oh no," said Garcia. "We can just take a swab of saliva and get your DNA." She looked at me. "Mr. Stein?"

I shrugged and looked at the table. "Sure. Anything to help."

"Great. I'll send someone in to take the samples." Garcia stood up to go.

Mo stood and smiled and shook Garcia's hand. I was slow to get up, and still felt either hungover or confused and upset at being shut down by Mo.

We left the building and walked out to the car. I didn't look at Mo until we were inside and I had started the engine. It was only when I pulled back onto the highway that Mo explained.

"My DNA is already in the database," she said, reaching for a cigarette. She handed me one as well. "So if they had found my blood at the scene, I'd be in a holding cell right now."

"Why are you in the database?" I said, and lit my cigarette.

Mo smiled. "I was picked up for something minor a few years ago in one of those states that takes a DNA sample from anyone who's been arrested."

I laughed. "Arrested for what? Being a slave-driver at work?"

"Ha ha. Very funny. No, something stupid. They dropped the charges, anyway. But it sucks that I'm now in the system."

"What was it for?"

"Never mind." Mo smiled and turned away from me and looked out of the window. She put down the glass a crack and a gust of hot air blasted in.

I looked at her, and then decided not to pursue it.

"So you think Garcia was just playing mind games with us? She took a guess about the blood and wanted to see how we reacted?" I said.

Mo shrugged. She was checking something on her phone.

I went on. "But isn't it possible that after my reaction she'll have her people go back over the scene and test more blood samples? It's only been a day or so. They can still get DNA from dried blood, right?"

Mo nodded. "They can, but they won't."

"Why not? Would they have cleaned up the scene so quickly? Don't they block off the area for a few days so they can go back if they realize they missed something?"

Mo nodded again. "They do, but they won't find any dried blood."

I sighed and gripped the steering wheel hard. I hated it when Mo fed me the answers bit by bit.

She laughed. "Maybe you don't remember when we drove back to the hotel from Chester's on Friday night."

"Remember what?"

"The streets."

"What about the damn streets?"

"I love doing this to you," said Mo. She dropped her cigarette out of the window and put the glass back up. "The streets were wet, Frank. The damn streets were wet."

Now I laughed. "It rained when we were at Chester's?"

She nodded and clapped her hands. "There was a summer storm for about three hours. The whole area got pounded. We were both passed out at Chester's. I remembered noticing the streets when we drove back to Milwaukee that night, but I didn't connect the dots back then or even yesterday when we talked about the antifreeze. But just now, when I tried to figure out why they hadn't found my blood, it all came back to me." She laughed and held up her phone to show me the weather report from that night. "Maybe that bullshit about Allah being on my side is true."

34

When we got back to Chester's, Simone was taking a nap. Chester was dressed and seemed a bit annoyed that we had taken so long.

"We need to get going if we're going to make our slot at the range," he said. "We'll need at least three hours, and I want to be out of there before the drunk Brewers fans come in."

"Okay," I said. "You want me to drive?"

"Yep."

"Let me hit the restroom first." I hurried through the living room and towards the first floor bathroom.

Five minutes later I was back outside. Mo and Chester were standing near the car. The trunk was open, and Mo was holding two baseball bats. She looked pissed.

"Where's the knife?" she said.

"What?" Then I remembered. At the restaurant, along with the tire irons, we had placed a knife on the ground in case we needed it. "Shit."

"Shit is right. No wonder Garcia figured there was someone else at the scene. That knife would have been too far away to fit into the story." Mo didn't wait for my reply. She turned and went back inside without another word.

I was mortified and speechless. Too many mistakes. This

next assignment had to go perfect. I didn't want to disappoint my new family.

Chester shrugged and started walking towards the garage. "How about we take my car," he said. "Come on."

35

Four hours later I wasn't sure what hurt the most: my head, with all the names and numbers of the weapons we used; my shoulder, from being unprepared for the surprisingly violent kickbacks from even the handguns; or my ego, from being yelled at and called a sissy by a gay plastic surgeon.

Still, after adjusting to the sound and motion associated with firing a weapon, it turned out I actually had pretty good aim. The shooting range was what they called full-service, which meant it had a course with moving targets. My first two passes, one with a Glock .22 and the second with a Smith & Wesson 9 millimeter, were adequate. But my third run, that time with a mini-Uzi submachine gun, was stellar. I had found my gun.

I was glad Chester had driven, because my right shoulder was sore as hell. But I felt good, almost prepared. Almost.

"So you're sure our guys have the same Uzis in their armory?" I asked.

Chester nodded. "Yep. At least three or four that I could see. Maybe more farther back."

"Good. That's what I'm using then."

Chester smiled. "I figured. Just don't spray Simone or me. That little beast dispatches almost a thousand rounds a minute."

I laughed. "Damn. Trust the Israelis to come up with something this slick."

"Yes. I love the double-irony of a Jew killing some neo-Nazis with their own Israeli-made weapons. Too bad those Neanderthals won't appreciate the poetic beauty in it."

I looked at Chester. "Oh, I'm sure you can read out a few choice verses before you plug those murderers."

He laughed. Then he looked at me for a second and got back to staring at the road.

We drove in comfortable silence for the next twenty minutes. Then I noticed him glancing over at me and smirking.

"What?" I said.

He gave me an odd smile. "You have something going on with Mo?"

"No way. She's my boss, you know. In multiple senses of the word. Why do you ask?"

"No reason."

We were quiet for the next few minutes. As we pulled towards the highway exit for Port Washington, I smiled. "Did Simone ask?"

Chester smiled, but didn't say anything.

"No need to say anything," I said.

36

That night we took it easy. Dinner was light, and no one drank anything. We spent several hours in Chester's basement going through the plan over and over and over again. Every detail was talked about, with every conceivable deviation from plan addressed and assigned an appropriate remediation action. By midnight I was exhausted. I was also impressed with the thoroughness and professionalism of our group. I could now see Mo's point about what happens when you bring ambitious and driven people together and get them past the mental barriers that make them live in lockstep with the law. That ambition and passion is easily diverted and harnessed. Perhaps too easily.

I didn't sleep well that night, but I woke up clear-headed and alert. By seven we were in the kitchen and dressed to kill. Mo was in black, and the rest of us were in red. Chester had suggested red because the walls of our targets' house were a dirty red. We weren't in matching outfits or anything—just regular street clothes. Of course, I had to borrow a pair of Chester's red jeans. Turned out he had plenty.

We drove in silence, each of us holding a cigarette. Janesville is almost two hours southwest of Port Washington, so it was a long time to be quiet. Still, nobody noticed. We were all too deep into ourselves. This was a time for solitude, a time to come to terms with what we were about to do, a time to stomp out any last-minute personal doubts, a time to convince ourselves that the job was already done and this was just the paperwork.

It was close to ten when we stopped at the rest-stop which was to be Mo's perch. It was an unmanned rest area. No gas or fast food—just restrooms and vending machines. There was a large expanse of lawn behind the small brown building, and I could see the steel railing that marked the edge. There were two other cars at the stop, but both had people in them, and it looked like they'd be gone soon. We waited, and the other cars soon left.

Mo got out of the backseat with the gun case. She was wearing those sheer surgical gloves and looked reasonably normal. She didn't look around at all, and walked straight past the restroom-building and towards the bushes that lined the area around the railing. We waited to make sure she couldn't be seen from where we were. Then I sent her a confirmation text, and we drove off.

It took another seven or eight minutes before we were under the highway and on our targets' street. Chester drove right past the house, turned the corner, took another left, and parked near what seemed to be a church combined with a homeless shelter. The church was a straight shot across the vacant lots behind our targets' house. Also, the church was the only possible spot where a strange car would not seem out of place in that neighborhood. If the timing worked out, the few homeless people milling about would soon be inside the building for the next few hours, and the street would be clear when we came back to the car. Besides, the majority of the shelter's patrons looked at least one parent shy of thoroughbred Aryan, and Chester was betting that in the unlikely event we were seen, the potential number of cooperative witnesses would be fairly low.

I heard the sound of metal on metal come from the backseat. When I turned, Simone smiled and handed me one of three shiny new chef's knives. The knife was heavy, and it had a firm rubber grip. The blade didn't look like something that would bend or snap easily. A great knife—perfect for paring, slicing, dicing, chopping. And yes, maybe a little stabbing.

"Slide it through the outside of your belt and drop your shirt out over it," said Chester. He grabbed his knife and showed me how. "Make sure it's pointing behind you and is loose enough to swing if you fall. That way you won't lose a kidney if you get surprised and knocked down."

I nodded, and did what he said. Then I looked back at Simone. I couldn't see her knife, but I figured she knew what she was doing.

Chester looked at his watch. It was just past ten. "The meeting is probably just getting started. Another five minutes, and we walk."

I took out a cigarette, but Chester stopped me from lighting up. I didn't argue. This wasn't the time to get into a frivolous conversation.

The five minutes passed in what seemed like thirty seconds, and I had only just drifted off into a daydream when I was interrupted.

"Let's walk," said Chester.

And we walked.

37

The overgrown grass and weeds in the vacant lot behind the first house was good cover, and we moved across it fast. The second lot was almost as sheltered, but the lot across from our targets' house had been cleared for what seemed to be a stalled construction project. So we waited at the edge of the second vacant lot.

Chester pointed at a small square window that looked to be just above the basement. "That gets us into the stairwell. Wait for Mo to send some rounds through the front windows, then give it ninety seconds for everyone to grab their guns. They'll probably gather in the stairs at that point, since there are no basement windows that face front. Then Mo will go quiet for thirty seconds."

I nodded. "Right. Then our targets will move up the stairs and onto the main floor. And Mo will wait until they're up there, and then she'll lay down a couple more shots to keep them busy."

Simone grimaced. "It's got to be perfect, though. If she fires too much, they may start back towards the stairs. Too little, and they may hear us busting through that basement window."

I smiled. "It'll be perfect."

Simone gave me a funny look that I didn't quite get. I

thought to ask, but Mo interrupted us by blowing out the front windows of the house.

We could hear glass and ceramic shattering, and then we heard shouts. The shouts got louder, and I guessed the men had gathered along the staircase that lined the back of the house. I felt calm, almost like my body saw no reason to kick me some adrenaline just yet. I hoped it was saving the rush for when we stormed.

Then everything went quiet. Mo had stopped shooting, as was the plan, but it was disconcerting that the shouting had also stopped. We could do nothing but wait. We were blind at that point—Mo was our eyes. Her next shot would be a signal for us to move.

Now the wait was excruciating, and the adrenaline started to gush into my bloodstream. I tried to will the precious hormone to retreat, afraid that I would use it up. Of course, this only pushed me closer to panic level, and my mouth suddenly went dry and I could feel my throat begin to pucker up like I had swallowed half a lemon. I tried to spit, but nothing came out.

Simone looked at me and touched my hand. I could feel her warmth even through two layers of sterile rubber gloves. For an instant, I had a vision of the two of us moving to a small town in Texas and settling down to raise some kids and maybe some cows. I smiled at her and squeezed her hand. I wanted to tell her I loved her. Not because I really was in love with her, but because in that moment I had an urgent need to express that sentiment. Maybe it was the fear of death that brought it out in me. Or maybe it's the wonderful logic of the human brain—since it realized that I wasn't going to physically remove myself from this stressful situation, it was trying to compensate by flooding me with positive emotions of corresponding intensity. Now I felt my throat loosen up, and I began to speak.

I'll never know what I was about to say, because Mo interrupted yet again with a three-shot volley that took out the remaining first-floor windows. Chester raised his hand.

"Go," he said, and sprinted towards the window.

We raced after him. He had kicked in the glass by the time I got there. After the briefest of glances to make sure we were behind him, he ducked down and slid feet-first through the square opening.

I dropped down onto the stairs and froze for a minute as my eyes adjusted to the darkness. Chester was already at the bottom of the stairs, and I knew he was making his way to the armory door, which was around the corner. The armory itself was built into the space beneath the same wooden stairs. I waited for Simone, and reached out to help her when I saw her legs come through the window.

But I should have been watching the stairs.

I didn't have much experience with guns, but everyone knows the sound of a shotgun being cocked. I slowly looked up to the top of the stairs, and into the twin circles of a twelve-gauge. My eyes refocused on another circular object farther up the barrel. It was the round shaved head of a smiling man. I blinked away the sweat from my eyes, and I may have even volunteered a pathetic smile.

The man turned his head slightly and made as if he was going to announce his catch to his comrades. I blinked again, and when I was done, it was as if I were watching an old film reel and had missed a few frames.

The man's eyes were as big as the double barrels of his gun. I gasped when I noticed the rubberized handle of a chef's knife peeking innocently out of a spot just to the right of his adam's apple. I stared at Simone, and then looked back up at the man.

A steady stream of dark liquid oozed from his cut, and the man sat down on the step above him, placed the gun next to him, and then slowly rolled head over heels towards us.

Simone reached out and stopped his fall. Then she grabbed her knife, stuck him with it once more, looked up at me, and shrugged.

"Come on," she said.

I stared at the lifeless body near my feet. I wanted to feel shock and horror, but all I felt was relief. I smiled at Simone and followed her down the stairs.

38

Mo's shots were getting more spaced out by the time we had armed ourselves. Of course, we couldn't actually hear the shots; just the impact. It did appear that there were enough breakable targets in Mo's line of sight, and she was hitting these so that we'd know she was still firing. Details, details, details. The mark of a good consultant.

"We need to move quick," said Chester. "That's twenty-one shots, and Mo's only got three cartridges. Nine more shots and she can't help us anymore."

I nodded as I tightened my grip on the mini-Uzi. Simone was using two Glock .22s. They looked good in her hands. Chester had a shotgun slung low across his back, a Glock in his waistband, and another shotgun in his hands. He opened the armory door. All quiet in the basement. We started to move, but then the noises made us stop.

A loud shout, then heavy footsteps on the wooden stairs above, followed by several low voices and multiple cautious movements. The boys had discovered their slaughtered brother. And with the broken window glass halfway down the stairs, it couldn't have been a stretch to figure out what was going on: they were being flanked.

Of course, being flanked doesn't mean so much if your target knows about it. So from our perspective, the situation had rapidly turned into us being cornered. Cornered in a room full of guns, but cornered nonetheless.

Chester looked at us. "I'm sorry, guys." He smiled. "I'll go first."

Simone nodded and looked at me. I was ready. My adrenaline was at a steady level, and my heart was pumping strong and hard.

"Let's do it," I said. If I was going down, at least I should act a little macho.

But then I grabbed Chester before he could charge out the door. He turned, and I think he was expecting me to be freaking out or whimpering to go home. His annoyed expression turned into a smile of realization when he saw me point to the wooden ceiling of the armory.

The footsteps had slowed, which meant almost everyone would be directly above us, creeping down towards the door. Now Simone got it, and she smiled too.

I spread my legs to brace myself, and then pointed my Uzi at the ceiling. Chester looked like he was about to laugh. He put one hand over his mouth, and tapped me on the shoulder with the other. He pointed at a set of old, well-used guns that looked sort of familiar. Chester mouthed the words, and I understood that they were AK47s. I guess they were a better bet for blasting through wood.

We each traded our weapon for one of the Russian-made classics. Each had a full magazine, and Simone pointed out the safety as well as the setting for fully-automatic fire. She gestured that I should wait for her sign before flipping the safety.

The small armory was big enough for the three of us to stand side by side with plenty of elbow room. We waited while Chester carefully placed a bulletproof cover on a box that contained several grenades and some ammo. Then he looked at Simone and nodded. She did a finger-countdown from three. On zero we let loose.

The sound of three AK47s reverberating in a small wooden room is something that has to be experienced to be truly understood. Full, throaty, and blood-curdling, like three four-stroke Harley-Davidson engines kicking to life in an echo chamber. The AK is called an *assault* rifle for a reason: this is not a gun intended primarily for self-defense—not unless you're one of those that says offense is the best defense.

The initial shouts of surprise and pain were drowned out by the thundering drones of our three barrels, and soon the air was heavy with gunsmoke and disintegrating wood and plaster. We sprayed every inch of ceiling like a maintenance team doing the waterproofing. I had no idea how many bullets came in a magazine, but it was a lot, because I could feel the empty cartridges gather around my shoes.

We hit empty at roughly the same time, and each of us gracefully reached out for a new magazine as if we were a synchronized swimming team performing in the gray fluidity of the smoke-and-dust mixture. The feeling was sublime. Perhaps the thick vibrations of the AKs had resonated with something deep in our spiritual centers, bonding us with our weapons, turning us into life-forms that were more than human. We were above logic and reason and common morality. There was no doubt about what we were doing, no consideration of whether it was right or wrong. We simply took in the bliss of the moment. If we had crossed a line, that line was no longer anywhere in sight.

Finally Simone raised her hand and lowered her weapon. Chester and I did the same, and we all stood absolutely motionless, listening for anything that wasn't dead.

After the last splinter had fallen and we were satisfied

that the only things moving were our three pumping hearts, Chester put down his weapon, whipped out his knife, and slowly moved out of the armory. We followed him as he moved towards the stairs.

The staircase looked like a battlefield on the morning after. No, it looked like one of those massacre scenes with bodies piled haphazardly and with arms and legs and heads intertwined as if it were a mound of parts that you could mix-and-match to create your own action figure. The blood was fresh, and I was glad the walls had been red to begin with.

We took care not to step on anyone. I'm not sure why, but it seemed disrespectful, even more so than pumping them full of metal projectiles from below. I pushed open the back door, and held it for Simone and Chester. Simone stepped out, but Chester didn't. He was counting.

"Eleven," he whispered. "There may be one more."

He raised his finger to his lips and slowly crept to the top of the stairs. When he got there he spun around the corner, and I heard a shout of surprise. I started up the stairs, and then stopped when I saw the back of Chester's red denims. He was hunched over and dragging a bleeding man towards the stairs. The man looked like he was in his late twenties. He had taken several bullets to his lower body and was barely conscious.

Chester pulled the man about a quarter of the way down the stairs.

"Remember me?" said Chester.

"No," said the man. "Who the fuck are you?"

"It doesn't matter. All that matters is that I remember you." Chester forced the man to turn around and lie down facing the stairs. Chester pushed the man's shaved and tattooed head towards the top step.

"Eat it," said Chester.

"What?"

"You know what. Eat it, you piece of shit."

"Come on, man. Why are you doing this?"

"You remember Tom Sullivan?"

The man was quiet for several long moments. "We made a deal with the DA for that. The guy who did it is in prison. What more do you want?"

Chester spoke quietly. "Tom was my husband. And you were there that night. And you know what I want. So eat it."

The man turned his head for an instant and looked up at Chester. "See you in hell," he said. Then he bit down on the edge of the hard wooden top step.

I didn't stop Chester, but I couldn't watch. The sound was awful, just awful. Chester brought his foot down several times, and there was a dull cracking sound each time.

Then, after a pause, I heard another cracking sound. But this crack was different. It was the crack of a small caliber pistol, like one of the first guns I had used at the range. I turned in panic, and saw Chester frozen at the top of the stairs. He was facing me, his mouth wide open. He was in pain, but I couldn't figure out why—I could see no living creature anywhere. Then I heard five more cracks followed by a clicking sound, and Chester fell forward into my arms. Only then did I realize why I hadn't seen the shooter earlier.

He couldn't have been over four feet tall or more than eight years old. He was shaved bald, and if I hadn't known this was a house of skinheads, I might have thought he was a victim of childhood cancer and suffering the effects of chemotherapy. His face was twisted into a grimace of anger, but it was still the face of a child. We had left our guns in the basement, but it didn't matter. He was out of ammo, which was good, because I wouldn't have attacked him.

"Out," said Chester. He was draped over my shoulder, and his voice was a gurgle near my right ear. "Leave me. Out now."

Simone had come back to the door, and she shouted and reached for Chester's legs to help carry him.

Chester kicked at her. "Now, goddamn it. Now!"

Simone looked at me, and back at Chester. She touched his cheek. He tried to smile, but his jaw started to convulse and rattle. Then he went still, and his face relaxed. Simone nodded at me, and we lowered him to the ground.

I left without looking at the kid again. But as I ran back to the car, I knew I would never forget his little white innocent dome. How many would he kill when he grew up? Did we turn him into a monster, or was he already well on his way? I almost smiled as we pulled away in Chester's car. At least I was no longer asking those questions about myself.

39

We picked up Mo as planned. She heaved the gun case into the open trunk and then came around to the rear door. She flinched when she saw only two of us in the car, but she didn't say a word. There wasn't anything to be said. Even with all the possible deviations from plan and allowances for improvisation, there was only one situation that would cause us to leave someone behind.

We drove in silence, that loud kind of silence where your ears feel like they might explode. Simone was at the wheel, and I was riding shotgun.

After lighting a cigarette, I turned and offered one to Mo. She refused.

"Hey," I said, pointing at the red on the white car seat. "Is that you?"

"Shit," said Mo. She grabbed the corner of her thick black tee, and I could tell it was soaked in blood. "Shit. Shit."

There was a box of tissues in the glove box, and I handed it to Mo. She plucked out a fistful and mopped up the blood. It was a leather seat, and the tissues worked well. She leaned over onto her good side so that no more blood would drip. We all knew that the police would search this car before the day was over.

We all went quiet again. Just a day ago we were a happy

family. Chester's death felt no less tragic than losing a brother or uncle or cousin.

But the silence didn't last long.

"Why didn't you take out that little Nazi bastard?" said Simone as she leaned to her right to get a look at Mo in the rearview mirror.

"He was out of my line of sight," said Mo. "Not that I would have shot a child. You know better than that, Simone."

"Where was the kid to begin with? If he came from the second floor, you would have seen him walk through the living room." Simone's voice was getting louder.

"I saw him earlier, but he was alone, and I didn't see a gun through my scope," said Mo. "Besides, I told you. I wouldn't have taken out a kid. You guys should have been backing up Chester."

I gulped. "That would be on me, I'm afraid." As it hit me, I started to choke up. "Oh God."

"It's not your fault, Frank." Mo paused. "It's hers. She knows you're just a beginner."

"Screw you," said Simone. "You had that murderer in your sights, and you let him go. You let him shoot Chester in the back."

Mo had calmed down now. She just smiled. "I can't make the call to shoot a child when I'm half a mile away."

Simone stared at the road. "Don't want to add to the list of dead children on your conscience? Why? What's one more? And this one wasn't even yours."

Mo let out a surprised laugh. "Are you serious?"

"Okay, stop. Please." I waved my hands. "Look, I'm not a beginner anymore, so that can't be an excuse. You guys trusted me enough to put me in there. And now Chester is on my conscience."

Simone sighed and went quiet. We drove for another ten minutes before pulling off the highway a few exits before Port Washington to dump the rifle. Then we got back on the road and drove in silence for the next twenty minutes.

Finally Simone looked over at Mo. "I'm sorry, babe."

Mo smiled. She tapped me on the shoulder. "I'll have that cigarette now."

40

Simone almost hit the front steps of Chester's house as she screeched in. I raced inside and ran upstairs to gather my and Mo's luggage. When I got back down, I heard Mo calling me out to the backyard.

She was sitting on the grass a few feet away from the fountain. I could see some medical supplies near her, and I guessed she wanted me to patch her up outside so that any blood would drip into the ground. I ran over and took a look. The stitches hadn't torn, and the blood had come from a small opening at one end of the wound. We taped her up tight, and I gathered the bloody swabs and placed them in a plastic bag to carry with us.

We went out front and loaded up our rental car. I could see Simone's rental, but there was no Simone. It was another twenty minutes before she came back down. She removed her rubber gloves as she walked up to us.

"Trash, dishes, bathrooms, and I put all the bed linens in the washer," she said. "I'm sure there's some other trace of us here, but if I can't think of it, it means it'll take a while before the police figure it out. Hopefully they'll see it as a one-man act of revenge."

"Until they find the three recently-fired AKs," I said.

Mo shook her head. "The place is littered with guns. And

Chester could have used two of them, maybe even all three. Doesn't mean anything."

"What about the kid?" I said. "He definitely saw me."

"We can't be certain what he saw. There was too much smoke and dust, and all the lights had been shot out. Even if he's able to tell the police that someone besides Chester was involved, there's a pretty low risk of him giving a sketch artist anything useful," said Simone. "Maybe he'd recognize you if you're caught by some other means and they put you in a line-up. But even then, a good lawyer can cast doubt on it, especially if some time passes."

I looked at Mo. "So what now?"

"Now we go home, back to New York."

I nodded. It was perfect. Our consulting project got done on Friday, we took the weekend to wrap up the paperwork, took Monday off for travel, and then we're back in Manhattan by Tuesday. A completely normal, explainable, and verifiable weekend schedule.

"What about you?" I looked at Simone. "Back to Texas? Walker-Midland?"

"Probably. Maybe a vacation first." She smiled at me. "I've taken a leave of absence from Walker. Personal reasons, I told them." She shrugged. "Dealing with the repressed emotions related to the untimely death of my ex-husband."

"Oh, right," I said. "Your last husband was killed. How did it happen again?"

Simone came up to me and kissed me gently on the mouth. "Boating accident."

41

The steep approach into LaGuardia Airport usually results in a solid bounce during landing, but we must have had a good pilot, because I didn't wake up until the stewardess shook me. I was startled, and stood up so fast that I hit my head on the baggage compartment above the seat. It didn't hurt. Those surfaces are designed to give way, so although it doesn't really hurt, it makes a loud sound, and everyone looks at you with shock and pity like you've just suffered a major head injury. I returned each and every look with a cold hard tough stare of my own. Don't pity me, my expression said, I'm a goddamn *killer*. Fear me, and thank me for doing this for you.

Mo had been upgraded to Business Class, and she was waiting for me in the terminal. We didn't have any checked luggage, of course, and so we headed straight out to the street. Mo's car service was waiting, and she gave me a nod and a smile before handing her luggage to the driver and disappearing into the black tinted Towncar.

As usual, I had forgotten to schedule my pickup in advance. If I called now, it would take twenty minutes before they got a car out to me. I looked over at the taxi stand—the line snaked all the way through the layered waiting area and was now blocking the terminal exit. As I was doing the mental calculation of whether the taxi line would take more or less than twenty minutes, the M60 bus pulled up to the green bus stop in front of me. I lived on 109th Street and Amsterdam Avenue, and the M60 ends at Broadway and 106th, so I was pretty much on the way. I checked for my Metrocard, and then jogged to the bus. It was empty, since LaGuardia is one of the terminals for the route. I slinked to the back and took one of the single seats that lined the left of the vehicle.

I loved the view when coming back into Manhattan via the RFK-Triborough bridge. You got to see the majestic towers of midtown, and then you exited right onto 125th Street in Harlem. The M60 takes 125th Street clear across Manhattan, and the layers of double-parked cars and hordes of scurrying jaywalkers means it can take forty minutes to cross just two miles of street. But the crowds and the lights and the horns and the music and the other indescribable sounds of Harlem's central artery usually made the trip go quick.

Almost too quick this time, and before I knew it I was the last one on the bus. I pulled the cord so I could hop off at 110th and Broadway, just two blocks from my building. The walk was quick and nice.

And she was waiting for me outside my apartment building.

"Simone? What the hell?"

She smiled. "Told you I might take a vacation first."

My shock wore off, and I laughed and kissed her. Within minutes we were inside my first-floor apartment and stumbling towards the bedroom.

42

The sushi delivery guy got there just after midnight. It was his last run of the night, and I gave him a thirty percent tip. Simone was already in the kitchen when I closed the front door. She wore a long green shirt and nothing else. After stubbing out her cigarette, she grabbed the food parcel from my hands and gave me a smack on the lips in return.

"I love that you can order fresh sushi to be delivered at midnight on a Monday," she said. "Maybe I'll just move up here."

I smiled.

She laughed at my expression. "Just kidding. Don't look so terrified."

"I'm not." I reached around her waist and put my face close to hers. "I just don't believe you. There's no way you're leaving your Texas ranch to move into a Manhattan shoebox."

"Well, it wouldn't be a shoebox. I'm pretty loaded, you know." She moved away from me and reached into the kitchen cabinet for two plates and a couple of bowls. "You have chopsticks? I hate these cheap wooden ones that come with the sushi."

I pointed at a drawer. "You know it's a million dollars per bedroom for a condo in the city, right?"

Simone didn't flinch. "Two bedrooms should be enough,

I think. One for guests, one for us." She turned to me and smiled. "Unless you're thinking kids. Which is possible, I guess. But I'm not sure I want to go down that path again."

I laughed. I wasn't sure if she was kidding, but I got the sense that she wasn't sure either. It was a playful conversation, and it felt good after the seriousness of the past day, not to mention the intensity of the past hour on my bedroom floor.

"So you're going to sell the ranch, buy a two million dollar apartment in Manhattan, and keep me as your boy-toy?" I shrugged. "I've heard of worse ideas. When can we move on this?"

Simone laughed as she emptied out the last of the *edamame* into a white ceramic bowl. I grabbed the plates of sushi, and we moved to the two-person table in the small dining alcove nestled between the living room and the kitchen.

We ate in silence for a little while, not because of any awkwardness, but because the salty soy sauce and fresh fish and pungent *wasabi* monopolized our attention. It was still Monday night, and it was hard to imagine how much energy we must have burned over the course of our very full day. The juxtaposition of geography and setting and mood from a neo-Nazi cave in Janesville, Wisconsin, to my cozy pad in Uptown Manhattan felt so natural that I became worried that it didn't seem surreal enough. In fact, the lack of surrealism itself was surreal. Maybe this was what psychiatrists call "compartmentalization"? But no, I wasn't blocking out what we had done earlier that day. In fact, I could think about it quite calmly. There was no trauma, no guilt, no regret—at least not in the usual sense of those terms. Sure, thinking about Chester caused a little flutter in me. I knew I was partially responsible for his death. I couldn't deny there was a part of me that felt some guilt about that.

But there was also another part of me, a part of me that had looked into Chester's eyes as he died in my arms, a part of me that understood that Chester didn't blame me. In some way, I knew that Chester had never planned to leave that house. I understood that he blamed himself for Tom's death, and I was suddenly certain that Chester would have taken his own life had the entire crew of murderers been put away to begin with. I had no doubt that if the kid hadn't finished it, we'd now be reading a news article about how a local plastic surgeon did the murders and then committed suicide in his Port Washington mansion. Of course, I had no way of knowing any of this, and in all likelihood it was just a defensive reaction to my own mistake. But still, it's hard to explain how certain I felt about it.

I snapped out of it when I felt Simone's hand on mine.

"Hey," she said. "You okay?"

I smiled and nodded and looked down at my empty plate.

"It wasn't your fault," said Simone. "Even if you had seen the kid, neither of you would have killed him. You know that."

"Yeah, but maybe we could have stopped him. Taken the gun away."

"He was too far away. You wouldn't have gotten to him in time. And both of you could have been shot." She shook her head. "Mo should have taken the shot when she had the chance."

"What? How can you say that? Especially after you just conceded that neither Chester nor I would have killed a child. Would you have taken the shot?"

Simone laughed and looked away. "You don't want to know the answer to that."

I leaned forward on the table. "I do."

She looked at me. "Yes."

"Bullshit," I said.

"Why don't you believe me?"

"Because." I reached for my pack of cigarettes and lit one.

"Because I'm a woman?"

I shrugged. "I don't know. Maybe."

Simone sighed. "I know I shouldn't make a big deal out of this, especially since it makes life easier for me." She lit her own cigarette. "But most people don't realize that women are better equipped than men to handle the psychological repercussions of murder. Especially when it comes to a random murder, or the murder of a child."

I burst out laughing. "Come on. I'll go so far as to grant women equal rights to that trauma. But you can't convince me that women are *better* suited to be wanton killers."

"I don't care about convincing anyone. The prevailing belief structure favors killers like me." She leaned back in her chair and blew a puff of smoke into the hanging paper lantern. "You know, there are a ton of unsolved serial-murders—and I'm talking every country in the world—which are unsolved precisely because no one would seriously consider the possibility that a female may have been the killer."

"Fine, maybe. But that's still different from the murder of a child. I mean, what about the whole maternal instinct thing? Wouldn't that make it much harder for a woman to kill a kid?"

Simone shook her head. "First of all, you obviously don't know what postpartum depression is. Many women fantasize about killing their children soon after birth." She took another drag from her cigarette and was quiet as the smoke rolled out into the dimly lit room. "But that usually passes quickly, of course. And my argument isn't really connected to postpartum."

"Okay." I put out my cigarette and reached for another. "Let's hear it."

"Well, I don't know if any psychiatrist would back me up on this one, but here's what I think." She paused for another moment, and shut her eyes briefly before continuing. "It's hard to explain, but I think it's an odd emotional sense of entitlement. I think the knowledge that we can bring new life into this world gives us an irrational sense of leeway when it comes to taking life out of this world."

I stared at her. "Nobody thinks like that. You're insane."

She laughed and shook her head. "No, I'm not saying any woman makes that calculation. Not even a woman who has killed her own children would make that explicit argument. But it's something that's buried deep in the psyche. And I think it would take the edge off any lingering psychological effects."

I looked away. "Okay, we're out of my area of expertise here. Even as an all-knowing management consultant, I don't feel prepared to speculate on this topic." I looked up at her and smiled. "All I have to say is that I'd like to see documented psychological studies on this before I start repeating the theory at cocktail parties."

Simone laughed and blew a puff of smoke directly at me. "Okay, I concede. I'm full of shit. It's just my own pathetic rationalization for why I don't feel anything when I kill someone. And I'm not sure if I ever did." She ran her fingers through her hair. "God, it's been so long now, I don't even remember what it felt like the first time."

"When was the first time, anyway?" I asked. "How did you get pulled into this craziness?"

Simone didn't answer. She gave me a look that seemed to say be careful about asking questions that you don't want to know the answers to. She stood up and began stacking the empty plates.

I grabbed the glasses and followed her to the kitchen. As we loaded the dishwasher, I nudged her and whispered into her ear.

"The boating accident?"

43

"My daughter from my first husband was twelve at the time," said Simone. She lay down on the right side of the bed and turned to me and I could smell the mouthwash on her breath. "One evening she told me that her step-dad had grabbed her and . . . propositioned her, I guess is one way of putting it."

"Damn," I said.

"So I asked him about it the next day. Of course, I expected him to deny it, but I figured maybe he'd get the message and at least stop."

"And?"

"And . . . the bastard just shrugged and said he didn't see what the big deal was. She wasn't his flesh and blood, he said, and so it was perfectly natural for him to be attracted to her." Simone turned and lay on her back and stared up at the ceiling.

"Holy crap," I said. "So you planned a boating trip and pushed him overboard?"

"No," she said. "I kicked him in the throat right then and there. In my goddamn kitchen. He went down right away, just like they described in my self-defense classes."

I sat up in bed and stared at her. I was somewhere between shocked and amused. "And he died?"

"No. At least I don't think so. It didn't matter. As soon as he went down, it seemed like I knew exactly what to do, even though I had never thought about it before." She looked at me and shrugged. "I took a metal rolling pin and smashed his head in. Then I dragged him out to the garage, loaded him into our boat, which was already hitched to the truck, and drove out to the lake. It was all done in less than two hours. I was finished with the police report before my daughter got home from school."

"Damn, Simone." I laughed. "What did you tell her?"

"The truth," she said with a shrug. "He was drunk and hit his head and fell off the boat and sank like a stone."

"Nice." I lay back down. "But how did that lead to you the Network?"

Simone laughed. "My sister-in-law."

I sat up again. "Wait, your dead husband's sister? She was in the Network?"

"Yup. And she had staged enough accidents to see right through my story."

"And instead of turning you in, she recruited you?"

Simone nodded. "Almost ten years ago now."

"That's a long time to be a super-secret assassin-chick." I kissed her on the neck.

She sighed. "Tell me about it. I need to retire."

"Yeah, I was wondering, actually. What are the retirement options for us?" I was still kissing her neck.

"There aren't any. This is a lifestyle choice. A permanent one."

I looked up. "Well, not all of us had a choice."

"Whatever. You had a choice. And you damn well made it. You're a born killer just like I am. Just like Mo is. You just needed help recognizing it."

I didn't argue, but just returned to making my way down

her neck. "But I guess when you're an Omega, you aren't necessarily out there as much. Isn't your job now making assignments and running validations or whatever? Managing the various cells that roll up to you?"

"That's part of it. But we're all expected to do field work. We're not detectives or investigators. We're killers, and we don't stop killing until . . . well, until we stop."

"And when do we stop?" I murmured. My eyes were closed, and my hands were sliding down in search of the bottom of Simone's long shirt.

She grabbed my hand. "I don't think you're listening."

I moved up on the pillow and looked at her. "Sure I was. You said we stop killing when we stop."

"And what does that mean?"

I shrugged. "When we decide it's enough, we leave. Resign. Retire. Quit. Whatever you call it."

Simone laughed. "I don't think Mo has explained things well enough."

"What do you mean?"

"Frank, there is no resigning or quitting. This is a one-way street."

Now my stomach raged with that feeling I had hoped would never come back. The intensity of the last few days had made me temporarily forget about the practical aspects of my new life. I thought Simone's emergence had freed me—after all, Mo didn't have anything on me anymore. She couldn't turn me in for killing Takahashi and Yoshi, because it would implicate her as well. I guess I had assumed I could now walk away whenever I saw fit, whenever I decided I couldn't handle the killing. Not that I wanted to walk away just yet, but still, knowing that I didn't have the option of walking away was not a small matter.

"But what does that mean? If I decide I'm done, what happens?"

"What do you think?"

"No way. That doesn't make sense. That's against everything this group stands for. Even soldiers get to go home after their tours, or get honorable discharges, or resign, or retire."

Simone ran her fingers through my hair. "But we aren't soldiers, honey. In some ways, what we do is more stressful because we need to keep it a secret from those closest to us. If we had the option to quit, we'd never be able to keep this thing going. Everyone would just stop sooner or later; more likely sooner. We'd have to keep recruiting new people, and there'd be more mistakes, more chances for leaks. The Network would turn into an inefficient, clumsy organization of half-assed murderers." She shook her head. "Noble intentions and motives aside, the reality is we need some external constraints to keep us locked into this lifestyle, into this life."

I took a deep breath and rolled over to my side of the bed. "Well, death is a pretty good constraint."

Simone crawled towards me. "Or a pretty good opportunity."

"And what does that mean?"

She sat up in bed and leaned over to the bedside table for her cigarettes. "Death can be our way out of this."

"You mean fake our own deaths?"

Simone shrugged as she lit a cigarette. "That's one option: fake deaths."

"And what's the other?"

"Real deaths."

I stared at her. "You mean suicide?"

She laughed. "Not our deaths, silly." Then she stopped laughing. "Remember, our organization is structured so that part of it can break off without exposing the rest. We also have some time-lag rules. Since I just started as a Beta Omega, my Alpha Omega wouldn't have revealed my identity to his peers quite yet. So it's just him. And I can get to him."

I swallowed hard. "But aren't there Alpha members from other cells that know about you? Alphas that report up to you?"

Simone spoke softly. "Just two cells in total. One of those cells was Chester's, and because of our protocols his Beta doesn't know me." She waited for a moment. "The other cell is yours."

I stared even harder. The smell of cigarette smoke mixed with peppermint mouthwash made me want to throw up. Or maybe it was just the dawning realization of what Simone meant, of whom she meant.

Simone looked at me through the rising cloud of white smoke. "What's the matter? You don't think you could do it? You in love with her?"

44

Simone probably didn't believe me when I said I was too sleepy to think. I didn't care. I buried my face in my pillow and pretended to be asleep. But I was terrified. What could I say? Faking my own death wasn't an option. I had thought about that enough when Mo had me backed into a corner, and I knew I would never put my parents through the misery. But I couldn't kill Mo. I thought about suggesting that we include Mo in our mini-revolution, but I knew it would be a mistake. Mo was in this for a deeper reason. For her, leaving would mean betraying the memory of her daughter.

But for me, leaving would be betraying Mo. And I was done betraying Mo. I buried my head deeper into my pillow and wished for it all to go away. For an instant, I wondered if Simone would snap my neck while I slept. But I was almost too sleepy to care. As long as it didn't wake me, a broken neck didn't sound so bad.

Then it was morning. I woke up and rubbed my neck and took in the fresh smell of cigarette smoke and coffee. Simone was sitting at the foot of the bed, her hair tied up, holding a steaming cup and reading on her BlackBerry.

She turned when she felt me stir. "Hey." She smiled at me. It was a warm, beautiful smile, and I felt it pass through me.

"Good morning," I said.

She put down her phone and touched my leg. "I'm sorry about last night. I wasn't serious. It had just been a long day. Maybe I am getting a bit too old and too crazy for all this."

"No problem. I barely remember what we talked about, anyway."

"Good. But I'm still embarrassed about it. Especially about asking if you're in love with her. I don't care about that. And it's none of my business. I have fun being with you, but if that ever needs to change, it's fine."

I smiled and nudged her with my foot. "I have fun with you too. And we're not in a line of work where romance is an option, right?" I stood up and stuck out my chest and pretended to flex my biceps. "We are superheroes. And all superheroes run into trouble when they fall in love. All of them: Superman, Batman, Spiderman—you name it."

Simone laughed. "Okay, Mighty Mouse. Get dressed. We have a date in an hour."

I looked at my biceps. "Mighty Mouse? That's harsh." Then I shrugged and walked towards the bathroom. "What are we doing on our date?"

"We're meeting Mo."

I stopped just before closing the bathroom door. "You told her you were here?"

"Yes. Why? Is that a problem?"

"No, of course not." I wasn't sure why I was surprised, but I guess when you're sleeping with the assassin-boss of your assassin-boss, the emotions can be hard to interpret.

45

We arrived at the 96th Street entrance to Central Park just before ten. The sun was out, and so was half of Manhattan. I wondered why it seemed like no one had to work that day. Then I remembered that we weren't working either—no consulting, and no killing. Just a walk in the park with my assassin-boss and her assassin-boss. Life was good.

"Hey," said Mo. She jogged up to us and gave Simone a hug. "What a surprise." She winked at me. "You guys get any sleep last night?"

I didn't answer. For some reason, I was uncomfortable with Mo's casual remarks about my relationship with Simone.

Simone looped her arm through mine and laughed. "Well, I tried to get romantic, but Mighty Mouse here said that superheroes can't afford to fall in love."

Mo smiled. "Is that so, Frank?"

I shrugged and forced a smile. Simone let go of me and walked ahead towards the park. I looked at Mo and shrugged again. We strolled after Simone without making any serious effort to catch up with her.

Mo nudged me with her elbow. "Mighty Mouse, eh?"

"That's me," I said awkwardly.

Simone was waiting for us near the playground at the entrance to Central Park. She seemed distracted, and was staring at the noisy kids when we reached her. She gave us an embarrassed smile when she noticed us looking at her.

"Come on," she said. "Let's walk uptown. If I remember correctly, there's a nice waterfall at the top of the park near 110th Street."

"I always found that waterfall creepy," I said. It was true. When I went running in the park, I'd always run a bit faster past the spot with the waterfall. Maybe it was because you couldn't really see it from the main road, but you could hear it, and you could feel the temperature drop right around that area.

"Come on, Mighty Mouse," said Mo. "All the more reason for you to come along and protect us from the evil that may be lurking near the waterfall."

"Yeah, right," I said. "Either one of you could kill me without even breaking a sweat."

Simone looked right at me with a serious expression. "No. It's sunny and humid. I'd probably sweat a little."

Mo laughed, but I didn't. Instead, I lit a cigarette, much to the disgust of a super-fit jogger who happened to be passing us right then. I glared at the runner. I resented his resentment.

The walk uptown was reasonably pleasant, and even the waterfall wasn't so bad. Actually, it was the first time I had really ventured off the main road and into the secluded waterfall area. It was a lot higher than I had expected, and much more than just a stream trickling over some rocks. There was no one else there, and the three of us stood quietly and soaked up the gentle roar of the falls.

Mo had her arms crossed over her chest, and she walked up to the edge of the falls and peered over. I happened to notice Simone looking at her, and it sent a shiver up and down my spine. I shook my head and looked down at the ground and smiled at my own paranoia. When I looked back up, Simone was staring at me. I smiled at her, and stepped up close to Mo.

"Be careful," I said. "I'm not a very good swimmer."

Mo smiled. "Well, I'm an excellent swimmer."

Now Simone moved near us and leaned out over the drop. "I don't think drowning would be your primary concern if you fell down there."

"I'm hungry," I said quickly. "How about we get some lunch?"

"Sounds good," said Mo. "Maybe somewhere in Midtown? I need to stop by the office at some point this afternoon."

I sighed. "Right. Work." I smiled at Mo. "I think I'll be working from home today."

Mo shrugged. "That's cool with me. Has anyone in the office called you about another project?"

"No. My schedule shows me as booked on the Milwaukee deal until the end of this week. And I haven't felt the need to update the staffing coordinator yet."

Mo smiled. "No hurry. You can hide out for a week or so. It might work out well, actually. I think this California gig I've been trying to sell may go through soon."

"Cool," I said. The prospect of flying under the radar for a week and then shipping out to California sounded nice. And judging by Simone's lack of interest in our conversation, I was optimistic that it would be a murder-free consulting job.

Soon we arrived at Central Park's west exit on 110th Street. Mo went out into the street to hail a cab, but Simone stopped her.

"Let's take the subway. I love the New York Subway," she said.

"Okay," said Mo.

We all walked to the end of the block and entered the stairs leading down to the 110th Street stop for the Central Park West subway line. It was a small station, and since there was another subway line a few blocks over on Broadway, this line wasn't used as much for local traffic. The platform was almost empty, and it stank of human piss.

Simone walked to the end of the platform and stretched out her arms and took a deep breath. "Ah. The funk of New York City. I love it."

I laughed. "Maybe you are cut out for city living, after all."

"Maybe I am." Simone turned to me and smiled.

"You thinking of moving to a city?" asked Mo. She walked up to the edge of the platform and leaned over to check for a train. The tunnel was dark, and Mo turned back to Simone. "Houston? Dallas?"

Simone laughed. "No. I was just talking shit. I like my country home. I have horses, you know." Suddenly her expression changed and she looked sad for a moment.

Mo looked at me and then back at Simone. I could tell Mo knew something was up. Maybe it was her jungle sense or whatever she called it. Or maybe it was just my paranoia again. It must have been, since Mo casually strolled past Simone and leaned out over the tracks once more.

"Train coming," she said.

The train sounded a bit too much like that waterfall, and I became alarmed as Simone took three steps to her left until she stood directly behind Mo. The roar became louder, and my paranoia screamed for me to do something.

I looked around, but there was no one else in sight. There was a camera monitoring us, but I suddenly became certain that Simone had been standing so as to keep her back to the camera at all times. And in a flash I remembered her opening up her hair and letting it fall across her face just as we had walked underground, which seemed odd to me, because the subway station was hot and humid.

The sound of the train was now deafening, and the blaze of its headlights disoriented me. For a second I thought I was shouting out loud, but I must not have been, because Mo was still facing the tracks, oblivious to what was about to happen.

I looked at Simone, and she was staring at me with a half-smile that I couldn't understand. Her smile made me want to fall to my knees and cry.

And she shrugged, turned away from me, and ran at Mo.

46

This time I could hear myself shout, but Mo still couldn't. She just stood there as Simone rushed towards her.

But my depth perception must have been off.

Simone ran straight past Mo, straight past the yellow line that says *Do Not Cross*, and straight into the path of eight hundred and fifty-two thousand pounds of moving metal.

Now, if you haven't seen something like this and aren't familiar with Sir Isaac Newton's simple law that says the total force exerted is equal to mass multiplied by acceleration, you might think that if a train is slowing down to stop, it's probably not fatal to step out in front of it.

And you'd be wrong. Dead wrong.

Obviously Simone remembered her high-school physics, because although it was a heartbreaking and traumatic sight for us, it was probably as quick a death as one could hope for. It is not an uncommon way for a New Yorker to end it, but it was not something I had witnessed before, and it is not a sight I'd wish on anyone.

And now I remembered Simone watching the children in the playground, and I thought of her sad eyes when she mentioned her horses, and I realized that her odd smile was just a simple goodbye.

And so I fell to my knees and cried, and for the second time, I grieved for Simone.

47

The police and paramedics and MTA staff came and went and I don't remember what I told them or if they even asked me anything. I cried the whole time. Mo was shocked at how upset I was, and I couldn't figure it out either. It wasn't guilt, that much I knew. Simone's choice had nothing to do with me. She wasn't lame enough to kill herself over some guy, and I wasn't arrogant enough to imagine that she would.

It was only later, in the privacy of my bedroom, with my head on the pillow that still smelled like cigarettes and peppermint, that I realized I had also been grieving for myself. My last hope of getting out had died in that subway station.

And then suddenly I was no longer sad. I felt liberated. I now had no choice but to embrace who I was and what I did. The process of my transformation was complete, and it felt wonderful and exhilarating. Lying there in my empty bedroom with all the lights on I began to laugh out loud. It was a sudden manifestation of the surge of ecstasy that whipped through my body, a wave of power, cold power, like a callous that covered my emotions, shielding me from their rawness.

I was alone, and free because of it. I was now worthy of my full name, middle initial included.

And I couldn't fucking wait until my next assignment.

48

Sadly, I did have to wait. Mo was still finalizing the sale of the California job, and she was busy as hell. I didn't go in to the office for the rest of that week. Truth is, I don't remember what I did, other than work out, smoke cigarettes, and watch Mighty Mouse cartoons. My enthusiasm for a raging killing binge had died down by the weekend, and I even began thinking about my regular job.

The following Monday I went in to the office. I hadn't been there for a couple of months now. Not particularly unusual for a consultant—in fact, partners look at you funny when you're in the office, because it usually means you're not on a project and hence you're not billing a client for your time. If you're not billing, it means that the consulting partnership is directly funding you from their own take-home. Hence the funny looks. What they're really saying is, "Get billable, you loser. I need to buy a new set of snowmobiles for my mountain home."

At first I laid low in the office. Then I checked my schedule on the intranet, and noticed that although it showed me as available that week, Mo had booked me for a month starting the following week, which meant she expected the California project to start up soon. That was good, because it meant I wouldn't get picked up for anything else for the rest of the week. Not unless someone needed last-minute help on a sales proposal or some internal research.

I took the time to catch up on some of the news from the Midwest. The "Janesville Massacre," as the *Milwaukee Journal-Sentinel* called it, had been chalked up to the work of Chester, the "vigilante plastic surgeon" who was seeking revenge for the District Attorney's leniency with the perpetrators of the hate-related murder of his partner. Apparently the act had received praise from several left-wing bloggers, and even the larger white-supremacist groups had not had much to say in defense of their fallen Aryan brothers. Obviously the child hadn't said much. Poor little guy. But he did know how to handle a gun awfully well, so I didn't lose too much sleep over him. He'd probably be better off in foster care than in that environment.

They obviously hadn't found the sniper rifle. And the only thing in the news reports that troubled me was the mention of FBI involvement. Not just the involvement in general, but the name of the agent in particular: Special Agent Ramona Garcia.

Still, it had been a week since the Janesville murders, and no one had tried to contact us. It seemed to be a pretty good sign that there was nothing to connect us to Janesville. I silently thanked Simone for cleaning out the trash and bathrooms at Chester's.

Mo called me on Thursday that week. She sounded upbeat.

"Hey. We sold the California project. I'm getting a small team to start here next week. You're on the team."

"Awesome," I said. "What kind of work is it?"

"Supply chain optimization for SpacedOut Clothing."

"Oh, shit, cool. They're a super-trendy company. I didn't know they were based in California, although I guess it's kind of obvious now that I think about it."

Mo laughed. "Yes. Trust me, their offices are as California as you can imagine."

I thought for a second. "Supply chain optimization. So we're going to be looking at how they get their textiles and other raw materials? And figure out ways to make that more efficient?"

"You got it. I knew you were an expert. At least, that's what I told the chief operating officer. He wants to see the resumes of every consultant we plan to include on the team. So make sure your resume has some related stuff."

I chuckled. "Well, that one sentence is the extent of my knowledge about supply chain optimization. But it's only Thursday. I'll take an online course via our intranet, and I'll also look at the knowledge-database and pull down reports that C&C has done for other clothing manufacturers. I'll be an expert by Sunday morning."

"Perfect," said Mo. "And book yourself in at the San Francisco Hilton."

"Hell, yes. The one at Union Square? I love that place. Are we working in downtown San Francisco?"

Mo sighed. "No. We're going to be working out of Spaced-Out's operations center in Burlingame, near the airport. But I got clearance for us to stay downtown, so we can at least enjoy the city a bit. The downside is we need to wake up an hour earlier every morning and drive through rush hour on highway 101."

"A small price to pay for staying at the area's flagship Hilton."

After a few years in consulting, every professional ends up with his or her preferred hotel, airline, and car rental company. It's often just luck—the first lengthy out-of-town project tends to lock you in to a particular vendor because of the perks you get for being a preferred member of a rewards program. I had ended up in the Hilton camp. Although the younger crew of consultants liked the Starwood Hotels, especially the W, I was fine with the Hilton group. I had always thought the W felt a bit like staying in a nightclub: everything was black, dance music played in the bathrooms, and the receptionists wore purple suits with black ties. Cool, no doubt, but a little too overstated for my tastes.

I spent the next few days learning about the global clothing industry, reading SpacedOut's annual SEC filings, and devouring all the information I could find about textile sourcing and production. I wasn't surprised to find out that India was a major producer of raw textiles, especially cotton. India was also a top manufacturer of clothing, and virtually every large garment company had operations there.

According to its annual reports, SpacedOut's offshore manufacturing was almost exclusively based in India. They had gone through a multi-year restructuring effort, and had consolidated their operations by shutting down facilities in Mexico, Ecuador, Indonesia, and Pakistan. That in itself seemed like a supply chain optimization effort, and I wondered why they wanted to hire C&C *after* they had completed the work. The answer came to me when I looked through SpacedOut's latest quarterly report.

Production costs had actually gone up over the past year, and the previous chief operating officer had been fired. The new COO, a hotshot who had effected miraculous turnarounds at several large garment makers, had been brought in to stop the bleeding and figure out what needed to be done. Of course, he had gone ahead and brought in a consulting firm to help him do just that. This way, if costs didn't come down, he could blame us, kick us out, and maybe get one more chance to fix things before he got fired. It was a good strategy, and one that kept firms like C&C in business.

By Sunday afternoon, I felt like a management consultant again—smart, confident, and articulate. I got a haircut in the early evening. After clipping my nails, I went out to Central Park and did the six-mile circuit all the way around. I slowed when I ran past the waterfall, but I didn't stop. There was nothing for me to see there.

When I got home, I did a few loads of laundry. As I stripped the sheets and pillowcases, I took a deep breath and fought back tears. Then, as I watched the machine spin away the last hints of Simone, I let myself cry one last time for her.

49

The consulting team assigned to the SpacedOut job had its first meeting at the San Francisco C&C office. Since most consulting jobs involved ad-hoc teams that were put together with staff from different offices around the US, it usually made sense to first connect away from the client site. That way we could meet each other, figure out roles and responsibilities, and get a little more background on the project so that we looked like a well-prepared cohesive team when we showed up at the client's offices. As consultants we were all accustomed to sizing up our colleagues quickly and integrating ourselves into new teams without much fuss. I had always liked that feeling of meeting a C&C consultant for the first time and instantly forming a bond because each of us understood that we'd be working together in an intense, high-pressure environment.

And consulting for SpacedOut turned out to be as high-pressure as anything. If I had thought that the work-ethic at a California company that made skinny jeans and pre-torn shirts would be as laid-back as their public image, that thought was quickly dispelled. Perhaps the new COO was feeling the pressure and passing it on to us. Fair enough. We were costing SpacedOut's shareholders a lot of coin. We should be feeling the pressure.

Our team was made up of me and five other consultants,

all from the San Francisco C&C office. It wasn't odd that I was flying in from New York—since Mo was the managing partner, it made sense that she'd want to bring in at least one consultant from her home office. And, of course, after a weekend of prep I was now a supply-chain optimization expert.

We spent the first few days in typical consultant mode, frantically working to impress our new clients while simultaneously struggling to get our heads wrapped around what the hell we were supposed to be doing for them. After several interviews with key operations personnel, we were directed to their repository of sourcing contracts. We love data, and now we had a mountain of it. Mo had three of the junior consultants start to read through the contracts line by line and extract any and all numbers. I worked with the other senior consultant, an Indian guy called Swami, to read through the biggest contracts to look for any clauses that might be loopholes for the other party to take advantage of SpacedOut.

The contracts were mainly with Indian cotton producers and processing plants, some of which also served as clothing manufacturers. The terminology was confusing at best, and I would have been lost without Swami, who had a law degree and was familiar with some of the standard clauses dictated by Indian labor law and other rules governing contracts with foreign entities.

The first week went by without us even noticing that we were staying in the heart of San Francisco. We car pooled out of the Hilton's underground garage before 7 AM, and we only drove back into town around 10 PM. All our meals the first week were consumed in the sterile cafeteria of SpacedOut's unmarked operations center in Burlingame. Apparently, SpacedOut's cool factor only applied to its corporate headquarters in downtown San Francisco.

We worked through the first weekend, but I didn't care. I

was learning a ton about contracts in general and also about the various components of the cotton textile business. The hard work and close companionship with the other consultants felt good, and I almost forgot about the Network and the fact that I was a murderer. Almost.

Not that I wanted to forget it. My jungle sense was developing well, and I found myself evaluating everyone as a potential target. The feelings of power and righteousness that had previously come and gone as surges had by now settled into a steady emotional buzz. I was now passing judgment based on rules that were independent of the law. The arrogance inherent in that statement did not escape me, and I took myself very seriously. It was getting easier for me to kill, and I knew I had to balance that with additional prudence when selecting a target.

Mo hadn't been expecting an assignment from the Network. Even though it turned out that Simone's death wasn't an unusual exit strategy for a Network Omega, our little branch was going through some temporary restructuring as Mo got familiar with her new Omega contact.

So you can imagine her surprise, and to some extent delight, to find that I was the one who unearthed our next target.

50

Gujarat State in western India is one of the larger cotton producing and processing regions of the country. The promise of low labor costs makes India in general an appealing candidate for cotton-sourcing. But the other appeal, perhaps particular to Gujarat at the time, was a streamlined local bureaucracy. Of course, in the context of Indian politics, streamlined simply meant that the system of bribes and kickbacks worked exceptionally fast and with very little mystery. Your Indian counterparts knew exactly whom to bribe and with how much and in what form.

Bribery wasn't a particular focus of the Network. We didn't view it as being objectively evil or undesirable, especially if it was rampant enough for all interested parties to get an equal shot at bribing their way in and out of government concessions. If we had a problem with that concept, the Network would be all-hands-on-deck to take out the thousands of well-paid Washington, DC, lobbyists. And I've always held the view that DC lobbyists make the political process more efficient.

And efficiency was the primary reason SpacedOut had restricted its cotton production to India. Although labor costs were lower in Indonesia and Mexico, India's well-established bribery infrastructure was unmatched. But still, as Swami and I dug deep into the piles of verbose contracts SpacedOut had signed with Indian companies, we could tell that something wasn't right with the labor numbers in Gujarat.

Firstly, we found several instances where SpacedOut had terminated dealings with certain local producers in favor of others with significantly higher labor costs per bale of cotton produced. We initially assumed that this was a way to account for the cost of bribery. However, when one of the executives we interviewed casually mentioned that bribes were paid in cash and accounted for as simple miscellaneous expenses, it became clear that there was no need for SpacedOut to be artificially inflating labor costs to hide money paid as bribes. So we dug deeper, and by the end of week two, we had it figured out.

Over the past two years, SpacedOut had systematically shifted its business away from local Indian cotton producers that used Muslim labor. Of course, this was not obvious from the contracts themselves, but I had done some research after Swami noticed that two of the cancelled contracts had been with cotton mills located in predominantly Muslim areas. After an evening of cross-checking demographics against the list of counterparties in SpacedOut's broken contracts, I ended up with a one hundred percent match between the list and Gujarat's Muslim-dominated regions. Now there were two burning questions: why, and why.

The first question was why Muslim labor was so much cheaper in Gujarat. And the second question was why SpacedOut, a corporation that seemed to clearly believe in equal rights and opportunity, would systematically avoid Muslim labor even though it resulted in higher costs.

Swami helped me with the first question, which was related to Gujarat's history of ethnic tension between the majority Hindus and the Muslim minority. Indeed, the tension was prevalent throughout India, but it seemed like Gujarat had made an art form out of the economic and social isolation of the Muslim community.

Swami explained how Muslims in Gujarat were being treated in ways eerily reminiscent of how Jews were boycotted in 1930s Germany. In fact, many local Hindu right wing leaders had taken to citing Hitler and Mussolini in their rhetoric. And recent terrorist attacks in India and around the world had made it easier for the more militant of the politicians to spread an anti-Muslim message and discourage local businesses from hiring Muslim labor.

And so, because most Hindu-owned businesses in Gujarat were shying away from Muslims, the labor costs were driven down as desperate Muslims were willing to work for next to nothing. And we were talking about some of the poorest of the poor.

So that was the answer to the first question. I didn't discuss the second question too much with Swami because I had an idea of where it would lead. SpacedOut's clothes were largely cotton-based, and so the Indian cotton contracts represented the single largest piece of the company's supply chain. The contract cancellation decisions had to have come from someone high up, someone in the California offices. The obvious choice was the previous COO, and if that turned out to be the case, the Network's protocol would be for Mo to pass the information up to the Network Omega, who would put out an assignment to the cell best positioned to take him down.

By the middle of the third week I had an answer. The previous COO would be off the hook, and Mo and I would be on it. Fine with me. I was ready. If I was going to be killing people like it was my job, I didn't want to get too rusty.

51

Modern enterprise-wide computer systems are data-hogging monsters. You'd be amazed at the details that can get captured and fed into a single company-wide database. While a dinosaur like Walker-Midland used old mainframe-based systems that captured only the basics, and that too in a form that no one except an MIT grad would understand, Spaced-Out used cutting edge integrated systems in which no one got to keep his or her full name out of the record books. And since my consulting team had been given access to the contracts database, it wasn't so hard to look at the usernames associated with the contract changes. I was starting to appreciate the obvious synergies between my dual roles as a management consultant and freelance killer.

To make it even easier for me, there was a single username associated with the thirty-plus cancelled contracts. Since SpacedOut's contracts database was linked with the human resources database, I was able to link to the employee's personnel record. Of course, I didn't have access to salary information or home addresses due to access restrictions, but I did manage to get a full name and corporate phone extension: Theresa Miller at extension 4460.

I wasn't surprised to find out that Ms. Miller was an administrative assistant. I didn't expect an executive to be keying in the changes himself. Ms. Miller wasn't at her desk when

I called, so I left a message introducing myself as a consultant and explaining that I was looking for some details about contracts related to the Indian cotton suppliers.

She called me back after lunch. It turned out that her boss, a vice-president of operations, was indeed the right person. He had been informed via a broadcast e-mail from the COO that a consulting firm had been hired to look into the supply-chain strategy, and to provide any assistance requested. And so I requested a meeting with Mr. Raghu Patel, Vice-President of Operations – India Region.

Patel was a short, skinny man. He looked like he had been sweating all day, even though the air conditioning seemed fine. He smelled like a mixture of body odor and Indian food, and he did not seem happy to see me.

When I sat down at his desk, I realized why I smelled Indian food: there were two open containers of some delicious-looking curry on his side table. I had interrupted his lunch, which was probably why he wasn't too pleased at my presence. I understood that. It was almost a policy of mine not to mess with a client's food-time.

"I'm sorry, Mr. Patel. I didn't mean to interrupt your lunch. We can reschedule this meeting, if you like," I said, putting on the warmest smile I could without appearing unprofessional.

That seemed to break Patel's funk, because he immediately smiled and shook his head violently and waved away my suggestion.

"No, no. Please. In fact, you must forgive my own rudeness for eating while we talk. My schedule is packed, just packed." He stopped chewing and swiveled his chair so he was facing me. "But all the VPs have been informed that this project is top priority. So you will have my full attention."

"Okay, great."

"Sorry, what is your name again? Theresa did not pass on

that information. She simply said that she had scheduled one of the C&C consultants."

"Oh, how rude of me not to introduce myself. I'm Frank Stein."

"Mr. Stein." He paused and gave me a half smile. "Jewish?"

"Yes."

He nodded, and then he turned to his food and stuffed some *roti* and curry into his mouth. "So, Mr. Stein, what can I help you with?"

"Well, my team is looking at some of SpacedOut's supplier contracts. And I noticed that a number of contracts have been cancelled and replaced with others that seem to be at a higher cost." I paused, and then I shrugged. "Is that one of the strategic moves that got the previous COO into trouble?" I said this in a somewhat joking manner, so that Patel could play it any way he wanted—he could use it as an out and simply pass the buck, or he could dismiss it as a joke and try and explain the business rationale for what I was seeing. This was a standard technique employed by consultants when interviewing client executives. Give them a chance to blame someone else, and you're more likely to get to the bottom of the problem.

But Patel didn't dodge it. He chewed his *roti* and calmly made eye contact with me as he dabbed his mouth with a paper towel. Then he leaned back in his chair and gave me that half smile again.

"Frank. Sorry, may I call you Frank?"

"Of course."

"Okay, okay, great. Well, Frank. Do you know much about how business is conducted in India? Especially when tie-ups between foreign and Indian companies are involved?"

I nodded and gave him a half smile of my own. "Yes, I do." I let out a small laugh and nodded again. "Yes sir, I do."

"Okay then. So you follow that the Indian government is always—how shall I put this—a partner in every transaction." He paused. "You follow?"

"Of course, Mr. Patel."

"Call me Raghu."

"Raghu. Yes, of course I follow. That's not uncommon, and it's not isolated to India either. Some would say that the United States has its own channels and methods for lubricating the wheels of commerce."

Patel laughed out loud. "Very well put, my dear Frank. You are a poet." He closed the plastic food containers, which did nothing to reduce the smell of turmeric, chili powder, and ground cumin seeds. "So anyway, some of those numbers in the contracts are padded as a result of precisely what you said—costs of the lubricant itself." He seemed pleased with the slight twist he had given to my analogy.

I cleared my throat. "That's what I figured at first. But after interviewing a few of the other VPs, it appears that the lubricant charges are simply allocated as cash withdrawn from the 'miscellaneous items' accounts. And that's fairly standard for US firms that do business in other countries. It's well recognized that greasing the skids is part of the costs, and so it doesn't create any serious legal scrutiny here."

Patel was quiet, but he didn't seem worried. He placed both elbows on his desk and leaned forward, propping up his chin with his fists. His eyes were opened extra-wide, and he showed that half smile again. It was like he wanted me to say something more, to ask him something more. I thought back to his earlier inquiry about whether I was Jewish, and I guessed where he was going. Of course, he wanted me to go there first. It was like a politically-correct game of chicken. Which one of us would say it first?

I decided to play innocent a bit longer. "So, are you saying that the new contracts have inflated labor costs because they are padded with expenses that, in the actual ledger books, have been allocated to the miscellaneous expenses account? And if I adjust the numbers in the contract to account for what's in the expenses account, we'll find that the new contracts are in line with or cheaper than the old, cancelled contracts?"

Patel leaned back again. The half smile was gone. "Probably. I haven't seen those numbers matched up. There are a lot of charges that hit those miscellaneous accounts. Feel free to do the analysis and let me know." He turned to his computer monitor and began scrolling through his e-mails.

I almost kicked myself. Patel was slipping away from me. He knew as well as I did that I'd never be able to do a clean analysis. The cash transactions would be labeled as random generic line items that could be explained in a hundred different ways. My theory was based solely on the unlikely coincidence of all the cancelled contracts being with suppliers from Muslim-dominated areas of Gujarat state in India.

So it was I who would have to blink first. "Well, actually, the reason I wanted to talk to you was because I noticed a pattern with the cancelled contracts." I paused and took a deep breath. "A pattern that made me think that you are a man with principles, a man who likes to make decisions that are morally correct even though they may not be financially sound."

This hit home. Patel turned back to me, and now his half smile had widened into a beaming grin. "Yes, my Hebrew friend. Without principles, what else is there? You understand this, no?"

I gave him a serious look that I hoped would convey sympathy with his bigotry. "Of course. I understand it as well as anyone. Better than most, I like to think." I was quiet for a few moments. "And that's the reason why I came to talk to you alone. You see, one of my fellow consultants is Indian, and my boss is a Muslim. I'm worried that it's only a matter of time before they notice the same pattern."

Patel caught his breath and I thought I saw a flash of panic in his eyes. Then it seemed he understood what I was suggesting, and his half smile slowly returned. "You have some recommendations?"

I rubbed my chin. "Well, not yet, but I think if we brainstorm a bit, we can come up with either a good explanation, or a way to reconfigure some of the information in the database."

Patel stood up and walked to the large tinted glass window. He stared out over the concrete parking lot and nodded. "Yes. But not here." He turned and smiled. "Do you like Indian food?"

52

"So you're going to Raghu Patel's *house* for dinner?" Mo was aghast.

We were sitting in the sprawling lobby of the San Francisco Hilton. I looked up at the frescoes on the ceiling and then back down at Mo. "Yes."

"Since when do you know so much about Indian Muslims in Gujarat state?" she asked.

I shrugged. "I'm learning. Been reading about the anti-Muslim riots that happened there in 2002. Some terrible stuff—murder, rape, people being burned alive. Just because they had been born into a certain religion." I sighed and looked at the thick blue carpet. "I'm not particularly religious or anything, but as a Jew, I can't help but flinch when you see the obvious parallels."

Mo smiled. "I'm not particularly religious either. But I remember reading about the Gujarat riots. Made me want to go out and do some killing myself. Still, what's our rationale for taking out Raghu Patel? We have a new Omega contact, and I want to be able to make a solid case for this."

I nodded. "My first reaction was disgust, which should be a good enough reason, but I know it's not. Then, after my meeting with Patel, I did some digging into the Muslim situation in India, and it turns out that there's been a systematic boycott of Muslim labor in many rural areas of India, and especially Gujarat, which shares a border with Pakistan. There's a lot of propaganda being spread by militant right-wing Hindu extremists in Gujarat—pamphlets and speeches about how the local Indian Muslims are secretly supporting Pakistan's terrorist activities and hence should be excluded from social and commercial activities."

"Which is bullshit. Most of those so-called terrorist supporters are poor and illiterate and don't even know a single Pakistani." Mo shook her head.

"That's what I'm getting from what I'm reading. But here's the problem: even the real terrorists, the foot soldiers in Pakistan and Afghanistan, are just poor people who have no reasonable job opportunities besides joining the militia. It comes down to simple economics. It's like so many Americans who join the army for no reason other than it's the best career choice for them. Think about some poor eighteen-year-old kid in a village in Pakistan. He has nothing going for him. Then the Taliban recruiters come in and give him a rifle and a paycheck. It's the best deal he gets."

Mo smiled now. "I see where you're going with this. If economics is the driving factor, then poverty-stricken Muslims in India could become prime targets for recruitment simply because they need to eat, and the best job they can get is to be a terrorist."

"Exactly. And people like Raghu Patel are perpetuating this. So in some way, their decisions are breeding new terrorists."

Mo nodded. "Okay. But are you sure he's doing this voluntarily? If the economic boycott is systemic, then isn't it possible that corrupt Indian politicians are the ones that forced the changes to the contracts?"

I thought for a minute. "You're right. His bigotry isn't enough reason to kill him if the decisions weren't his." I nodded and leaned back on the yellow and red pin-striped couch. "I'll have to flush it out of him over dinner." I looked at Mo. "But if I confirm it at his house, can I go ahead and take him right then and there?"

Mo sighed and shook her head. "I doubt the Omega will get through the validation process soon enough. I'm not even sure how it'll get done. I mean, I'm sure the Network stretches into India, but who knows."

I didn't want to wait. "But *I'm* doing the validation. Who else is in a better position to do it? If the Network had Patel in its sights, then we'd have been given the assignment already, right? Didn't you say the information flow was two-way? The Omega trusts that we're not just killing people because they smell funny. Or am I missing something?"

Mo was quiet, but I could tell she was holding back a smile. "Yes, Frank. It is a two-way deal. But I don't know much about the new Omega. More importantly, he or she probably doesn't know much about us. And two Network members connected to us have just died." She sighed again. "I just want our next job to be clean and by the book."

I snorted. "The Network specifically picks people who are willing to do things outside the rulebook. And you're arguing that this new Omega is going to be impressed by how obedient we are?"

Mo finally let her smile break. "Fine. Leave the authorization to me. The more important question is what's your plan? And how am I supposed to get into Patel's house? The way you've positioned yourself, this meeting is supposed to be happening without my knowledge, correct?"

I nodded. "I'll do it alone."

Mo laughed. "Getting a little bold, are we? No. That's unacceptable. I can't allow it. Not so soon."

"How's that knife wound healing for you?" I had noticed Mo's stiffness over the past few days, and had guessed that the travel and long hours hadn't done much for her.

"Screw you. I'm fine."

"I'll do it myself. I already have a plan." Of course, I didn't have a plan, but now I'd have to come up with one in about fifteen seconds.

"Okay." She looked at me with a smirk. Mo could read me like I was one of those books with extra large print. "You going to stab him with a fork at the dinner table? In front of his wife and kids?"

I hadn't thought about Patel's family. I gulped, and then I looked up and smiled. "Poison," I said with confidence. "I'll get the information out of him over a pre-dinner drink. And if it's a go, I'll put something in his food. Indian food should be able to mask the taste of pretty much anything." I shrugged. "Maybe get something that'll take a few hours to kick in so I'm long gone."

Mo smirked some more. "Do you know much about poisons?"

"What's to know? I'll do some web browsing from a public computer that can't be traced back to me, figure out what's easy to get a hold of in the next couple of days, and that's that."

"That's that, eh?" Mo shook her head. "Okay. Do your digging and let me know."

53

Digging was indeed the correct term. After some light browsing, I settled on one of Mother Nature's finest killers: *Amanita Ocreata*—the Death Angel, an all-white mushroom, half a cap of which is enough to kill a man. Symptoms would only emerge after several hours, by which time severe internal damage would have taken place. And given that the symptoms are vomiting and diarrhea, chances were that Patel would try and get through it without going to the hospital. If he did go to an emergency room, it was unlikely they'd diagnose the problem as being *amanita* poisoning—after all, Patel wouldn't know he had eaten a strange mushroom.

Best of all, the mushroom could be found on the outskirts of wooded areas. Like some of the areas across the Bay, around the Berkeley Hills. So it was settled. I would spend the next three evenings picking mushrooms.

I told Mo about this, and she laughed at first but then came around when she read up on the deadly fungus. It was no joke. The toxins destroy the liver, and once the symptoms are visible, the treatment of choice is an emergency liver transplant. Just imagine: you eat a tiny bit of a beautiful, pure white mushroom, and soon your only chance for survival is to get your liver replaced. And that's only for a chance at survival—the mushroom's kill rate is over forty percent, and even then only if you're lucky enough to get a new liver in time. Good lord. I thought back to the "magic" mushrooms I had eaten without question at a Phish concert during college. I shivered, and then pushed my morbid thoughts aside and focused on work.

That evening, after the team drove back to San Francisco and ate dinner together, I took the shared rental car and drove out across the Bay Bridge, past Oakland, and towards the hills. I had taken some directions to a state park that would be open, and I had photographs of the Death Angel mushroom.

I felt silly poking around in the bushes looking for a mushroom to use as a murder weapon. It was like I was some insane evil genius planning an unnecessarily complicated way to kill my target. Like in those old James Bond movies, where the bad guy designs an elaborate machine for the one specific purpose of killing 007. I shook my head when I remembered that Bond always got away. Then I reminded myself that I wasn't the bad guy. I was only the killer, and those two terms were no longer synonymous in my world.

About an hour after sunset, I called off my search. The trees looked scary at night, and I wasn't thrilled at the idea of looking for something called the Death Angel while alone in the woods. It also occurred to me that dawn might be a better time to go mushroom-hunting.

So I woke before dawn the next morning. It was Tuesday, and my dinner date with the Patels was set for Thursday. I was in a pleasant sleepy haze as I drifted across the Bay Bridge and towards my hunting grounds. I stopped at a gas station on the way so I could relieve myself and pick up a second cup of coffee. Cash only, of course.

The sun was breaking when I got to the state park. The

night had been cool, and the trees and shrubs still glistened with morning dew. I was feeling lucky, and I even did a little hop as I scurried towards the tree line. I felt like Nintendo's Mario or Luigi, out looking for a hidden mushroom that would give me superpowers. I pictured myself with a full Italian moustache and little red overalls, and I giggled like a madman as I poked around the underbrush.

Then I saw her. She sat innocently under a majestic oak tree, and her soft white body called out to me. I smiled and nodded in greeting. Good morning, my lady. May I have this dance?

The Western North American Destroying Angel. The Death Angel. *Amanita Ocreata*. Color: white. Edibility: deadly. Hell yes.

I slapped on a fresh set of my sheer rubber gloves, a pair of which were almost always on me these days. Although I knew that *amanita* wasn't deadly to the touch, I didn't want to take any chances. There were two of them on the ground near a bulging tree root, and I grabbed both and placed them in a sandwich bag. Then I put the sandwich bag into another sandwich bag, and hurried back to the car.

It was almost seven when I got back to the hotel. My frequent-guest status at Hilton Hotels entitled me to a suite, and my gigantic living room had a good-sized fridge in it. I put the mushrooms in the vegetable tray and took a shower, humming the Super Mario Brothers theme as I shampooed.

54

The next two days were business as usual. I tried to avoid Swami just in case he wanted to bring up the contract cancellation pattern again. But there was no need. We were busy running analyses on the transportation segment of SpacedOut's supply chain, and so our attention was on some of the shipping companies that brought finished product from third-world manufacturers to SpacedOut's retail warehouses in the United States.

Mo didn't spend much time with the consulting team. There were a few other C&C partners visiting that week—a common occurrence in the early stages of the first project for a new client. Consulting partners are salespeople first and foremost, and a new client meant that new relationships needed to be developed and old sales pitches could be reused and positioned as if they were exclusive to the client.

Thursday came, and I didn't see Mo at all until the very end of the day. We crossed paths as I was leaving the office, and since a few of the junior consultants were still around, we didn't talk much. She wished me luck and motioned for me to call her. She meant call her when I was done with the evening. By now it was clear that the time leading up to a kill was personal time. Like how those downhill skiers plug their ears and close their eyes and visualize the course before the final run, I was playing out the various possible scenarios for that evening's meal.

The Patels were childless, which was a huge relief. That left the wife as the only other person to worry about. I figured that if Patel was guilty, his wife couldn't be innocent. Still, although that would make her a bigot, she wasn't the one who made the decisions that were unjustly keeping thousands of uneducated Muslims in crippling poverty in one of the world's densest breeding grounds for Islamic fundamentalists. Good. Call me sexist and old fashioned, but I wasn't ready to kill a woman just yet.

But that complicated things, because it meant I couldn't just poison the entire vat of a particular dish. I'd have to mix the *amanita* into the food on Patel's plate itself. I'd have to do it at the dinner table.

After having pondered the question all week, I came up with what seemed to be a reasonable plan. First, I chopped and ground up the mushrooms into a paste. After thinning out the paste with water, I loaded the mixture into a small syringe that had a thick spout and no needle. The syringe was small enough that with some practice I was confident about masking it in my hand and using the base of the same palm to depress the plunger.

The actual delivery couldn't be planned beforehand. I didn't know the layout of his place and the setup for dinner. Would we formally sit at a table with the dishes laid out? Would we serve ourselves from the kitchen and eat in the living area? Or would the Patels surprise me by grilling spicy *tandoori* chicken in their backyard? I rehearsed each option in my mind until I felt comfortable that I would find a way to squirt the deadly paste into Patel's food. But of course I would make sure he was good and drunk first.

55

It turned out that getting Patel drunk wasn't a problem. When I pulled up at his single-storey house in Fremont, California, he walked out to greet me holding the dregs of what must have been a stiff whiskey-soda. The sun was setting as I locked my car. I looked around before I entered the house. The house lots were small, but the neighborhood seemed very quiet. No sounds of children, and I figured that perhaps the houses belonged to young busy professionals who weren't at that stage yet. Patel's was a corner house at the beginning of the street, and so he had, in effect, just one neighbor. I took note of the dark windows of the neighbor's house, and guessed that they were out. This meant they'd be coming home at some point, and I'd have to check for their car before exiting so I wouldn't run into them. The fewer people who saw me, the better. After another quick scan of the block, I entered the house.

It was a simple home. A full carpet that was thin but not worn. Cane and bamboo living room furniture. A dining table that looked like it came unassembled from Target. And reasonably tasteful wall art that looked Indian enough to me.

Shalini Patel was a quiet, quick woman. She spoke excellent English, but didn't seem to have much to say. I got the sense she was a bit annoyed with her husband for inviting me over, or perhaps she was uneasy with the reasons for my being there. Probably both. After pouring me a drink, she said something about having to finish up some work, and then disappeared into a back room.

Patel and I chatted aimlessly for the first two drinks. He could certainly hold his alcohol, and I began to worry about whether I'd be able to hold mine. As he walked to the bar to measure out my third Johnnie Walker Black along with his fourth or fifth, he looked over his shoulder at me and I could tell from his expression that he was ready to talk business.

"So, my Hebrew friend. How are things with your consulting assignment?"

"Busy as hell." I smiled. "We're trying to justify our billing rates, you know. And your boss, the new COO, is a real hardass. We're up half the night every night preparing to give him his daily status updates." I nodded as Patel handed me my fresh drink.

Patel laughed. "Yes. He is quite a tough man. Very good, though. He will do well for the company."

I nodded again and took a sip. "So," I said.

Patel smiled. "So," he said.

"So you and your wife are from Gujarat State, originally?" I asked.

"Yes. I am from Ahmedabad, and Shalini is from Baroda."

"How are things in Gujarat these days?"

Patel shrugged. "Peaceful. And optimistic. The local government is pro-business, and has put a lot of money into infrastructure like roads and telecommunications. It's good for the people."

I took another sip. "So things are back to normal after the 2002 riots?"

Patel smiled. "What do you know about the 2002 riots?"

"Only what I've read."

"And what have you read?"

"That it all started in a town called Godhra, when a train carrying mainly Hindu families was attacked and burned by Muslim militants." I knew that the cause of the train fire was still a topic of dispute. Many said it was an accident, and some said that it was a setup by the right-wing Hindu movement to make a push with its anti-Muslim propaganda. Still, I had to stoke Patel's fire here.

Patel nodded. "Good. At least you got the facts right. The leftist media in many places is denying that the rail car could have been set on fire in the way it was. Some are saying it was an accident." He laughed. "There are no accidents like this."

"Of course not. Anyway, after word got out about the innocent Hindus that were killed, there was naturally some retaliation against the Muslims." I shrugged. "Tit for tat. They were basically terrorists, after all."

"Exactly. And it was a long time coming, anyway. The Godhra incident was just the final straw. The Muslim situation was a time bomb waiting to explode, and we brave Hindu warriors were the ones who shielded the world by throwing our bodies on the bomb to smother its effects." Patel spat an ice-cube back into his empty glass and made himself another drink.

"So you were in India during the riots?"

Patel nodded. "Indeed."

"In Gujarat?"

"Yes." He turned and flashed a proud smile. "Yes. Shalini and I both. We worked with some of the organizers."

"Oh, really?" I nodded at him as a show of respect. I thought about the reports claiming that the mob attacks were far from spontaneous uprisals and closer to well-planned strikes on

Muslim residences and businesses. The mobs had been given lists of Muslim targets. The circumstantial evidence pointing to an organized genocidal effort was hard to ignore.

"Yes," said Patel. "We did what we could to help. Muslims have no place in India. They have their Islamic countries like Pakistan and those places in the middle-East. They should live there in isolation. Then they can have their loud prayer calls and marry their four wives and do whatever the hell they want. You understand all this, of course. The Jews and Hindus have a common enemy in Islam."

I nodded and raised my glass. "And you are continuing to do what you can even though you're now in the United States. I respect that."

Patel smiled. "Yes. If I can starve even one of those bloody butchers by taking away his livelihood, then I will do so. It is my duty as a Hindu warrior."

That was enough for me. I couldn't tell if it was the alcohol or the conversation, but I was feeling a bit queasy, and I figured it was time to move on with the evening. I excused myself and went to the restroom. As I had hoped, Shalini was bringing out the food when I got back. I went up to the dinner table and smiled politely. Shalini gave me a sharp look and nodded and forced a smile. After placing a stack of fresh hot *rotis* on the table, she gestured to a chair and then called out to her husband.

"Come on now, eat. Enough drinks for you." She waited until Patel had walked to the table, and then she left the room.

"Your wife isn't joining us?" I asked.

Patel waved his hand towards the door to the back room in a flippant gesture. "She must have eaten already. Let it be. We have some private matters to discuss, anyway."

I nodded. "This food looks amazing. The smell itself is making me full."

Patel smiled. "Yes. Shalini is a superb cook."

The spread on the table really did look appetizing. There were at least three main dishes: chicken in a thick yellow gravy, shrimp that had been fried in a red spice, and a vegetarian dish that looked greenish-brown. I stared at the vegetarian entrée. Yes, that would be my delivery mechanism. The consistency seemed right—vaguely mashed, but with lumps that protruded through the thick pasty exterior.

"What is that?" I asked.

"*Guchi*," said Patel. He was busy serving himself some chicken, and didn't notice my puzzled expression until he was done. Then he smiled at me. "Sorry. That's the Indian name. It's just mushroom in an onion and tomato gravy."

My heart jumped and I was afraid that my change in expression would give me away. I couldn't help but smile at how perfect this was. I was certain that my intense visualization of the evening's plan had generated a cosmic shift that was making things flow exactly as I wanted. The mushroom dish was the universe's way of giving me a hint that I was destined to succeed without a problem.

"So," said Patel as he tore a piece of *roti*. "You have some ideas of how to handle the paper trail of the cancelled cotton supplier contracts?"

I pretended like my mouth was full, and just nodded. I hadn't thought too much about it, but I wasn't worried. "Electronic trail, you mean."

Patel smiled, but he wasn't amused.

"Sorry," I said. "Bad joke."

Patel smiled again, and reached across the table for the vegetable dish. I felt my breath catch as I watched him heap the sticky mush onto his plate. As he reached for a fresh *roti*, I knew I had to act soon. This was my chance. I felt into my pocket for my syringe, and cupped it in my right hand. I slowly plucked the cap off the tip and positioned the syringe so that I could squirt it in one quick motion. After glancing at Patel's face, I decided he wasn't drunk enough to not notice my hand over his plate.

I drained my glass of water and then inhaled loudly through my mouth. "Can I trouble you for a fresh glass of cold water? The food is excellent, but it's a bit spicy."

"Of course," said Patel. He looked over his shoulder as if he was hoping his wife would be waiting there to serve us. Then he slowly wiped his hands with a paper napkin and grabbed my glass and walked to the kitchen.

I stood up fast and leaned over the table and squirted the deadly juice into Patel's plate and immediately sat back down. After carefully replacing the cap on the empty syringe and putting it back into my pocket, I looked around in panic, half expecting Shalini to be standing there, quietly watching me while dialing 911 to report an attempted murder. But no, the universe appeared to be firmly on my side. I heard the sound of the bathroom door closing, and guessed that Patel had gone to hit the head. I relaxed and thanked the universe one more time.

As I casually looked at Patel's plate again, I noticed that my poisonous paste had been deposited as a white, bubbly, grainy patch on the surface of the food. That wouldn't do. After looking around and then holding my breath to listen for approaching footsteps, I picked up his fork and gently pushed the *amanita* solution deep into Patel's helping of the mushroom dish. Then I stirred the mixture to remove the depressions that my fork had left. Satisfied, I put the fork down and polished it with a napkin. Not that anyone would check, but I couldn't have my fingerprints on Patel's fork. Paranoia is king, I remembered. Mo would be proud.

Then I realized that too much paranoia can sink you.

Shalini Patel looked shocked as she approached me from the doorway that led to the back rooms. Although she couldn't have seen me use the syringe, anything she saw after that would have looked equally suspicious. Perhaps she saw nothing, but it didn't matter. My startled reaction would have left no doubt that I had been up to no good. I jerked back in my chair so hard that its two front legs briefly left the ground. I felt my face warp into an involuntary look of absolute panic. I was like a McDonald's employee who's just been caught in the act of pissing in the mustard.

56

"I thought there was a bug or something in his food, so I used the fork to poke around," I said. "Please don't be offended. The food is all wonderful. You really are an amazing cook."

Shalini was quiet as she came up to the table, but I could see the tightness in her lower jaw. She looked me in the eye, and I shrank under her gaze. Her stare was cold and heartless, and in those dark pits I could see the images of blood-soaked men, women, and children begging her for mercy. If she was capable of compassion, I didn't see it. I'd like to say it was my own guilt that made me feel this way, but there was no guilt at play here. My only thoughts were towards self-preservation. That, and completing my assignment. I was a professional, and I would get the job done. That's what professionals do, even if things go wrong. In fact, that's what defines a professional: the ability to go to work even if you're having a bad day.

And right now it looked like I was going to have a very bad day indeed.

"What did you put in his food?" she asked in an accentless deadpan.

"Are you serious? Why would I put anything in his food? I told you, I thought I saw a fly or something sit on the food and I was checking." I could feel the sides of my jaw hurt as I forced a smile.

"I didn't trust you the moment I saw you. You are a bloody liar. I don't know what you're trying, but I know you're trying something." She moved closer to the table.

Now I stood up and raised both hands in protest. "Look, there's no need for this. I'm probably a little drunk as well, so perhaps I lost track of what I was doing and just felt like mixing his food up with a fork. It sounds ridiculous, I know, but it's kind of a habit of mine. I used to do that to my brother's food to annoy him when he was a kid, and maybe I just unconsciously felt at home here." I shrugged and shook my head. "God, this is so embarrassing. Please forgive me."

She smiled, but it was not a comforting smile. "Nice one. But I read your bio on that social site. It said you are an only child."

I gulped as I remembered the cute, upbeat, self-deprecating paragraph I had written to describe myself on my public social networking profile. Universe, why are you abandoning me now, I thought.

Then Patel walked back into the room with a glass of water. "What's happening?"

Shalini folded her arms across her chest. "I told you this guy was up to something. He put something in your food. Maybe some drug. Or poison."

I laughed. "You're insane." I looked at Patel and smiled and shook my head. "You don't believe this, do you?"

Patel looked at his wife. "What's going on, baby?"

Shalini didn't respond. She was focused on me. She smiled and motioned towards Patel's plate.

"Eat it," she said.

I laughed again. "Come on. This is getting a bit too much. Let's just all sit down and finish up before this wonderful food gets cold."

Patel nodded. He gently put his arm around his wife. "Yes. Come, baby, why don't you join us now."

She pushed his arm away. "I want him to eat some of that. He eats three bites, and I will apologize and then make you all some tea."

"This is insulting," I said, and put on a stern expression to cover up my frustration for not having brought a knife with me. It had seemed too risky to carry one, but now I longed for its warm handle and cold blade. As I moved away from the table, I began to look around the room for a possible weapon. The situation was escalating, and the likelihood of Patel eating the poisoned food seemed to be dropping fast. My heart began to pound as I realized I would have to kill both of them.

57

Shalini wasn't backing down, and now Patel himself was eyeing me with suspicion. I had to get better with controlling my facial expressions. Perhaps I'd take an acting class after this assignment. I shrugged and smiled, hoping to defuse the situation or at least buy some time.

"Okay, fine," I said, and slowly moved towards the table.

I reached for the fork and gripped it hard and imagined myself flipping it around so I could stab with it. First Patel in the throat, making sure to pull the fork back out so the blood would flow free. Then I'd have to improvise with Shalini, since she'd in all likelihood attack me with whatever weapon was handy. Or perhaps she'd run out of the house. Or worse, try and call 911. No, maybe I do her first, and make the bet that Patel tries to stop me instead of running for the door or the phone.

"He's not going to do it," said Shalini. "Go bring a plastic container from the kitchen. We'll get this stuff tested."

Patel shook his head in disbelief and walked out of the room. Shalini stared at me, and I was surprised that she didn't seem afraid in the least. That's too bad, I thought. She should be afraid.

Then as if she could read my mind, her expression changed and she turned and made a dash for the cordless phone that sat on a chest-high shelf against the wall. I went after her, and lunged to grab her shoulder and spin her around. But, to my surprise, she turned before I could touch her.

It must have been as confusing for her as it was for me. There was no sound except for a dull thud and the whisper-like splash of the red sprinkles that spontaneously appeared on the white wall behind her. Her body whipped around and my eyes stared into hers. She looked puzzled for a second, and then she fell down hard, dragging the phone to the floor with her.

Patel came running in just as the second bullet slammed into Shalini's body. He screamed, and then I was on him.

All my well-practiced moves didn't count for shit right then. It was a street fight, and we clawed and wrenched at each other, each of us grappling for leverage. I took him down to the carpet and turned him so I could lock his head and snap his neck, but his short hair was saturated with coconut oil and I couldn't get a grip. Patel was howling like a rabid beast, and I couldn't tell if my punches were hurting him or not. Finally I managed to bury my right fist deep into his gut, and I heard his lungs empty as if they were balloons that had just been popped. He doubled over, and I went to the table and grabbed the fork.

"Not as professional as I would like. But it'll have to do." My vision locked in on the bulging vein in his neck as I walked towards him. He was kneeling down, almost in an execution-style position, and I felt a tiny surge of emotion. Not pity or remorse. More like when you have a sudden urge to cry because the aesthetics of a scene or situation are overwhelming.

Here were two people, man and wife, both of whom had repeatedly made conscious decisions to effect the murders of innocent people. And here I was, a man who was once innocent, but who had since chosen to become a murderer in the name of a twisted form of justice. In that moment I wondered if I really was different from Patel or Shalini. Didn't they believe in the righteousness of what they were doing, just as I was finding it so easy to justify my own acts of violence? Who makes that call, I wondered.

Then I smiled.

I do, I thought. I make that call.

I raised my fork and stepped forward to complete my act of arrogant judgment, but perhaps I moved too slow. Or perhaps Mo just had an itchy trigger finger.

This time there was no second shot because the first one left no doubt. The bullet went clean through his head, burning a straight line through the gray matter just behind the eyes. He stayed there on his knees for several seconds, his blank dead face begging my forgiveness. I shook my head and smiled and thought of that cliché: forgiveness is up to God; our job is simply to make sure you meet Him.

58

Although I did take a quick look out of the open living room window, I didn't expect to see Mo. I was slightly embarrassed, but thankful. Also, I understood why she came. She was experienced enough to know that I wasn't experienced enough yet. I had made several mistakes—some in planning, and more during execution. Mo had spent years developing young consultants, and she knew that the best way to grow someone into a leader is to let them go ahead and lead something even if they're not quite ready. For some things, the only way to get ready is to actually do it. Murder is one of those things.

As I snapped on my surgical gloves and methodically cleaned away all traces of my presence in the house, I wondered about the risk Mo had taken. You have to assume that the feds pay attention to certain kinds of weapons purchases, and you'd think a sniper rifle is on that list. I shook my head as I thought about Ramona Garcia.

After flushing the toilet and covering the bowl with an overdose of that blue stuff, I took one final look around the house and nodded to myself. I paused and stared at the rapidly drying food on Patel's dinner plate, but then decided there was no need to take the poisonous entrée with me. I peered through the side window to make sure the neighbors weren't around. They weren't, and I walked out the front door.

I polished both doorknobs with a paper towel, and then walked to my car while humming a melancholy variation of the Mario Brothers theme. Sorry, Miss *Amanita*. Tonight was not our night. But please don't sulk. We will dance together another time.

59

"Ramona Garcia," said Mo.

It was after midnight, and we had just eaten a spicy meal at a hole-in-the-wall Thai restaurant a block from the San Francisco Hilton. We were strolling towards the beautifully lit Union Square when Mo mentioned the name.

I turned to her in surprise.

Mo smiled and nodded. "Yes. We go way back."

I coughed out some cigarette smoke and stared at Mo. "Back like how?"

"Back to the beginning. Garcia used to be at the FBI's Houston field office. She had her eye on Simone for many years. And when Simone recruited me, Garcia began to watch me too."

"So she's questioned you before? You didn't act like you knew her when she interviewed us in Milwaukee."

"No. I had never met her before. Simone and I just knew about her." Mo smiled. "Anyway, she was getting pretty close. At least Simone thought so."

"Close to getting some hard evidence?"

Mo nodded. "Yes. On some of Simone's early jobs, including her husband's boating accident." Mo smiled at me. "I assume she told you about that?"

"Yes." I was stunned, and my thoughts raced as I began to re-evaluate Simone's reasons for suicide.

"In fact, Simone was pretty sure that Garcia could nail her for her husband anytime she wanted."

"So why wait?"

Mo shrugged. "Our best guess is that Garcia thought she'd be able to get both of us if she allowed Simone and me to continue our work. But then . . ." Mo took a deep drag and slowly blew the smoke up into the cool, clear Northern California night.

I sighed. "But then you stopped working with Simone when I came along. I was too good to pass up—your words, not mine."

Mo laughed, but it was a sad, wistful laugh. "Well, you were. The Network is bigger than any one of us. We're all guilty of murder, and we all know we're going to have to pay. We're killers, but we're not hypocrites."

My voice wavered. "And so . . . Simone . . . with the train . . ."

Mo nodded. "Yes. Simone knew her time was up. Garcia was going to cut her losses and bring Simone in for her husband's murder. No way was Simone going to jail." Mo smiled, and a tear rolled down her soft skin. "We had talked about it many times."

We circled the square in a shared trance of heightened silence. I could feel Simone around us, embracing us, letting us know she was okay. As we walked back towards O'Farrell Street and the Hilton, I smiled at Mo.

"Well, doesn't it mean you're in the clear? I mean, with Simone gone, there aren't any witnesses to your early work. And if there was hard evidence, you'd be arrested by now."

Mo nodded and then looked at the ground. "Yeah, but it's not the early work I'm worried about."

"What? Janesville? But you weren't even in the house. Chester and Simone are both dead, and if there's any physical evidence in that house, it'll point to me."

Mo shook her head. "No. You'll be okay. In fact, that's why I bought the sniper rifle under my own name."

I looked at her. "I don't understand."

"It's only a matter of time before they figure out that shots were fired into the Janesville house from outside. They'll dig the slugs out of the wall and realize it was a high-powered rifle. Then they'll extrapolate the trajectory and calculate that the shooter was positioned at the rest-stop on the highway. And then they'll—"

I snorted. "That doesn't prove shit."

"You didn't let me finish." Mo smiled and touched the tender spot on her side just above her hip. "And then they'll find my blood."

60

I refused to believe her. "But you can't be certain about the blood. Didn't you check the area before we picked you up?"

Mo sighed. "Yes, but I wasn't looking for blood. The area where I set up the gun had a blacktop patch, and I wouldn't have noticed." She turned to me and smiled. "Frank, when I saw I was bleeding in the car, I realized the bloodline was all the way down my leg. I had felt the wetness earlier, but since it was hot and humid that day, I assumed it was sweat."

"But still. You don't know for sure." I thought for a moment. "What about the weather? They must have gotten some more rain over the last couple of weeks."

"Not enough. Plus, the area had heavy tree cover."

We entered the hotel lobby. It was empty, and we stood in the middle of the gigantic open room and stared at each other.

"Okay. Let's think worst-case scenario," I said, putting on my consulting risk-management hat. "Say Garcia finds the blood and matches it to you. The gun is long gone, and they wouldn't be able to connect it to you anyway. So it's all just circumstantial, right?"

She nodded.

Now I was puzzled and angry at her most recent decision. "So why the hell did you buy a rifle under your own name and use it to kill two people? Especially when it'll be easy to prove that you were in California at the time and connected to the victims?" I shook my head and tried not to curse out loud. "I don't get it. You just turned dismissable coincidence into convincing evidence. Now they would have a case against you even if there's no blood at that reststop. Or they could lie about the blood and try and get you to confess, and you have no way of knowing whether or not they're bluffing." I was getting worked up, and I began to pace on the thick carpet of the Hilton's lobby. "Goddammit, Mo. What is going on?"

Mo smiled. She didn't look me in the eye. "Frank, it's getting to the end of the line for me." Now she looked up. "And I wanted to leave you in a position where you have a chance to get out."

I was furious. "What the hell do you mean?"

"Let's step back outside," said Mo. "I need a smoke, anyway."

We walked back out onto O'Farrell Street and stared up at the moon. We lit cigarettes and I waited for Mo to explain herself.

Mo laughed. She didn't take her eyes off the moon. "Well, the timing is working out pretty well. See, the new Omega doesn't know who you are yet—we have a protocol that requires a waiting period before I reveal your identity. So for another ten days or so, I'm the only living person in the Network that knows about you."

I stared at her in disbelief.

Mo turned to me and smiled. "And Garcia's got nothing on you. So once I'm gone, you're free."

I refused to think about what she was saying. "Screw this freedom crap. What's this shit about 'once you're gone'? What the hell does that mean?"

"I told you, Simone and I talked about it. We knew we'd have to pay for what we've done. But we also knew that jail wasn't an option."

I dropped my cigarette and crushed it with my shoe. "Then you can run. Resign from C&C and disappear. You have money. After things cool off, we can continue our work."

Mo laughed. "Frank, my job as a management consultant is what allows me to do the work in the first place. Without that, we won't have access to the same people or the same information. We'd just be putzing around trying to clean up street trash, and there are others much better suited for that work." She shook her head. "No. I'm not going to run."

I thought she was going to say something else, but then Mo just stared back up at the moon and went quiet. The answer was so obvious now that I was appalled I hadn't figured it out earlier. In fact, I should have guessed it the moment she told me about her daughter. After all, Mo had turned herself into a killer in order to understand what her daughter had gone through. How could I think she wouldn't replicate her daughter's final act? Mo would want to go out the same way. She had perhaps decided this even before her entry into the Network. All that killing was just delaying the inevitable. The last life she took would be her own.

Mo snapped her fingers in front of my face and I jerked my head away.

"Hey. Don't look so sad. I'm still here, you know." She smiled at me and punched my shoulder. "It's not over yet. We've got one more to do."

A tiny dart of optimism and hope shot across my synapses. "One more? You mean . . ."

Mo shrugged and started to walk back towards the hotel. "It seems only right that we do a farewell run."

I scurried after her like a child who's just been told he can go back to the playground for another turn on the merry-go-round. Hell, yes.

61

Our farewell run, it turned out, would be meaningful in another way. It would bring closure to some unfinished business.

C&C would be hosting an invite-only symposium for a select group of hedge funds. It's something that the New York offices of many consulting firms like to do. Any time you can bring current and potential clients into a closed discussion, it's good for your sales pipeline.

And yes, my old friends from MacroResearch, Charter Capital, and The NationFirst Fund were all on the invite list. They had accepted, which surprised me at first, but I soon understood. After the 2008-2009 meltdown, the Securities and Exchange Commission, along with its international sister organizations, had increased regulation and oversight of hedge funds. Although funds still wouldn't have to disclose their proprietary investment strategies, the introduction of any sort of oversight to a previously unregulated industry creates worry for the incumbents. And this would be especially so for small funds that might have something to hide.

Although MacroResearch, Charter, and NationFirst were packaging and distributing their holdings in ways that weren't technically illegal, they couldn't risk any of their investments becoming public. Even if they didn't get into legal trouble, they would undoubtedly lose investors if the finance departments of America's largest public companies realized they were indirectly providing working capital to rogue nations and despots who were issuing highly suspect—and therefore highly lucrative—treasury bonds. And since the interpretation and handling of the new SEC requirements was one of the hot topics for the C&C Hedge Fund Symposium, we had a high acceptance rate on our invites.

It had been easy to get our three target funds on the list, since Mo was one of the main partners sponsoring the event. She'd be giving a keynote speech, and was also scheduled to appear on several panels.

And as with any such event, consultants clamored to be involved because it meant getting some face-time with senior partners, and so there were at least a dozen C&C analysts, associates, and seniors handling everything from the catering menus to conference room reservations to preparing content for the discussions and breakout sessions. Naturally, I was brought in to work with Mo to prepare her PowerPoint slides as well as anything else she needed—like planning ten murders.

The symposium was to be held over a three-day weekend at the Ritz Carlton near Battery Park at the southern tip of Manhattan island. It was a corner lot, and had views of the city, the Statue of Liberty, and the open Atlantic Ocean. Seemingly perfect for a massacre to end all massacres. Literally speaking.

Still, the idea of doing the kills at a C&C event bothered me. No matter how discreet we were, if Ramona Garcia had any doubt left, this would take care of it. For someone watching Mo, the correlation of kills, C&C clients, and her presence would be impossible to dismiss.

I had suggested to Mo that we pose as investors and visit

the offices of each fund on separate days, but she had refused to entertain the option. She didn't seem concerned about the blatant connection between C&C clients being killed and our proximity to those murders. Mo was confident Garcia would get no evidence on me. As for herself, well, Mo wasn't worried. "We'll both be free after this one," was all she said to me.

I had spent the past few days meditating on my imminent emancipation. After initially revolting against the idea of stopping, I soon realized I'd be ready to quit after this last assignment. Although at some level I felt like I was at the beginning of a long and happy career as a killer, at another level I knew that Mo was no small reason why I was doing this. And if she wasn't going to be with me, I didn't really want to do it.

I couldn't begin to explain why I felt this way. It wasn't something as simple as saying I was in love with her. Well, maybe that was part of it, but if so, certainly not a conventional romantic kind of love where I imagined us cuddling together or raising babies. Neither did I fantasize about having mad, passionate sex with Mo. That was Simone, and that wasn't the kind of love I had for Mo.

No. This was something different. An overarching love that seemed to connect us at a level beyond that of the world around us. Like we had fought together and loved each other over many lifetimes and in many different times and places. Not that I was a believer in reincarnation or anything like that—I wasn't, and I'm not. But it's the only way I can describe it in terms that even begin to ring true.

I felt like a lovesick puppy as I walked towards the taxi line outside LaGuardia Airport late Thursday night. Mo had taken an earlier flight, and so I had been left alone with my pathetic self-pity and overly dramatic analysis. I lit a cigarette, and as the hot smoke fired up my nicotine receptors, I reminded myself that I wasn't a goddamn puppy.

I nodded and smiled and stared at the clueless people around me. I could feel confidence and power well up like a fluid filling my inner being. No, I wasn't a puppy at all. I was a big dog, and I was a killer.

And big dogs bite. And killers kill.

62

The Ritz was surprisingly understated for a hotel whose name had morphed into a common noun. Understated, but still elegant. The C&C Hedge Fund Symposium was to be held in the main ballroom, which had been carved up into a large common area surrounded by private sections for breakout sessions. Each of the three days was to begin with a keynote speech in the main space, followed by several smaller workshops or lectures in the walled-off areas. The final day would end with Mo's keynote speech.

Naturally, Mo wanted the symposium to go well, and so we'd only move on the final day. The plan was simple enough, and somewhat reminiscent of my suggestion for killing the fourteen Walker-Midland employees. Mo would schedule private meetings with each of the three funds to discuss "innovative marketing techniques designed to reach untapped segments of the institutional investor universe." It sounded good, and would be ideal for our three funds. After all, the word "innovative," when used in the world of finance marketing, simply meant "deceptive and misleading but perfectly legal."

Mo had asked one of the other consultants to reserve a suite on one of the high floors. Her only requirement was that it have a door to the separate bedroom and a view of the water. We'd use the bedroom as our makeshift morgue, and I figured the view was so that no one from the neighboring buildings could see inside.

This room was by no means a secret. Mo had informed her colleagues that it was available all weekend for private meetings as well as for a quick nap or shower for the C&C folks, many of whom would be working late into the night to prepare for the next day's sessions. We'd make sure to place the "No Maid Service" sign on the doorknob at the end of the second day. Mo wanted the room to be covered with random fingerprints and DNA by the time Sunday afternoon rolled around. She also made sure that neither of us spent any time in there before Sunday. That wasn't a problem, because we had our work cut out over the next couple of days.

Our immediate task was to figure out who was who at each of our target firms. There was a chance that one or more of the funds had brought a young analyst with them, perhaps someone who didn't know exactly how those commissions were being made. If that were the case, we'd have to figure out a way to keep those individuals out of the Sunday meetings.

Of course, we had a list of attendees, but it didn't tell us much more than how many people were attending, what their names were, and which funds they worked for. No titles or biographies were available, and my internet searches didn't come up with anything useful about their backgrounds. To top it off, hedge fund folks are secretive by nature as well as necessity, and many of the symposium attendees weren't wearing their nametags, so we had to do some mingling before we could even match the names to the faces.

Luckily, mingling is something consultants learn early in their careers. From analyst-training bootcamps to the various networking events organized by C&C for its consultants to meet colleagues from other branch offices, mingling was encouraged and expected. Alcohol was always present, but the best consultants quickly learned how to minimize their own consumption while maximizing someone else's. This asymmetry in drunkenness usually resulted in an information advantage, since the other party was happy to talk. I also found that talking to someone who was plastered had the benefit of making my own limited comments seem extraordinarily witty and engaging.

I grabbed the final list of attendees and looked up my targets' names. One person had cancelled, so I needed to track down a total of eleven people—three from Charter Capital, two from MacroResearch, and six from the NationFirst Fund. The size of the NationFirst contingent scared me. Mo wanted to schedule them last, anticipating that it would be the messiest. I had disagreed with her. I figured we'd need to be at full strength if we hoped to kill six people, so I thought it'd be best if we did that first. Descending order of difficulty, is what I told Mo. Of course, Mo didn't budge, and so I gave up and focused on my snappy cocktail party conversation.

The NationFirst contingent was easy to spot. One of them had a nametag, and he was standing with five others who I could tell weren't C&C folks. And since this was the first evening of the symposium, most of the attendees were sticking to their cliques. My nametag identified me as part of the C&C organizing committee, and I was about to go up to them when Mo stopped me.

"No, let me," she said. "I don't want too many people seeing you chatting up the future murder victims. Just mingle around and locate the other five and point them out to me when I'm done with these guys."

She didn't wait for my response, but walked up to the NationFirst group. I couldn't hear what she was saying, but I knew she was dishing out her best charm, and that would be enough to put anyone at ease. I turned away and continued my covert scoping mission.

After several false alarms and polite conversations, I got a hit. MacroResearch's Jake Jessup and Paul Chin were sitting at a table with one of my C&C colleagues. All three of them had beers in hand, and they seemed to be having an actual conversation. I nodded at my colleague, and waited for a break in the dialogue to get myself involved.

I stayed long enough to figure out that MacroResearch was a small shop, and Jake and Paul were the co-managers. This meant they would both know exactly what they invested in. I asked a few casual questions, which they evaded, and so I backed off and slumped down in my chair and simply observed.

Jake was mid-forties, with thick black hair that could have benefited from some combing. His accent was odd, and I wondered if he was the guy I had spoken to in my failed attempt to extract information over the phone. The more I listened, the surer I became, and I was glad I had remained quiet. If he recognized my voice, it might have put him on guard.

Paul was younger, with cropped hair and something that resembled a soul patch under his lip. Only after getting a closer look did I realize it was a heavy scar from an old injury. Although I was becoming quite good at inflicting creative damage to the human body, I couldn't figure out the scar's origin.

Jake and Paul had met at business school in London, and had dropped out to start MacroResearch. After two years in Europe, they had moved to New York, apparently to be closer to a broader pool of potential investors. The way they talked, I could tell they were the kind of people that liked to make money for its own sake. Money was how they kept score. As the conversation began to get edgier, graphic details of how they spent their money began to emerge, and I made an excuse and took my leave. Mo hadn't wanted me to spend too much time with these guys just yet, and I had enough information to know that if MacroResearch was indeed packaging and reselling the securities of rogue nations and unrecognized self-proclaimed sovereigns, Jake and Paul were the ones responsible.

I stepped out onto the terrace for a smoke and watched the room through the glass French doors. Mo seemed to be in top form, and the NationFirst crew were nodding and smiling at her. Whatever she was selling, they were buying. It wasn't for nothing that Mo was a top partner in the New York office of a global consulting firm. I smiled to myself, and then got back to work examining the six members of the NationFirst delegation.

There were four men and two women. All the men wore suits—three in black, one in gray. Good, no individualists here—unless you count the one dude who broke from the pack and went with gray. Two of the men were early thirties and white and, by their mannerisms, almost certainly American. The guy in the gray was maybe fifty, also white, but more Mediterranean, and I couldn't help thinking he was French. The last guy was clearly younger, maybe mid-twenties, and looked like he was from the Indian subcontinent.

The French guy was paying attention to Mo's pitch, but I could tell he was also evaluating her, like he was trying to figure out how much of what she was saying was bullshit consulting sales stuff and how much was actually something that could benefit his fund.

The two American men were completely enthralled by

Mo's spiel. My guess was that they were the day-to-day traders and managers with a stake in the firm, while the French guy was the founder. No doubt all three of them were well aware of their fund's investment strategy.

The Indian-looking guy I wasn't so sure about. He appeared self-conscious, and I could tell he wasn't particularly interested in Mo's talk, but was trying hard to make sure he looked earnest and professional in front of his colleagues and boss. Yeah, this guy was a low-level analyst. They probably used him as an analytical gofer—someone to whom they'd assign bits and pieces of research. I doubted that he had a full view of the actual investments. We'd have to keep him out of the room.

Now my attention shifted to the two women. One was maybe late twenties-early thirties, and she wore a dark green pant-suit that didn't fit so well. Perhaps she had lost some weight recently and hadn't bothered to downsize her wardrobe. It couldn't have been an illness, because she looked alert, clear-eyed, and fit. Maybe she just didn't wear suits much and hadn't for a while, so didn't realize this one'd be too big. Based on her age and her mild interest in what Mo was saying, I guessed she was somewhere between analyst and manager, but probably not a partner. Maybe she handled sales or dealt with clients along with her French boss. Either way, no way of telling how much she knew. Mo would have to make the call.

The second woman was older, maybe mid-forties. She was heavy, and her white blouse and matching long skirt made her look heavier. As I looked at her, I realized that she was the only one who wasn't laughing. Sure, she could have just been bored, but I knew what bored looked like and that wasn't it. No, she was staring right at Mo with a distant yet condescending look on her face. Perhaps she was an ex-consultant and could see right through Mo's dog-and-pony show. Or perhaps Mo had brought up the topic of the Sunday sessions and this woman didn't like the idea.

I sighed and turned away from the glass-paneled door. The moon was out, and the Statue of Liberty looked greenish-blue and very pretty. I dropped my cigarette and was debating whether to have another before embarking on my search for the Charter Capital people when I heard a thick female voice behind me.

"You have an extra smoke? I left mine in the car, and it's with the valet."

I turned, and was startled to see the large woman from NationFirst standing in the doorway. Now that she was close, I could see that it wasn't flab that had made her seem large. It was muscle. Her biceps were well-formed, and I could tell they had been worked recently. The wings above her shoulders and near her neck told me that she used a rowing machine often, or perhaps she was on a crew team. The top three buttons on her blouse were undone, and I almost gasped at the muscle definition on her pectorals. This woman could probably bench press me while smoking a cigarette.

She smiled as I held out my pack. "Thanks," she said.

I stared at her in silence before realizing she was patiently waiting for a light. After fumbling for my matches, I thankfully managed to light her smoke with some degree of composure. But that didn't last long.

"Wow, you are in great shape," I blurted out, and immediately turned red. "Sorry. That sounded crude."

She laughed. "Don't worry. It's still okay to tell a woman she's in great shape."

I smiled and looked down at my nametag. "I'm Frank Stein."

"Lori Hildebrand." She shook my hand. "From NationFirst."

"I'm with C&C."

Hildebrand nodded. "Do you work with a lot of hedge fund clients then?"

"Not really. I'm just here for the free food and booze." I shrugged.

Hildebrand laughed. "At least you're honest."

I was quiet.

Hildebrand stopped laughing. "Sorry. I just have a low tolerance for bullshit consulting sales pitches, and my tolerance levels have already been exceeded after ten minutes with what's-her-face." She waved towards the ballroom without turning.

I knew she meant Mo, but I didn't ask. I just nodded. "Well, our partners are partners because they sell new work. And sure, there's always some bullshit involved in a sales pitch. But our clients are all well-informed and intelligent, and no one pays millions of dollars for services unless they know they're getting something out of it."

"Fair enough. NationFirst sells stuff, too. Of course, it's a lot easier for our clients to measure what they're getting out of it." She smiled.

"So you're on the sales side of things? You deal with the insurance companies and other institutions that invest in your funds?"

"No. That would be Henri and Shanaya." She turned and peered through the glass door. "There. The French-looking guy and that skinny thing with the long black hair."

I nodded. "Then you're a portfolio manager? You allocate money?"

Hildebrand shook her head. "Nope. I do field research. And I do deals."

I paused for a moment and pretended to be trying hard

to remember something. "Now, you guys are a macro-fund, right? You invest in sovereign debt? The securities of other countries?"

"Very good. I guess you do know something about the hedge fund world."

"So when you say field research and deals, you mean you go out and investigate the creditworthiness of a country? And if you think the interest rate they offer on their bonds is commensurate with the country's stability, you work out the terms and conditions with that country's treasury department?"

Hildebrand laughed. "That's a very professional explanation. But 'treasury department' is too glamorous a term for some of our counterparties. 'Dude with an army and a craploud of diamonds or minerals or oil to use as collateral' is more like it."

My face was turned away from the light, so Lori didn't see me go flush. I swallowed hard, and then nodded again. "So you lend money to small countries? Third world types? Up-and-comers that can pay high interest rates but have enough collateral that you feel the loan isn't too risky?"

She nodded. "Yep. But don't ask me which countries. Those are trade secrets, you know."

I laughed. "Of course. Besides, I'm not very good with geography. Especially of places that seem to change borders and rulers every couple of months."

Hildebrand smiled. "Those are the some of the best opportunities for exactly that reason. People can't keep track of who's who and which group owns what. You can't figure this stuff out by searching the internet. You need someone down on the ground. See, the debt business is all about collateral. And since many small, unstable countries are rich in natural resources, they actually have excellent collateral. All you need is a clear contract with the ruling party of the country." She paused and took another cigarette as I handed her the pack. "And, of course, a way to enforce the contract in case the rulers start to miss the interest payments or seem to be in danger of being unable to pay back the full loan."

I was quiet as I lit her cigarette. Then I smiled and spoke nonchalantly. "So NationFirst has its own group of mercenaries that you dispatch when some African despot you lent money to is overthrown in a coup? And your people either get your cash back, or take his diamonds or gold or whatever other valuables you can?"

Hildebrand laughed and then winked at me. "Something like that."

I nodded and shrugged. "Well, it's not much different from how the American loan industry works. Or US foreign policy, for that matter." I dragged on my smoke and looked at her. I had suspected she was ex-military, but now I was sure of it. How else to explain her knowing her way around war-torn nations that no one wants to lend money to? Not to mention her authoritative manner of speaking. Oh, and those serious GI Jane muscles.

Hildebrand smoked quietly. She turned away from me and walked to the edge of the terrace and stopped and stared at Lady Liberty. She seemed lost in thought. Her body was straight like a post, and as I looked down at her feet, I saw that her heels and toes were perfectly aligned. With the exception of her smoking hand, Lori was standing at full attention.

For a second I thought she was going to salute the statue, but then she turned back to me. "All those years in the army. All those years fighting and killing for Miss Liberty, the great bitch." Then she smiled. "But now I'm cashing in. Damn, I love this country."

63

Mo and I met for breakfast at the Ritz at seven on Saturday morning. She had tracked down the three folks from Charter Capital the previous night while I had been on my extended smoke break with Lori Hildebrand. Mo wasn't happy about me talking with Hildebrand. She was even unhappier when I told her about Hildebrand's military service.

"It doesn't matter. She's a civilian now. If anything, it makes what she's doing even more disgusting. She's directly channeling private American funds to countries that are all too happy to kill our soldiers, and if that isn't the greatest insult to anyone who's ever worn an American uniform, I don't know what is," said Mo. She gulped her coffee and stared me down. "Just stick with the goddamn plan. I told you not to spend too much time with any of these people. You should have given her the damn cigarette and walked back into the room and scoped out the Charter Capital people like you were supposed to."

I was a bit taken aback by Mo's hostility. So far she had been in a light-hearted mood, but that seemed to have changed over the past day. Not surprising, I guess. Her upcoming agenda items were eleven murders and one suicide. Of course, I still didn't really believe Mo would kill herself. Sure, I didn't doubt she had thought about it for years, probably planned it, and perhaps now it seemed more real to her after Simone's dramatic exit. In fact, it wouldn't surprise me if she did eventually take her own life. Just not yet. There was unfinished business, more killing to do. She couldn't bring me in and then just leave me here.

We stepped out onto West Street and lit our cigarettes in full view of the rising sun. After taking in some of the morning air along with our nicotine, Mo stepped in front of me and turned to face me.

"I guess there's no reason for me not to tell you this. I got a bit defensive earlier because I didn't want you to think this was personal." She smiled. "Well, I guess it is personal, but that doesn't change anything. She meets the Network's objective criteria anyway."

I didn't say anything. I was starting to suspect where this was headed, and my earlier optimism began to fade. Perhaps this last assignment would take care of Mo's unfinished business. Perhaps she really would leave me after it was done. Leave me and go join her daughter.

"You've guessed it, haven't you?" said Mo. She had turned away, but I could tell she was smiling.

"Jungle sense," I said.

She turned back to me and laughed. "Well, don't head out to join the great apes just yet. It couldn't have been that hard to figure out."

I laughed and flicked my cigarette into the street. The burning butt bounced into the path of an old tourist couple, and they looked at me as if I were one of New York's sights.

Mo went quiet for a bit, and then sighed before continuing. "Hildebrand was Sheila's commanding officer."

I had guessed it, but I still paused and swallowed hard. Then I nodded. "Didn't she recognize you last night?"

Mo snorted. "She would have if she had bothered to come to Sheila's funeral."

I looked at the ground.

Mo looked away and went on. "Still, I'm glad she didn't. Maybe Sheila's friends wouldn't have spoken to me as openly if Hildebrand had been there."

"Spoken to you about Sheila's tour? Iraq?"

Mo nodded. "Her last month there was unusually bloody in terms of mistakes."

"Mistakes like what? Killing civilians?"

"Yes. Which happens, of course." Mo shrugged. "It's a war, and war is messy. Soldiers make mistakes or get bad intelligence. Or both. That's part of the deal."

"So what happened?"

"Her platoon had taken out a couple of homes. Sheila wasn't on the front lines, of course, but she was one of the first in to survey the damage. Apparently one of the homes was full of young women, children, and a few infants. All were blown to bits." Mo sighed. "Sheila took it pretty hard. I mean, she had seen blood and death before, but I guess this really got to her."

"I don't doubt it. Can't say I'd be able to handle it either."

Mo nodded. "Anyway, after a week of nightmares and thoughts of suicide, she apparently went to Hildebrand and asked to see an army psychiatrist. Hildebrand wouldn't let her. She said Sheila was within a month of the end of her tour, and she needed to stick it out."

"But why? Hildebrand was worried about her own reputation? Didn't want anyone to think she couldn't manage her people?"

"Yes. 'For the sake of all the women in the service,' is apparently what she told Sheila." Mo shook her head. "Again,

I get it. I understand the mentality of a female commander being tougher in general and especially so on the women under her command. But there are limits, and from what Sheila's army brothers and sisters told me, Hildebrand was way over them."

I paused as I considered my next words. "You think it had something to do with Sheila being a Muslim?"

Mo shot me a look. "Absolutely not. Our armed forces are actually very sensitive about that. No, this had nothing to do with race or religion. It was just old-fashioned sexism." She slowly began to walk back to the hotel, and I followed.

I shrugged. "Either way. You were right. None of this has any bearing on what we're about to do. I told you about my conversation with Hildebrand. She's obviously using contacts from her army days to make deals with god-knows-whom in all kinds of unknown countries and fragments of nation-states. And you know that genocide is seen as the number one duty of all these little self-proclaimed prophets and leaders of military governments."

A few months earlier I might have tried to argue that we report Hildebrand to some kind of government agency, but now I knew better. I wasn't even sure what laws she was breaking, let alone how to prove it. The only thing clear was that she had forfeited her right to live in the land of the brave and free. Indeed, forfeited her right to live.

Mo smiled as the wood-and-glass doors of the Ritz slid open for her. She looked over her shoulder at me. "It just seems like a nice way to finish up. Like a cherry on top of the dessert that follows a long and satisfying meal."

The image of a red cherry gave way to thoughts of a blood spattered room with eleven bodies piled in the corner, Lady Liberty looking on and smiling at her two righteous warriors.

64

"No blood," said Mo. "At least not for the first two sessions. It'll be too hard to clean up."

It was late Saturday night, and we had just left the Ritz after an exhausting day of presentations, nauseating amounts of polite conversation and networking, and a reasonably enjoyable dinner followed by drinks and live music. Many of the symposium attendees were still in the Ritz's ballroom getting loaded, while others had decided to head out on the town. It was around midnight, and Saturday night in Manhattan was only just getting started.

Mo and I had noted the rapidly increasing pile of empty bottles of hard liquor behind the makeshift bars in the Ritz ballroom. Noted with pleasure, because it meant everyone would be groggy, cranky, and sloppy the next day.

But the "no blood" warning worried me. I looked at Mo as we walked out into the clear night. "So no knives? Then what? We strangle them all one by one? Maybe we can do that with Jessup and Chin from MacroResearch since it'll just be the four of us in the room. But Charter's got three people, and it takes at least a few minutes to strangle someone, doesn't it? That's plenty of time for the odd one out to run and get the police or call someone or attack us. And I don't even know where to begin with the six from NationFirst. One of those mini-Uzis sounds good right now."

Mo laughed. We had walked east along the top of Battery Park and had turned left onto Broadway. Manhattan's most famous street started down here, right near the equally famous *Charging Bull*—a sculpture which had appeared one night outside the New York Stock Exchange before being moved to the paved island near the city's first public park, a small round spot called Bowling Green. The area was fairly deserted, and we sat on one of the benches and looked up at the century-old US Custom House.

"Calm down," said Mo. "There's only going to be four from NationFirst. Shanaya and Arvind won't be there."

The sales woman and the Indian-looking analyst, just as I had guessed. "Oh?"

Mo nodded. "Henri, the managing director, didn't think they needed to be there. And I think that works fine. They don't make investment decisions, and probably don't really know what's going on."

"Okay. I guess that's better. But still, it's four of them. How the hell do we kill four people without any blood? Especially when one of them is ex-military. Did you see how big her biceps were?"

"Leave Hildebrand to me." Mo lit a cigarette. "And NationFirst will come in last."

"Oh, okay," I said. "So . . ."

Mo smiled. "So there'll be some blood."

"So you've got NationFirst scheduled at the end. And Charter Capital is coming in second?"

Mo nodded.

"I didn't really talk to that crew, but I did meet them." I paused and lit my own cigarette. "Three of them, right? All had southern accents. Maybe Georgia or North Carolina. I don't really know."

"The two men are from Tennessee," said Mo. "The woman is from Atlanta. Caitlin. She runs the firm, and the two guys are her day-to-day managers. Polite people. Hopefully they'll die politely as well."

I laughed involuntarily as I tried to imagine how someone could die politely. I looked up at Mo. She was red in the face from trying to suppress her giggles.

It looked like this was going to be fun after all.

65

Sunday morning came around, and I got to the Ritz by eight. Mo and I didn't meet for breakfast. She thought it would be good if we weren't seen together a lot, a strategy we had been following all weekend. Although I had been working on Mo's projects for several months now, the lack of time spent in the office meant that no one would know that we were particularly close.

As expected, most of the attendees were in rough shape after the long night. The breakfast buffet was virtually unattended, and there were almost as many Ritz employees present as there were symposium attendees. The morning's first general session was equally well-ignored. For a moment I worried that our targets had overdone it the previous night and would decide not to show, but I was wrong. By late morning, all nine of our soon-to-be victims were in the Ritz's ballroom looking exceptionally fresh and well-groomed. Perhaps it was the extra sleep. Or maybe they each woke up with a premonition of what would take place that day, and subconsciously wanted to look their finest. As someone famous once said, you should always dress as if you're going to get murdered in those clothes.

As we broke for lunch, I watched Mo greet each group separately and casually, and from the genuine smiles that broke out as she shook hands, I could tell she had made an impression on most of them. Now I understood why they were all bright-eyed and bushy-tailed this morning. They really were expecting to get something valuable out of the afternoon sessions.

Mo ate lunch with the NationFirst group, and I could see that even Hildebrand was yielding to Mo's charm. For a moment I thought I saw Hildebrand sneak a peek down the top of Mo's low-cut black blouse, but then I felt embarrassed at my blatant stereotyping. Regardless, if Mo was getting through to Hildebrand, my major cause for concern was being addressed.

I ate with a bunch of C&C analysts. As they discussed their hangovers and giggled with pride at how they popped some pills at a club, danced all night, and then watched the sunrise from the wooden boardwalk of the Brooklyn Bridge, I mentally rehearsed the afternoon's activities.

Jake Jessup and Paul Chin from MacroResearch would be coming in at two. We planned to meet in the living area, and the three-person couch and matching armchairs all faced the large window that overlooked Ellis Island, New Jersey, and the Statue of Liberty. We'd invite Jessup and Chin to sit on the sofa, counting on the fact that their attention would be drawn to the soft blues of the sky and ocean. Mo and I would circle behind them and use our super-high-tech murder weapons: plastic ties.

Yes, those stiff plastic ties that you use to bundle wires together. The ones where you push one end through a tiny loop at the other end, and there's an automatic one-way locking mechanism that only lets you make it tighter. The ones we had were extra-large, and they were permanently locking, meaning that the only way to remove them was with a serrated knife or thick scissor.

We'd be forming the ties into large loops beforehand, loops

big enough to go around a head. Then we'd slip them over the appropriate heads and pull the ends in tight. And that would be it. No trying to break someone's neck. No strangling someone with your bare hands while staring them down. Nothing else to do except make sure our victims didn't break too many things as they struggled and writhed and suffocated and died.

Not that we were looking for ways to emotionally separate ourselves from our acts. We were just being utilitarian. If we got into a close-quarters struggle, chances were good that we'd take a hit or two. And how to explain conducting a business meeting in the Ritz covered in sweat and blood and with a bruise or two on the face? Besides, watching people squirm and gag as they choked to death would be plenty emotional.

If we pulled the plastic collars tight enough, it wouldn't take very long. Perhaps three to five minutes, and then they'd at least be passed out if not dead. We'd leave the ties on their necks and simply drag them into the bedroom where they could complete the asphyxiation process in peace. Not so bad. Especially considering the misery their actions had caused. Actions that yielded fifteen-to-twenty percent—an obscene return for collateralized debt. The investment capital was being used to fund genocide in Africa and Eastern Europe, buy weapons to attack US and Allied interests, or fund the continuation of illegal regimes in South America or Asia. Sounds stereotypically dramatic, but there's a reason such stories are now stereotypes.

It all seemed so far removed from a place like the Ritz-Carlton in Manhattan. And it was, of course. That's why these people found it so easy to ignore the ramifications of moving some numbers across the screen and watching the profits pile up. As they say on Wall Street, if it's vaguely legal, then it's moral enough. And if you haven't been called on something, then it must be vaguely legal.

Well, these guys were getting called on it now. And that call would come from people who had their own beliefs about the correlation between law and morality. People like us.

I must have had an odd expression on my face, because one of my colleagues, an old business-school buddy, threw a piece of bread across the table at me.

"Hey, Frank. What's up, man? Long night? You still tripping on something?" It was Joe Fletcher, an amiable guy who seemed to have lost a lot of hair since the last time I had seen him.

I snapped out of my self-righteous daydream and smiled. "No, just thinking about all the shit I have to do over the next few days."

"Where're you working these days? I've been buried in this nightmare project up in Albany, so I never come in to the office anymore."

"California. SpacedOut," I said as I picked up and ate the piece of bread Joe had thrown at me. "Mo Hussein's project."

"Damn, everyone wants to get on that project. Supposed to be a cool company. And it may turn into a long-term gig, which would be nice once winter gets here."

I shrugged. "All companies look the same once you get inside."

Joe laughed. "Yeah, being a consultant for a brand-name company is like being an OBGYN—once you've seen it from the inside, you can never look at it the same way again."

I winced and looked apologetically at the two female consultants sitting at our table. They didn't seem to be as offended as I was.

Joe noticed. "Sorry. Been working on a New York State Government project for the last two years. Those old guys in Albany talk as though women still aren't even allowed to vote." He sighed. "I need to get out of there before I go totally native."

I nodded. "Going native" was a term used for a consultant who had spent so long with one client that they took on the culture and mannerisms of the client firm's employees. It was a bad sign, and it defeated the entire purpose of bringing in an outside consultant.

I stood up and headed to the buffet table to grab some coffee. Joe followed me.

"But since we're on the topic," Joe said as he motioned towards Mo, "you hit that yet?"

Mo was standing some distance away with her profile towards us. She did look especially good in a dark brown pantsuit and tight black blouse.

"You're kidding, right?" I said, forcing a smile.

"Why not? She's divorced. And I heard she messes around with other consultants."

I didn't say anything, but I felt a weird pit in my stomach when I realized I had never asked Mo about her husband. Or maybe the feeling was related to the comment about Mo messing around on the job.

I felt indignant for a second, but I wasn't sure if the emotion was directed at Joe or towards Mo. I grabbed my coffee and made a beeline for the terrace. I felt like a high school kid who just found out that the girl he likes is sleeping with some dude in class. I was pissed with myself, and glared at Lady Liberty and sucked down my cigarette so fast it made my lungs burn.

"Nervous?"

I whipped around. It was Mo. She was smiling and walking towards me with an unlit cigarette in her fingers. For the first time I noticed how trimmed her nails were. The nails of a murderer with an eye for detail. Someone who knew she'd be getting her hands dirty.

"It'll go well," she said. "The first two meetings will be smooth. The last might get messy, but we'll be warmed up by then. And I guarantee Hildebrand isn't as tough as she looks. No need to worry."

I smiled, but it was a fake smile. "I'm not worried." I took a drag and turned and looked out over the sea. "Maybe just a bit sad. I was just starting to get good at this, you know."

Mo laughed. "Well, well, well." She laughed again and walked up close to me and leaned on the terrace railing. "I love that I was so right about you."

I smiled again, this time for real.

Mo looked at me with a serious expression. "You know, I didn't mention this to you earlier because I assumed you'd want out, but there is another option."

"Oh?"

"I can give you a phone number."

I paused. "You mean for the Network?"

She nodded. "If you want to continue once I'm gone, they'll assign you to a new Alpha." She smiled. "Hell, after today, they may even make you an Alpha."

I laughed. The thought had crossed my mind earlier, but I hadn't found the right time to bring it up. But now that the topic was in play, I found myself not wanting to talk about it.

Mo shrugged. "Anyway, I guess you have a couple of days to decide."

A gentle warm breeze came in from over the water, and I suddenly felt sad. I turned to Mo, and for a second I was afraid I'd burst into tears. "Mo," I said.

She smiled and turned her face into the breeze. "Don't," she said.

"Don't what?" My sadness was quickly transforming into

rage, and I looked around when I realized how loudly I had said those last two words.

"You know what." Mo was calm.

"Mo, you are not going to kill yourself. It's insane. It's stupid. It's cowardly." I waited and took a deep breath. "And I don't think you're actually going to do it." Although I didn't believe my last statement, after saying it I began to wonder. What if Mo was in fact planning to run? What if she was planning to fake her own death like Simone had?

Then I sighed. Simone had only needed to fool me, not anyone else. It would be hard for Mo to fake her own death without leaving a body behind. Ramona Garcia wouldn't be fooled by a car crash or random explosion.

When I returned to the moment, she was smiling at me in that all-knowing way. "Frank, don't kid yourself. I'm not trying to fake you out."

I shrugged. "I don't know about that. After all, the best way to keep a secret is to tell no one, not even those closest to you. Especially not those closest to you."

Mo laughed. "True. But I'm not going to argue with you. You'll see for yourself."

"What do you mean?"

"Monday night. Stop by my place in Westchester."

I didn't get it until I remembered the lie Mo had told me about how Simone died—carbon monoxide poisoning. One of the most painless ways to go, and a common cause of death for entire families. Every winter there are stories of how a family tried to heat a house using a charcoal grill. Since the house is sealed for winter, the grill quietly sucks in all the oxygen and spews out carbon monoxide. And nobody wakes up.

Now I felt she was serious. I was quiet for a bit.

"What about your husband?" I said.

"Ex-husband." She shrugged. "He'll get over it. I'm leaving some stuff for him, and that should ease his pain." She nudged me. "I'd put you in my will too, but it might look weird. I want you to have a chance for a clean break."

"If I want it."

"If you want it."

We were both quiet now. Our cigarettes had long since burned out, and as we looked at Miss Liberty standing in her blue-green majesty, our thoughts began to drift back to the task at hand.

"Anyone got a light?"

The voice was thick, but distinctly female. We turned. Lori Hildebrand stood in the doorway. She was in a sleeveless blouse, and the sight of her sinewy arms cast serious doubt on Mo's earlier comment about Hildebrand not being as tough as she looked. As I moved close to her with my lighter, I noticed her nails. They were unpainted and closely trimmed. The nails of a killer.

66

"So how did you end up in the hedge fund world after the army?" said Mo.

We still had an hour before our first meeting, and Mo seemed to want to stay and talk a bit. I didn't mind. By now it no longer seemed sick and twisted to have a pleasant conversation with someone just a couple of hours before murdering them.

Hildebrand smiled. "Made a pit stop at Harvard Business School first."

I nodded. "Yeah, I've heard that HBS likes to accept ex-military."

Hildebrand shrugged. "Well, there's no bigger corporation than the United States Military. So we already come with a lot of management experience. And a knack for making decisions under pressure."

"I can't even imagine," said Mo. "You served in Iraq, right?"

"Most recently, yes. And in Somalia before that. Along with a few other places that I can't really talk about."

"Or you can tell us but then you'd have to kill us?" I laughed.

Hildebrand smiled. "More likely someone else would kill all three of us via overhead satellite."

We all laughed now. I looked straight up into the cloudless sky and pretended to be afraid. We all laughed again.

"But seriously," said Mo. "I can't imagine how tough it must have been in Iraq. Were there a lot of women there at the time?"

"Quite a few. Not so many officers, but now there are a decent number."

"Did you have a lot of women under your command?" Mo asked.

I glanced over at Mo, but her expression was casual and relaxed.

"A few. I was one of the first female commanders in Iraq, and some of my girls were the first women to see some real action. So yes, it was tough. It's not easy to gain the trust and respect of a bunch of men in that environment. You almost need to be tougher to be taken seriously as a woman in the army."

Mo nodded. "And tougher on the women under you as well?"

Hildebrand took a deep drag and smiled. She looked at the ground and was quiet as she flicked the ash from her cigarette. Then she looked up at Mo. "You're Sheila Hussein's mother."

Mo nodded like she knew Hildebrand had known.

I was surprised, maybe more so because I seemed to be the only one surprised. These women were way ahead of me.

Hildebrand continued. "I'm sorry about your daughter. It's hard on those kids out in the desert."

I held my breath and cautiously looked at Mo. But Mo could handle herself better than anyone. She didn't even flinch, but I could see by the inch of ash on her burning cigarette that she had been standing absolutely still for several minutes now.

Hildebrand sighed. "Look, I don't know what you've heard,

but I can understand what you must think. All I can say is that I was no tougher on Sheila than I was on anyone else."

Mo smiled and looked into the distance past Hildebrand. "Let me see if I can remember that comment . . . ah, got it: 'Just because you have a vagina doesn't mean you have to act like one.'"

Hildebrand looked grim. "As I said, I treated everyone in my unit the same. If we give in every time someone complains about the pressure, the army psychiatrists will be the single largest unit on the ground."

"But she was talking about suicide. The signs were there for you to see." Mo was still calm, but her voice had begun to waver.

"*Everyone* talks about suicide after a while. Once you see enough killing, death is no big deal. It's a normal psychological reaction that when you're in a stressful situation, your mind looks for escape routes. For example, if you're stressed at work, you fantasize about quitting. But when you're in the army and are already desensitized to death, the easiest way out seems to be suicide. And when you see people being killed in terrible ways out in the field, sometimes you can't help but feel it's better to die on your own terms." Hildebrand paused to stub out her cigarette. "Again, I can't say I wouldn't feel the way you do had it been my child. But I stand by my actions. There may have been signs, but so many others display the same signs and don't commit suicide. And Sheila killed herself while on leave. Weren't there signs for you to see as well?"

I stiffened.

Mo looked down and nodded. She touched her left eye and then looked up. "Well, anyway, I have to run." She smiled at Hildebrand. "See you at four upstairs?"

67

The conversation with Hildebrand had left me feeling uneasy. If the afternoon's plans had been motivated solely by revenge, I might have tried to talk Mo out of it. Hildebrand certainly didn't seem repentant, but her response was less defensive and more sensitive than it could have been.

But I also suspected that Mo wasn't burning to kill Hildebrand to avenge Sheila. The only person Mo really blamed was herself, that was obvious. In some perverse way, I think Mo wanted to bring herself to blame Hildebrand, but couldn't. Mo wasn't the type of person who hides from accountability. Now I began to worry about whether Mo would be able to kill Hildebrand at all. Perhaps she would question her own motives and hesitate.

And if she did, I'd have to step up. Although the thought of killing a woman still didn't sit right with me, I had no doubt that Hildebrand deserved it as much as anyone else on the agenda for that day. Perhaps even more. Of course, after spending some time with Hildebrand, I didn't really want to kill her. But I couldn't let that play into it. All of us in the Network were dancing on that line separating morality and insanity, and if we started to dirty up the objective criteria we had set for picking victims, then we'd be lost. If we started to segregate our victims and only kill the ones we didn't like, then we'd be nothing but common serial killers, and eventually we'd fall into that downward spiral where we'd start to kill based solely on our own tastes. Mo had once talked about Network members who fell into that hole. Such people quickly became Network "assignments" themselves.

As I took the elevator up to the 23rd floor, I had to remind myself that the sickening feeling rising within me was part of the deal. There was no glamour in our kind of righteousness. We all knew that murder was always wrong at some level, and each one of us would pay the price in any number of ways. One of those ways was to live with the knowledge that we had intentionally violated one of humanity's inviolable rules: live and let live.

I stepped off the elevator just as I remembered that humanity itself had violated that rule. More specifically, my own government and my fellow citizens and other voters had individually and collectively decided to violate that law. In some sense, Mo and I and the Network were ahead of the majority of the others because we were facing the consequences of those decisions. Yes, we were righteous after all.

That odd feeling of synchronicity hit me again as I snapped on my gloves and reached for the door handle just as my inner monologue had gotten me to the point where I no longer felt sickened at what I was about to do or sorry for my poor lot in life. Then my head buzzed as the adrenaline poured into my bloodstream, and I knew I was ready.

Nine more kills and it would be over. Nine more, and I would be free.

68

Mo was on the couch and the television was blaring. It was a strange sight, and I walked around her and up to the window so she could see me. She flipped off the TV and stood up. I noticed she had already donned her clear surgical gloves.

"You okay?" I asked.

She nodded and smiled.

"You handled that conversation with Hildebrand pretty well. For a minute there I thought we'd have to take her out on the terrace itself in front of about seventy people."

Mo laughed for a second, and then gave me a distant smile. "I'm sorry. I should have warned you I was going to bring up the topic. I wanted to get it out of my system before we got up here, because, to be honest, I wasn't sure how I'd react." She moved up to the large window and stood beside me. "And this can't be about revenge."

I smiled. "I don't think it will be. You're too strong and self-aware for that. I know you take full responsibility for Sheila. Not that you should, of course. But I know you do."

She smiled at me. "Thank you."

My smiled faded and I touched Mo's hand. "But you're still planning an act of revenge. A self-directed act of revenge. If this can't be about revenge, then it means you can't kill yourself either."

She ripped her hand away like I had burned her. "I'm well aware of my motives. And this conversation is over."

"Sorry," I said.

Mo walked over to the bedroom door and opened it. The room was large, with a king-sized bed, a writing desk, two chests of drawers, and an attached bathroom. I had noticed another bathroom connected to the living area, which meant there would be no reason for our guests to enter this room. At least not while they were still alive.

"So we're just going to dump the bodies in here? In a pile on the carpet and bed?"

Mo shrugged. "Why, you have some ideas for an artistic arrangement?"

I let out a dry laugh. "No." I looked down at the set of black plastic ties Mo had given me. "The murders will be artistic enough. Where are these from? K-Mart?"

"Rite Aid, smartass." Mo seemed to be cheering up a bit.

We prepared the plastic strips by positioning the ends into their loops so they could be easily slipped over someone's head. I stepped back to the foyer near the main door and surveyed the room. The large window was dead center, and was the first thing that would grab anyone's attention. The couch faced the window. A granite-topped table lined the back of the couch. Mo had cleared the table, and we placed the plastic loops on the cool black surface. The specks of gray on the granite provided just enough visual noise to render the ties virtually invisible to someone walking past and around the table to sit on the couch.

We quietly went through the suite and disconnected all the phones and hotel intercoms. Then we placed our own cell phones in a desk drawer so they wouldn't be accessible to anyone in a struggle. Due to the barely-legal nature of the meeting topics, the plan was for me to request our guests to leave their cell phones on the table near the entryway. I didn't expect anyone to resist the suggestion. After all, the thought of being murdered by a couple of management consultants was unlikely to have crossed anyone's mind, including Hildebrand's.

It was almost two. Jake Jessup and Paul Chin from MacroResearch would be arriving soon, and there was nothing else to do but wait. Mo and I stood near the window and stared out at the tug-boats and barges and tourist cruiseboats that were leaving little white trails of foam as Lady Liberty smiled at us. *Vive la liberte*, I thought, and then came the knock at the door.

69

Jake Jessup and Paul Chin were dressed in jeans and sport jackets, but their expectant and anxious expressions made it clear that they were taking the meeting seriously. When I asked them to leave their phones near the door, they smiled and nodded, seemingly thrilled at the air of secrecy. We stood far enough away from them that handshakes didn't seem necessary. We didn't want them to notice our rubber gloves, even though I'm sure we could have explained that away. Again, being murdered by a couple of management consultants in a sunny room in the Ritz is not something that even the most paranoid hedge fund guys would expect. This was going to be easy.

"Wow, nice view," said Chin.

"Damn. We should get some office space down here," said Jessup. "It's nice to see some water and sky instead of gray buildings."

They both walked up to the window and stood there for what seemed like a long time. I lingered near the entryway, and Mo stood casually off to the side, near the small bar.

"Please have a seat," Mo said. "We'll be with you in a minute. I'm just going to grab some water."

I noticed that Mo didn't offer them anything. She didn't want to risk them turning around or coming up to the bar.

She waited until they both sat down, and then she looked up at me and nodded. I moved forward at a normal pace. Mo timed herself so we got to the table at the same time. We couldn't afford to stall behind the couch, because our presence might make them turn. As it was, they were still enamored by the view.

My adrenaline had settled down to that steady level that I was getting accustomed to, and I picked up the plastic tie with neither hesitation nor haste. I was now oblivious to what Mo was doing, but had no doubt that we were in complete alignment.

The thin plastic loop dropped down over Chin's head like one of those rings falling over a prize at the carnival. I yanked hard on the free end, and then simply jumped back and out of the way.

After the initial muted gagging sounds, things were quiet except for the simple acoustics of their fingers clawing at the thin smooth lines of plastic that had reduced their windpipes to the size of threads. At first they turned violently around while seated, then they stumbled to their feet, tripped over each other and the low coffee table, fell down to the thick carpet, and finally began to writhe and thrash like those first two fish I had caught many years ago.

Of course, those fish stayed alive for almost thirty minutes. These two guys went limp after three. Mo and I were silent but unmoved. There was nothing to do but watch them die, and so that's what we did. As their movements slowed and finally stopped, I glanced back up at Madame Liberty through the window. She was still smiling, and I turned to Mo and shrugged.

We dragged the two bodies feet first into the bedroom and placed them at the far end of the room near the writing desk. We shut the door and walked back out into the living area. I grabbed their cell phones and turned them off before dropping them near the bodies in the bedroom.

When I rejoined Mo, she was looking at the wall-clock. It was seven minutes past two. Our first meeting had lasted eight minutes.

70

Next up was Charter Capital—the Southern contingent. Since there were three of them, things would be slightly more complicated, though not by much. The plan would stay pretty much the same. We'd ask them to leave their phones by the door and then come in and sit. Chances were that all three wouldn't sit on the couch, which meant that one of them would be on an armchair and would be able to see us dropping the plastic chokers over the other two.

Mo was betting that Caitlin, being the boss as well as the only woman, would take the armchair. James and Robert, the two men, would probably claim the couch.

We'd still drop the plastic ties over the men's heads from behind, but we'd have to move fast, since we'd expect Caitlin to start shouting and run for the hotel phone—which was disconnected—or the door.

Caitlin was probably in her early forties. She was slim, but didn't appear to be particularly strong or athletic. Mo wanted to handle Caitlin herself, with me blocking the path to the door in case something unexpected went down. The plan was to use a plastic tie for Caitlin as well, although there would probably be a struggle before Mo got it over her head. Still, I had seen Mo handle people far bigger than Caitlin, and I didn't expect it to take very long.

Mo and I didn't say much for the rest of the hour. It was a

comfortable silence, with each of us adrift in the semi-trance that I had come to recognize as a key element in the build-up to a kill. Although the window was sealed shut, I could imagine the sounds of the surf breaking gently against the Manhattan shoreline, the soft purr of the speedboats racing up the Hudson, and the comical horns of the tugs and barges and miscellaneous other watercraft that filled the blue space twenty-three floors below us.

As if part of the dream, a gentle knock appeared at the door. I snapped to attention and stood up in an instant. Game time.

Mo took her place by the bar so it would look like she was getting herself something from the small fridge. I went to the door and opened it, making sure to step back so that no one would offer to shake hands.

Of course, I had underestimated the warmth and politeness that had been bred into the two Southern gentlemen, and both Robert and James moved briskly towards me with outstretched hands. I greeted them both with vigorous handshakes, and prepared to answer the obvious question about my gloves. To my surprise, neither of them commented on it. As I said, I had underestimated their politeness.

I smiled and asked them to place their phones on the table near the entryway. Now, this did seem to offend them, and perhaps even concern them a bit. Caitlin's expression made it quite clear that she neither understood nor expected to understand the reason for my unusual request, and Mo stepped in to save me.

"Caitlin, please don't be offended. As you're aware, today's conversation could easily be taken out of context by anyone outside this room, and we just don't want to take any chances." Mo smiled. "I don't know if this ever happens to you, but sometimes when I think I've hung up or ignored a call, I find that the other person has been on the line for God knows how long."

That settled the issue, but the exchange had introduced a small amount of tension. I hoped the expansive view of the sea and sky and statue would smooth things over, but the group barely noticed. I felt myself getting a bit nervous, and I took a few deep breaths to bring my heart rate down. It didn't work, and I looked at Mo, my eyes widening. She was calm. Her expression calmed me a little, and as I saw Caitlin lean back in the armchair while Robert and James dropped into the corners of the couch, I exhaled and smiled. Things were falling into place after all.

Caitlin looked up at Mo and smiled. "May I ask what you use those plastic ties for? I noticed them on that table behind the couch."

I saw that Caitlin was staring at Mo's gloves, and I began to panic. Then I reminded myself that although Caitlin may have noticed the odd details surrounding our meeting, there was no way she could seriously think this was a setup to kill all three of them. This was the beauty of what we did, the beauty of the Network. We brought violence to the people who never in their wildest dreams expected to confront it.

Mo glanced at me ever so subtly and I moved forward in tandem with her. Our advance was casual, and we were both smiling.

"They're props for an ice-breaker exercise," said Mo. "We consultants have a lot of little games we use during conferences and in break-out sessions for people to get to know each other."

Robert and James had both turned to look at us. We were almost at the table behind the couch, and I looked at Mo for my cue.

"Here, I'll show you," said Mo. She pointed at the window. "Look straight ahead, you guys."

Robert and James smiled politely and turned to the window. Perhaps they were worried about being put on the spot and being asked to answer some dumb questions about their backgrounds or do some silly team-building trick.

And as Caitlin watched us, Mo and I placed the loops around the two men's heads, looked at each other, and in perfect unison pulled the ties tight. Then we politely stepped back to allow the Southern gentlemen enough space to react to the plastic cutting into their throats, squishing their vocal cords, airways, and oesophagi into single condensed tubes like how you might squeeze a large amount of tertiary pig matter into a slender string of sausage.

As Mo bounded over the couch to drop the stunned Caitlin to the floor, I stepped away and took up my position near the passage to the door and watched the proceedings.

Robert jerked back and forth on the couch while James threw himself forward, hitting the coffee table with his shin, and then slamming his head into the wooden base of the unoccupied second armchair as he went down hard on the carpet. Robert's rocking motion became more pronounced, and I saw him wildly look around the room, briefly making eye contact with me before turning his rapidly dimming eyes back to his immediate surroundings.

Then for an instant Robert seemed to regain his Southern composure, and I could see him trying to slip his fingers under the plastic tie to relieve the pressure on his neck. But Mo had pulled the tie tight and his stubby fingers couldn't get in there and soon he was out of air and then it was over for him. He slowly lay down on the couch almost as if he were going to sleep. And so he did go in a reasonably graceful manner.

I looked at James, who was also motionless by now, and was politely lying face-down on the carpet. Text-book perfect.

Meanwhile, I could see that Mo was having no trouble with Caitlin, who had mouthed a silent scream before standing up and backing away towards the window. Given more time, perhaps she would have gotten over the initial shock and run for the phone or the door, but as it was, she had less than five seconds from the time the plastic nooses went tight around her colleagues' necks to when Mo's strong arms were pulling her to the ground.

Caitlin struggled at first, but Mo had her on the ground in a headlock. I had some idea of the power Mo's petite body could generate, but was nonetheless startled when suddenly Caitlin's neck snapped and she went limp in Mo's arms.

"Damn," I said. "Is that what you call an ice-breaker?"

71

Eleven minutes. That's how long it had taken to clean up Charter Capital. We now had five bodies in the bedroom. We placed Caitlin and James on the bed to clear the floor space for the four bodies that would be coming through in the next fifty minutes.

We went back out to the living area. Mo straightened the couch cushions while I turned off the orphaned cell phones and dumped them in the bedroom. When I got back out, Mo had turned on the TV. As she pumped the volume, I looked at her in surprise.

"This one could get noisy," she said, and sat down on the couch.

I joined her, expecting that we'd sit quietly and wait for the last round of kills. But Mo wanted to go over the plan. She had apparently thought of a couple of changes since that conversation with Hildebrand after lunch.

"Hildebrand is obviously the wildcard. It's risky to go after her first, because it may take too long and the others would have a chance to run," said Mo.

I nodded. "And it's also risky to leave her for the end, because then she'd have time to stop us or get help. Or both."

Mo went into the bedroom. She came back out holding a thick metal pipe that was probably two or three feet long.

I recognized it as a curtain rod, a makeshift weapon that Mo had taught me to use in my solo practice routines. She walked over to the bar area and placed the rod just behind the counter.

She stood at the bar and looked at me. "Start off the same way: invite them in and ask them to leave their phones near the table. Then walk back towards the couch. Don't shake hands, even if it seems rude."

I nodded. Even Hildebrand couldn't possibly guess what we had in store, but there was no reason to arouse any suspicions that something out of the ordinary was going on.

Mo continued. "I'll call Hildebrand over to me near the bar and talk to her until the other three sit down. When they do, you immediately choke one of them—preferably one that's on the couch."

I smiled and nodded again. "Hildebrand will turn away from you."

Mo took a few practice swings with the curtain rod. "I'll drop her quick and then come and help you. By the time I get to you, one guy should be down and you should be in control of a second. So there'll just be one more for me to handle. Shouldn't be a problem."

I went to the desk drawer and pulled out a couple of new plastic ties and began to loop them in preparation. Mo stopped me.

"You'll only need one. For the first guy," she said.

I looked up, but Mo had gone back into the bedroom. She returned with two glistening chef's knives. I took one without saying a word. At least my last kill would be done the old-fashioned way.

"Okay," I said. "And I assume you'll go back and finish off Hildebrand."

Mo nodded. "At my leisure." She turned up the television volume some more.

I wondered if I should say something, but then decided against it. I wasn't sure what she was planning, but I couldn't believe Mo was capable of torture. Besides, we had talked about her feelings towards Hildebrand. This last assignment would be handled professionally. Mo wanted it that way, didn't she?

There was no time to discuss it, anyway, because just as I slipped the knife into my belt and dropped my jacket over it, a loud knock came at the door. I checked the clock—it was four in the afternoon. NationFirst was on time.

72

Henri, the founder and managing director, was the first to enter. I stood back and held the door open. I nodded, but was careful not to make eye contact until they were all inside. I didn't want to invite a handshake. Henri introduced the rest of his team to me. Andy and Mickey were the other two besides Hildebrand.

All of them were dressed in formal business attire. Henri was in a dark blue suit and an orange tie, Andy and Mickey were in black, and Hildebrand wore dark red. Mo smiled and called them in while loudly apologizing for the television.

"I'll turn it off in a second," she said, pretending to look for the remote behind the bar. I knew Mo had hidden the remote in a drawer.

Andy and Mickey took seats on the couch, and Henri took an armchair. It was funny how people chose their seats relative to their standing in the company. Henri, being the boss, gravitated towards the single-seater armchair, while Andy and Mickey, both junior partners, were happy to share the couch.

So far things were panning out. No one had balked at the request to leave the phones near the door, and I wondered if it was perhaps not such an unusual request in the secretive world of hedge fund folk.

Mo had subtly invited Hildebrand over to the bar. She

was quietly—and genuinely, it seemed—apologizing to Hildebrand for the awkwardness of their earlier conversation. Hildebrand was all smiles, and I wondered if speaking with Mo had taken a load off her shoulders as well.

I turned my attention back to the three men in the seating area. Andy and Mickey were staring out of the window and muttering to each other. From their bobbing heads, I guessed they were talking about the view. Henri, on the other hand, was glaring at the loud and offensive television set that hung on the wall to his right. He did not look pleased, even when accounting for the general French expression of disapproval at all things American.

As I walked towards the back of the couch, my attention shifted from Andy to Mickey. Andy was slightly taller, and had a thick mop of red hair. Mickey looked stronger, and had short hair that highlighted his bald spot. Since Mickey was on my right and Henri was to Mickey's right, I decided to go that way.

There was no need to look at Mo. She'd be paying attention. With cold focus I snatched up the plastic cord and slipped it over Mickey's round head and pulled it in so hard that his entire body slammed back into the couch cushion. He immediately stood up and reached out his hands at nothing in particular. As he turned, I could see the confusion in his bulging eyes. To my amusement, Henri and Andy seemed equally confused. The blaring sound of the television was adding to the chaos, and since it was drowning out any cries of pain or alarm, the entire scene looked comical, like when you walk past the glass window of a nightclub and you can see people twisting and shaking as they dance to music that you can't hear.

I must have hesitated, because I heard a metallic clunk

followed closely by the dull sound of a heavy body hitting the carpet, and then I felt Mo push me towards Henri as she ran at Andy.

Henri had snapped out of his shocked paralysis, and had reached the hotel phone that sat on the thin table against the far wall. It was disconnected, and when he realized it, he made a dash for the doorway.

I hit him with a classic diving tackle. My arms locked his knees, and my body weight forced his legs to buckle. He went down flat on his face, but turned and started to pump his legs furiously. I couldn't keep his knees locked, and his black leather dress shoe hit me on the forehead. I reeled, more out of surprise than anything, and that was enough for Henri to kick me once more, this time in the chest.

Now he was on his feet, and I was still down. By the time I got to my knees he was at the door and fumbling with the chain and deadbolt. I whipped out my knife, but I was probably eight feet away from him and still not upright. I took a deep breath, changed my grip on the blade, and flung the knife with all my strength.

Any professional athlete will say that you know how good your stroke or shot or drive is by the smoothness of your follow-through, and I finally got to understand what that meant. My arm had swung all the way back down after my throw, and since I was still on my knees, I fell forward onto my face. I didn't see the knife tumble through the air, but I knew it had struck gold.

When I looked up, Henri was leaning with his cheek against the door, his right hand desperately trying to reach for the knife that was buried deep in the center of his back. After admiring my aim, I walked up to him and grabbed the rubberized handle.

"Here, let me help you," I said, and pulled the knife straight out.

Then I grabbed his hair, yanked back his head, and sliced clean and deep across his throat. I let him drop right where he was. He slowly sank to the carpet, one hand against the door, the other hanging limp to one side. The bright red blood oozed over his shiny blue shirt collar and carefully made its way down to the carpet where it pooled in a neat little maroon circle.

"Very elegant," I said. "You French people look classy even in death."

After taking one last proud look at my final kill, I turned back to see if Mo needed help.

She didn't.

73

Andy had taken it directly in the chest, and although his once-white shirt was now crimson, I could tell Mo had only struck once. I whistled when I saw that the knife was still in him. It had been buried so deep, I hadn't noticed it at first. She had driven it right through the middle of his sternum, probably the hardest entry point in the human body. I made a mental note to write down the brand of those chef's knives. They were certainly top quality.

Hildebrand was moving, but she was barely conscious and far from coherent. I didn't see any blood on her light brown hair. Mo had obviously not wanted to kill her with the blow to the head.

"Well, don't just stand there. Help me," she said.

I went over to Mo and helped her lift Hildebrand. We carried the heavy woman over to the armchair and placed her in a seated position. Mo grabbed a few more of the plastic ties, and I silently watched as she bound Hildebrand's arms and legs.

"Mo?" I said, as an uneasy fear took root in me.

"Shut up," said Mo. "And get out."

"What?"

Mo tugged on the plastic lines to test their strength. Then she stood up straight and looked at me. "Get out of here.

We're done. Come over to my house tomorrow evening if you want." She paused. "Or else this is goodbye."

I was stunned, and felt myself start to shiver as the adrenaline drained out of me, leaving my overtaxed muscles and nervous system to fend for themselves. I slowly moved to the couch and sat down and began to rub my eyes. When I looked up, Mo was gone.

She emerged from the bedroom with what must have been a long pillowcase. I watched in a daze as she used the white cloth to gag Hildebrand, who was slowly coming to her senses.

"Mo," I said again.

Now Mo stopped and looked at me. Her expression softened, and she sat on the couch and moved close to me. For a second we both looked straight ahead at the calm blue sky with its little fluffy clouds. Then I felt Mo's hand on mine. Even through our gloves, the feeling was electric.

"Hey," she said. "Go. I'll see you tomorrow evening, okay?"

I took another look at Hildebrand. She was wide awake now, and had begun to strain against her bonds. At first her eyes were wide with panic, but now I could see she was trying to assess the situation and find a way out. When I turned back to Mo, her expression and posture had lost their tenderness, and she was all business. No. There would be no way out for Hildebrand.

And there was nothing I could do. Hildebrand needed to be taken out just as much as the eight others who had died that day. Yes, I wasn't comfortable with what I feared Mo was going to do, but I knew that Mo would have to live with it, and die with it.

As for me, I'd have to live with walking away, perhaps forever tormented by allowing what I could only imagine would be torture. But there would be many other things that tormented me, so what was one more? The adrenaline-induced rush I had felt earlier was long gone, and as I went to the door and pulled Henri's lifeless body away, I felt like a pathetic, cowardly murderer again. I tried to remember that what we had done was noble and righteous, but somehow that didn't ring so true anymore. I was a low-life terrorist, no better, and possibly worse.

I looked out into the hallway to make sure it was clear, and then I stepped out. As I turned to close the door, I saw Mo retrieve her knife from Andy's chest. I took a deep breath and shut the door and took the elevators straight down into the parking garage so I could leave the building unnoticed.

74

The SpacedOut consulting team wasn't scheduled to be out in San Francisco until later that week, so I spent Monday cooped up in my apartment, feverishly checking the news on television as well as the internet, panicking every time the phone rang or the buzzer sounded.

Naturally, the massacre was all over the news. Nine bodies had been found in a suite at the Ritz-Carlton in Manhattan, which meant Hildebrand was certainly dead. None of the news channels talked details, so I had no idea how she had been killed, or if there had been signs of torture. Mo sent me a text in the early afternoon, and it appeared that there was enough confusion as to what had gone down that the police hadn't reached out to her yet. We were still on for the evening, but I no longer gave a shit about what Mo was going to do to herself. I was in a deep hole, and suicide didn't seem like a bad way out. In fact, it seemed like a pretty good way.

I buried my face in the couch pillow when I realized what I was thinking. I tried once more to imagine what my parents would go through, and then my thoughts started to drift back down the path of faking an accident. Not faking my death, just faking how it happened so my parents might think it was an accident and not self-inflicted. A few cigarettes later, I calmed down and sunk back into the comfortable state of apathy that had consumed me for most of the day.

At four in the afternoon, I finally moved from the couch. I hadn't eaten or showered or even brushed my teeth yet. After stubbing out the last cigarette from what had been a fresh pack that morning, I dragged myself to the bathroom and got ready.

I took the subway down to Broadway and 86th and picked up a rental car. I drove back uptown and took the Hudson Parkway North. The ride to Westchester took almost two hours, but I barely noticed. In fact, the only thing I remember about the car ride was being annoyed that the rental company had somehow managed to remove all the ashtrays from the vehicle.

It was almost seven when I got to Mo's, and I was about as angry and depressed as I had been at any point that day. I felt weak with dehydration and hunger, and my throat was dry and itchy.

Mo lived in a beautiful house in what seemed to be an extremely well-to-do neighborhood. In New York City you always hear the rich people with families say that they lived in Westchester, and even with that hype I was taken aback by how upscale the neighborhood was. Mo's place must have been worth several million even in a down market, and it was one of the smaller lots.

My careless depression abruptly left as I walked up to the front door. Now I was apprehensive and sad and in that confused state of mind where all I wanted to do was shout out loud. What do you say to someone who's about to kill herself? Especially when you're the last person she's chosen to be with. Do I tell her I love her? Do I beg her to stay?

Mo answered the door before I could fall any deeper into my melancholy. She was in black track pants and a loose red shirt.

"Hey," she said.

"What's up," I said.

"Come in." Mo stepped back.

I walked in and looked around. The house looked spotless and smelled fresh. I remember reading somewhere that if you're feeling like killing yourself, you should first clean your home. Nine times out of ten, when your home is neat and tidy the desire to end it all diminishes. I smiled at her, and tried to feel optimistic.

My optimism disappeared when I noticed that all the windows save one had been closed and sealed with duct tape. The door to the passageway that led to the stairs had been closed and sealed as well. A charcoal grill stood near the open window, and the flames had already given way to a steady, dull red glow.

I turned to Mo with a desperate smile on my face. "This is ridiculous. You know this is ridiculous, right? If you're doing all this just to fake me out, then please tell me. You know I'd never let on that you're alive."

Mo smiled at my smile. "Frank. Let's not get back into this. I can't fake a carbon monoxide poisoning without a body. And besides, I don't want to run. This is what I want. This is the plan. This was always the plan." She sat down on the large green cushioned couch and beckoned for me to sit by her. "And I know you understand."

I sat next to her and stared at the shiny black grill. I turned back to her and felt like I should say something, but I couldn't think of anything to say. I wanted to say that I loved her, but I knew I would start sobbing if I tried to speak. I looked up at her and tried to tell her with my eyes, but she wouldn't look at me. Instead, she went to the last open window, shut it gently, and sealed it with tape. I stared as she picked up a prescription bottle from the mantel and swallowed a few pills. She still wouldn't look at me.

I stood up. I wanted to go to her and put my arms around her and tell her that we could maybe go somewhere and have a normal, happy life. I took a step towards her and reached for her hand. But she turned away from me and moved close to the grill and stared down at the whispering red coals.

"I'll see you in hell, Frank," she said. "Goodbye."

And I turned and walked out of the house and got into my car and drove back to Manhattan at ninety miles an hour with all four windows rolled all the way down. It was pitch dark and raining when I dropped off the car at the rental spot, but I didn't give a shit. I puffed on a cigarette until the rain put it out, and then I slowly walked home alone in the night.

EPILOGUE

Like I said, all stories about management consultants begin and end with a laptop. This laptop has a big blue sticker on it with some words in yellow print. The words say *Property of the Federal Government of the United States.*

Yes, part of my deal lets me finish typing up this rambling, self-indulgent account. It's not your typical confession, but the federal prosecutors can pull what they need from it.

And although I'm almost starting to fancy myself as a writer, I'm not going to take you through any heroic or guilt-ridden or philosophical explanations of why I turned myself in. I can tell you that there was no proof other than my confession, so I guess there is a sense of righteousness written into these pages.

Hopefully that feeling will be enough for me to keep it together while I sit on death row. I gave up my rights to appeal in return for being allowed to wait for the needle in solitary.

Small comfort, though, since I know I'll never be alone again. They're all watching me—Yoshi, Miroslav, Takahashi, Henri, Raghu, and the others. Watching, and waiting. Waiting for me to join them.

But I'm not worried, and I'm not scared. I know there's someone else watching. And I'd like to think she's waiting for me too.

∞

Thanks for reading.

If you'd like to get an email when the next installment is out, visit **www.frankstein.net/mailinglist**.

And please consider rating this book on Amazon, GoodReads, or your favorite book review website. Thanks again.